TASTING CANDY

'You're tight,' he breathed, grabbing my hips as he withdrew slowly. 'And very wet. How many men have fucked you since you married Rod?'

'Shut up,' I spat. 'Just fuck me and then get out of my life. For good.'

'You love it, don't you?' he asked me, ramming his knob deep into the tight sheath of my pussy. 'You love a damned good fucking.'

TASTING CANDY

Ray Gordon

This book is a work of fiction.
In real life, make sure you practise safe, sane and consensual sex.

First published in 2005 by
Nexus
Thames Wharf Studios
Rainville Road
London W6 9HA

www.nexus-books.co.uk

Typeset by TW Typesetting, Plymouth, Devon

Printed and bound by
Clays Ltd, St Ives PLC

ISBN 0 352 33925 X

You'll notice that we have introduced a set of symbols onto our book jackets, so that you can tell at a glance what fetishes each of our brand new novels contains. Here's the key – enjoy!

cp (traditional)

cp (modern)

spanking

restraint/bondage

rope bondage/hojojutsu

latex/rubber/leather/enclosure

fem dom

willing captivity

medical

period setting

uniforms

sex rituals

One

The photograph clearly showed my face, so there was no mistaking my identity. My naked body bound with leather straps, metal clamps biting into the ripe teats of my nipples, the scene was incriminating to say the least. But who had taken the photograph? Someone must have been at my lounge window, lurking, spying. There was no note attached and nothing in the hand-delivered envelope to give me a clue as to the photographer's identity. This was obviously the launch of a blackmail attempt.

I'll never forget that fateful day, my fifth wedding anniversary. The worry, the anxiety . . . Who the hell had taken the photograph and dropped it through my letterbox? What did they want? Money? I tried not to show my concern as I sat in the restaurant with Rod, my husband. Although fraught with worry, I did my best to appear relaxed as he reached across the table and squeezed my hand.

The flickering candlelight reflected in the dark pools of his eyes as he smiled at me. He looked handsome in his navy-blue blazer and white shirt with his dark hair swept back. He was 28, a good-looking man with a high-powered job and an excellent salary. I was four years his junior. And I was a lucky girl, so people told me.

1

This was our wedding anniversary, our celebratory meal. In his soft voice, Rod said that I'd made his life complete; that he'd never been happier. Looking down at my wedding ring sparkling in the candlelight, I slipped my hand out of his and toyed with my empty wineglass. After five years of marriage, Rod didn't know me. He knew half of me: the home-maker, the loving wife. But he had no idea that there were two sides to me. Did I know myself?

'More wine?' he asked me.

'No, no, I'm fine,' I replied, trying not to look at the young man hovering by the door to the cloakroom.

'Cindy, I . . . I meant it when I said that you've made my life complete.'

'I know,' I breathed. Did I feel guilty? 'It's been a lovely evening, Rod.'

'Yes, it has. We've got everything we could wish for. A lovely home, each other, happiness . . . You really have made my life complete. You are happy, aren't you?'

'Yes, of course I am,' I replied with a giggle. 'I've never been happier.'

'Would you like some coffee?'

'Mmm, please. I'm just going to nip to the loo.'

After leaving the table as Rod beckoned the waiter, I went out to the foyer and frowned at the young man standing by a yucca plant. He looked me up and down, licked his lips provocatively and grinned. He was in his late teens, good looking, rugged, rough, suntanned . . . His name was Ian. I'd met him in a bar a couple of weeks previously and we'd taken an instant liking to each other. But he shouldn't have been at the restaurant. This was my wedding anniversary; my special evening with my husband. Moving towards me, Ian reached out and squeezed the firm mound of my breast.

'You look great,' he whispered huskily.

'Ian, no . . .' I began, glancing over my shoulder. 'What the hell are you doing here?'

'I came to see you, Cindy. Aren't you pleased?'

'Yes, no . . . I mean . . . For God's sake, Ian. This is my wedding anniversary.'

'So?' Taking my wrist, he pressed my hand against the crotch of his trousers. 'I thought I'd give you an anniversary present.'

'No,' I returned firmly through gritted teeth, squeezing the bulge between his legs. I was becoming weak in my arousal. 'Not here.'

'Where, then?'

'Nowhere. Not tonight, of all nights.'

'In here,' he persisted, pulling me into the Ladies.

After almost dragging me into a cubicle, he unzipped his trousers and hauled out his erect penis. I looked down and eyed the veined shaft, the purple crown silky smooth. This was my wedding anniversary, I reminded myself repeatedly as I sat down and gazed longingly at his beautiful organ. My wedding ring caught the light as I wrapped my fingers around his solid shaft, and I pictured Rod sitting at the table sipping his coffee. This was wrong, I knew. But I couldn't help myself as I leaned forwards and took Ian's bulbous glans into my cock-hungry mouth.

'Happy anniversary,' he whispered, clutching tufts of my long blonde hair and rocking his hips. 'Like your present?'

'Mmm,' I moaned through my nose as I swept my tongue over the velveteen surface of his knob.

'You're a slut, Cindy. A cock-sucking slut.'

'Mmm.'

'Suck it and drink my spunk.'

I *was* a cock-sucking slut. The feel of a swollen knob bloating my mouth, the salty taste, the gushing

3

spunk jetting to the back of my throat ... I was addicted to cock sucking. I'd first taken a solid cock into my mouth behind the gardener's shed at school. I'd kneeled before a young lad and unzipped his trousers. He'd looked down in amazement as I'd sucked his purple globe into my wet mouth and tongued his slit. My first taste of salt, my pioneering spunk swallowing. It had been a bet, a dare. Did I have the courage to suck the spunk out of a boy's cock? I won the bet. From that day forwards, I'd sucked cock and swallowed spunk at every opportunity.

Ian stifled his gasps of pleasure as he clutched my head and rocked his hips gently. The purple globe of his erect cock glided back and forth between my full lips, massaging my wet tongue. I closed my eyes and sucked hard. I was desperate for the taste of spunk, the feel of the creamy liquid sliding down my throat. My juices of desire soaking my panties, I wondered whether to allow my hungry pussy the pleasure of Ian's cock. No, there wasn't time for that.

Ian came quickly, his creamy spunk bathing my snaking tongue, filling my cheeks and dribbling down my chin as my mouth overflowed. Repeatedly swallowing hard, I drank from his throbbing knob, revelling in the crudity of my adulterous act. My wedding anniversary, my special evening out with my husband ... And I was sitting in the ladies' toilets drinking spunk from another man's cock.

I hadn't planned this; I hadn't wanted this. But Ian knew how much I loved sucking his cock, swallowing his spunk. He knew that I couldn't resist an opportunity to take his magnificent organ into my mouth. I should never have told him where I'd be that evening. I should have forced myself to spend at least one evening with Rod without committing adultery. But I was weak, and Ian knew how to play on my weakness.

'You really are a dirty little whore.' He chuckled, finally slipping his deflating cock out of my spunk-brimming mouth.

'And you're a bastard,' I returned, licking my glossed lips as I left the cubicle. 'You shouldn't have come here this evening. I told you that I –'

'I'll bet you're pleased that I did come,' he quipped.

'Look, I . . . I have to get back to Rod.'

'Is he going to fuck you tonight? Is that what you've planned for your anniversary?'

'If I have to,' I sighed. 'It *is* supposed to be a special evening.'

'I'll see you tomorrow, OK?'

'No, not tomorrow.'

'Why not? Are you seeing someone else?'

'Of course not. It's just that I . . . I had a letter this morning. I have to go out tomorrow.'

'You had a letter?'

'Yes, a . . . I'll ring you, OK?'

After returning to the table with the taste of Ian's spunk lingering on my tongue, I sat down and gazed at the small box in front of me. Rod had bought me a present. Smiling, I opened the box and pulled out a diamond-studded, gold necklace. I looked up and smiled again, told him that he shouldn't have. He said that I was worth it. A perfect wife, one in a million. Did I feel guilty? I don't know how I felt. I suppose I felt sorry for Rod. He, like our families and friends, thought that we were the perfect match; soul mates.

'You were a long time in the loo,' he said as I tried on the necklace.

'Jilly rang on my mobile,' I lied.

'Is she OK?'

'Yes, yes. She called to wish us a happy anniversary. Rod, the necklace is beautiful. Thanks.'

'A beautiful necklace for a beautiful woman.' He

frowned as he lowered his eyes. 'You've got something down the front of your dress,' he whispered.

'Oh, er ... I must have spilled something,' I stammered, taking a napkin and wiping Ian's spunk from my dress. 'Ice cream, I expect.' Ian's present.

I didn't drink my coffee as I wanted to savour the taste of Ian's spunk as we drove home. I wanted to savour the taste of another adulterous act. How many cocks had I sucked? How much spunk had I swallowed during my five-year marriage? Did it matter? What Rod didn't know couldn't hurt him. He thought that we were happy. He thought that I was his faithful, loving wife. That's all that mattered.

The phone was ringing when we got back to the house. My stomach churned as Rod answered it in the lounge. Was it the blackmailer? Shit, if Rod discovered what I'd been up to ... From the kitchen, I could hear him, but I didn't realise who he was talking to until he mentioned Jilly's name. Why the hell had she called? If she said that she hadn't called earlier ... Rod finally came into the kitchen and frowned at me.

'That was Jilly,' he announced.

'Oh?'

'She called to wish us a happy anniversary.'

'Again?' I said, forcing a laugh.

'She didn't ring you earlier, Cindy.' He sounded suspicious.

'She didn't ring me?' I giggled. 'Has she lost her memory?'

'No, I don't think so. Why did you say that she'd called?'

'Because she *had* called. You know what she's like, Rod. A scatterbrain at the best of times.'

He stared at me and rubbed his chin. 'Alan drove past the house yesterday afternoon,' he said. 'Alan Johnson.'

'And?'

'When he got back to the office, he told me that there was a man at the door.'

'A man at the door? I'm not with you, Rod. What are you talking about?'

'There was a man at our front door, Cindy. You didn't mention that anyone had called.'

'No one called, for God's sake. If they did, then it must have been when I was out.'

'Alan said that you were talking to the man.'

'Rod, no one called . . .' It was time for an instant lie. 'Wait a minute. Someone came round about collecting for a jumble sale. That must have been who Alan saw.'

'What time was that?'

'I have no idea. What's this about?'

'Nothing,' he murmured, smiling at me. 'I'm sorry. I'm overreacting.'

'To what? A man came round about collecting for a jumble sale. It's not the sort of thing I'd bother to mention to you, is it?'

'No, of course not. I'll make some coffee.'

I walked into the lounge as Rod filled the kettle, and thought about Ian calling the previous afternoon. He'd come round for sex, as usual. Two afternoons each week, that was our arrangement. The chances of Alan Johnson driving past . . . Why had he mentioned it to Rod? Was he the blackmailer? He'd probably only mentioned it in passing, but why was Rod suspicious? And why the hell had Jilly phoned? The scatterbrain didn't usually remember what day it was, let alone our wedding anniversary.

In five years of playing around behind Rod's back, only once or twice had I roused his suspicion. But I was an adept liar and, when I'd come close to being caught out, I'd always managed to wriggle my way out of trouble. But now there was photographic evidence of my debauchery. How the hell could I wriggle my way out of that? Alan Johnson? Jilly? Who the hell was watching me? Not Jilly, surely?

As Rod brought the coffee into the lounge, I realised that I'd become complacent. I'd lost count of the men I'd fucked in the house; sucking cock in the lounge, screwing in the marital bed ... Rod never called in during the day or came home early, so I'd thought that I had nothing to worry about. Our house was surrounded by tall bushes, detached with a long driveway. There was no way anyone could see our house unless they stood at the bottom of the drive. Alan Johnson must have slowed down almost to a halt to see our front door. Or had he crept up the drive with a camera? Ian was going to have to come in through the back door in future.

I could almost feel Rod's suspicion as he sat in his armchair and sipped his coffee. His dark hair cascading over his unusually lined forehead, he looked worried. What else had Alan bloody Johnson said? How many times had he spied on the house? I didn't like the man. He had curly blond hair and long slender fingers – and he gave me the creeps. He'd only called at the house a few times to talk to Rod about work, so I didn't really know him. But I didn't like the way he looked at me. He had thin lips and narrow eyes. He'd stare at me, gaze at my blouse billowed by my firm breasts, gape at my naked thighs. He was a horrible little man. But I'd never have believed that he was a blackmailer. I wasn't being blackmailed, I reminded myself. Not yet, anyway.

'Did you give him any?' Rod asked me.

'Any what?' Rod had the irritating knack of assuming that I knew what he was talking about. 'Give any what to whom?'

'Jumble to the jumble man.'

'Oh, no, no.'

'Boy scouts or guides?' he persisted.

'What? Oh, er . . . he didn't say. Rod, I really don't want to discuss the jumble man on our anniversary.'

'I wasn't discussing him. I was interested, that's all.'

'Perhaps I should have mentioned that a gang of bible bashers called the other day. Just in case Alan happened to see them at the front door and –'

'Cindy, he was only passing,' he cut in with a laugh. 'Don't get so uppity.'

'I'm not uppity. I think I'll go to bed.'

'All right. I'll catch the news before I join you. I won't be too long.'

I was sure that something was bothering Rod. It wasn't Jilly's phone call or Alan driving past. Had he discovered something about my secret life? It was so unlike him to be moody, let alone suspicious. Had he seen the photograph? No, the blackmailer wouldn't have shown Rod the evidence of my debauchery. Not if he planned to take money from me. The worry was too much to bear. I needed some relief.

Slipping my hand beneath my pillow and grabbing my vibrator as I snuggled beneath the quilt, I lay on my back and parted my legs wide. Running my fingertips up and down my sex crack, I realised how wet my pussy was. Ian loved licking me there, lapping up my sex milk and teasing my clitoris with his wet tongue. He'd torture me, keep me hanging on the verge of orgasm until I begged and pleaded with him. He'd finally suck my clitoris into his hot mouth and allow me my pleasure. He was a bastard.

Rod wasn't into oral sex. Many times, I'd pulled my pussy lips apart and asked him to tongue my pussy. I loved the feel of a tongue delving into my sex hole, licking deep inside my cock-hungry pussy. After an hour of tonguing my pussy, Ian would drive his huge cock into my drenched pussy and fuck me senseless. Ian was rough, common, vulgar. He'd mumble expletives as he fucked me, tell me how tight my cunt was, what a dirty slag I was.

Rod always shied away from tonguing me and drinking my creamy juices. I'd often wondered whether he really liked sex. Many times, he'd turned his back on me in bed and left me desperate for an orgasm. Many times, I'd slipped beneath the quilt and sucked on his cock. But he'd come up with excuses. He was tired; he had an early start in the morning . . . Doubting that Rod would want sex, I switched my vibrator on and pressed the buzzing tip against my erect clitoris.

Sucking spunk from Ian's knob had turned me on, sent my libido rocketing, and I was desperate for the relief of a powerful orgasm. Sex with Rod was nothing exciting and far from satisfying. When we had any physical contact, he'd shove his cock into me, usually from behind, pump me full of spunk and then go to sleep. He'd mumble words of love and tell me how beautiful I was. He'd tell me that I was a perfect wife. There was never any variation, never any fun involved. Ian would tell me that I was a filthy whore-slut. We'd laugh and fuck, and then fuck again.

Sex with Ian was cold and loveless. But his crude words turned me on. He fucked me for the sake of fucking me. He used and abused me. No, we used and abused each other. We tried anything and everything: all positions, all holes. He'd drive his knob deep into my pussy and then ram his beautiful organ into the tight sheath of my bottom and spunk my bowels. Sex with Ian was extremely stimulating and immensely gratifying.

My clitoris teetering on the verge of orgasm, I reached beneath my thigh and thrust two fingers into the drenched sheath of my neglected pussy and massaged my hot inner flesh. The exquisite eruption came quickly, exploding within my pulsating clitoris and shaking my naked body to the core. The immense relief, the incredible satisfaction . . . I loved the beautiful sensations my vibrator brought me; the sheer gratification. My vibrator, my secret lover. One of my secret lovers.

Thinking of Ian, picturing his hard cock, I recalled his words. *Are you seeing someone else*? I was pleased that I'd put him off calling at the house the following day. Pleased because I *was* seeing someone else. Richard was in his sixties, wifeless and lonely. He needed a little comfort; physical contact. That's why he came to me. Despite his age, he had a big cock and amazing staying power. He was also kinky.

Slipping my wet vibrator back beneath my pillow, I recalled Richard spanking my bare bottom the last time he'd visited the house. He loved playing sex games. He loved anilingus, licking deep inside my bottom hole to lubricate me before fucking me there. After finally falling asleep, I dreamed my dreams of Richard. His huge cock shafting my tight pussy, screwing my bottom hole, spunking in my mouth . . .

'Cindy, you're brilliant,' Rod said as he came into the kitchen and gazed at the cooked breakfast on the table. 'Eggs, bacon . . . What would I do without you?'

'Grab a packet of biscuits, knowing you.' I laughed. 'Come on, or you'll be late.'

'What have you got planned for today?' he asked me as he tucked into his food.

'I might go and see Jilly. See how her memory is after last night.'

'Her memory might not be good, but it's odd that she should forget that she phoned you.'

'Jilly's an odd girl,' I said, making light of it. 'She was going to come round the other morning. When she didn't turn up, I rang her. We'd only arranged it the day before and she'd forgotten all about it. By the way, I'll tell you if we have any callers today.'

'Don't be silly.' He chuckled and gulped down his breakfast. 'Right, I'd better get going. I'll see you tonight, love.'

'Have a good day.'

'And you.'

Once he'd gone, I cleared the table and went upstairs. Richard wasn't due until ten but I liked to be ready well in advance. After taking the suitcase from the top of the wardrobe, I pulled out Richard's favourite clothes: a gymslip, white blouse, navy-blue knickers, white ankle socks, black patent shoes . . . He was the teacher and I the young pupil. I'd be a naughty little schoolgirl, and he'd put me across his knee and spank my bare bottom. My hair would be in plaits, tied with red ribbons. I loved our naughty games.

Once dressed up, I gazed out of the lounge window and I waited for Richard. Would the photographer turn up? Would Alan Johnson happen to drive past? Perhaps he was building up the courage to ring the doorbell and try his luck with me. Did he know that I was a dirty little slut who'd fuck anything in trousers? Almost anything. There was no way I'd fuck Alan bloody Johnson.

The thought of someone photographing me in my bondage gear was increasingly worrying. I couldn't stop thinking about someone hovering outside the lounge window with a camera. No doubt they'd make their move at some stage. But when? And what would they demand in return for their silence? I felt so helpless. There was nothing I could do, other than wait for the inevitable contact, the demand for hush money. Noticing Richard walking up the drive, I dashed through the hall and opened the front door. I had to stop worrying.

'Have you been a naughty little girl?' he asked me as I ushered him into the house.

'Very.' I giggled, leading him into the dining room. I felt that we were safer at the back of the house.

'This won't do, Cindy, it really won't do. Lift your gymslip up and show me your knickers.'

I lifted my gymslip and stood with my feet wide apart. He gazed longingly at the navy-blue material bulging over my full sex lips. I liked Richard. Dressed in a Harris Tweed jacket, crisp white shirt and brown corduroy trousers, he looked refined with his silver-grey hair and suntanned face. He was warm and friendly, a kindly man. His wife had long since gone, but his libido was alive and kicking. Although he was a sad old pervert, he was a nice man, and we got on extremely well.

I'd met him in the local supermarket. He'd helped me with my trolley and I'd suggested he come back for a coffee. Not intending to seduce him, I showed him around the garden. He seemed more interested in my short skirt than the plants so, when we sat on the patio, I parted my legs and showed off my tight panties. It was a test, and he passed with flying colours. Unable to drag his eyes away from the triangular patch of white silk between my thighs, he wasted no time when I asked him to kiss me there.

Why had I offered my young body to an old man? I don't know why. The thought of having sex with a stranger or a part-time lover excited me no end. Whenever I was in male company, I thought about sucking cock, drinking spunk. I couldn't help myself. I was a slut, a tart. I loved cocks; I loved sucking knobs, feeling spunk flooding my tight pussy, pumping deep into my arse ... I wallowed in my adulterous acts, relished the danger, loved the very notion of taking another man's cock into my mouth. I was a wanton whore.

'Have you been masturbating again?' Richard asked me, breaking my reverie.

'Yes, sir,' I confessed meekly.

'Then, I'll have to spank your bare bottom,' he returned angrily, sitting on the leather chesterfield. 'Come here, girl. I want you over my knee.'

Lying across his lap with my bottom jutting out, positioned for a good spanking, I grinned as he pulled my gymslip up and yanked my navy-blue knickers down. He ran his fingertips over the pert orbs of my buttocks, obviously admiring the view as I whimpered as if crying. Parting my bottom cheeks, opening my anal gully wide, he teased the brown eye of my anus with his fingertip. I quivered, my breathing fast and shallow as his fingertip ran over the delicate brown tissue surrounding my secret hole. Could he see the white stains in the crotch of my navy-blue school knickers?

He mumbled his words of fantasy as he stroked the sensitive ring of my anus. *Naughty little girl, bad girl* ... If only Rod had fantasies; if only he played sex games with me. The trouble was that Rod loved me. He didn't want to use and abuse me for crude sexual gratification. Why didn't he want to massage my bottom hole? Why wouldn't he finger me there? Was that crude? Whatever the reason, it didn't matter. I had my male lovers to assuage my feminine cravings.

Finally easing the tip of his finger into my bottom hole, Richard massaged the hot inner flesh of my tight rectum. I squirmed and gasped as the sensations permeated my pelvis. My womb rhythmically contracting, my clitoris swelling, my juices of desire oozing between the engorged inner lips of my pussy, I breathed heavily in the grip of the debauched act. He threatened to push two fingers deep into my tight hole unless I told him where and when I'd masturbated, then he slapped my naked buttocks with his free hand.

'In bed, last night,' I confessed.

'Did you use your vibrator?' he asked me, easing a second finger into the tight duct of my rectum.

'Yes, yes, I did,' I gasped.

'Did you come?'

'Yes, sir. Several times.'

'That's very naughty,' he admonished me. 'Young schoolgirls shouldn't masturbate. I'm going to have to punish you most severely.'

Managing to drive three fingers deep into the contracting duct of my rectum, he again slapped my buttocks as I squirmed on his lap and made out that I was crying. I loved anal abuse, the crude violation of my rectum. But the worrying thought of the blackmailer took away from my pleasure. I imagined him lurking in the back garden, his camera at the dining-room window, focused on my naked bottom as Richard fingered my anal canal. When would the blackmailer make his demands?

I quivered as Richard pulled his sticky fingers out of my arse. His wet tongue lapped at my bottom hole, teasing me, tasting me as he stretched my buttocks apart to the extreme. He'd once said that he was an anal lover. Was I an anal slut? I was enjoying his arse tonguing, the feel of his saliva running down between the cheeks of my bottom to the swollen lips of my bared pussy.

But my mind was elsewhere. Photographic evidence of my adulterous ways, blackmail . . .

'Where are you, Cindy?' Richard finally asked me. 'Where are your thoughts?'

'I'm sorry,' I sighed. 'I just can't relax.'

'Problems with Rod?'

'No, no. Well, I . . . I don't think so.'

'Do you want to talk about it?'

'No,' I breathed, sliding off his lap and standing before him. 'Fuck my arse, Richard,' I ordered him, leaning over the dining-room table. 'Fuck my arse and take my mind off my worries.'

Standing behind me, he dropped his trousers and stabbed at my saliva-dripping anal eye with his bulbous knob. I loved the feel of a huge cock deep within my tight little arse. I'd first experienced anal intercourse when I'd been at college. A young lecturer had had his eye on me for some time, and I'd been hoping that he'd ask me out. As the weeks passed, nothing happened. He was married, and obviously didn't want to commit adultery. But I was sex crazed, and wasn't going to be beaten.

One lunchtime, I almost dragged him into a stock room and dropped my knickers. Bending over a table with my skirt up over my back, I told him to fuck me. He fell prey to his inner desires and drove his beautiful cock deep into my hungry pussy. The thought of destroying his marriage vows fired my passion. I'd taken another woman's husband, desecrated their relationship. I could hear people milling about in the corridor as he fucked me. The danger thrilled me. If we were caught, he'd lose his job and his wife. And I'd be thrown out of the college. Was I the devil's daughter?

Before his spunk had jetted, he'd slipped his cock out and pressed his swollen knob hard against the tightly closed eye of my anus. My eyes were squeezed shut. I knew what he was attempting, and I tried to relax my sphincter muscles to allow his cock entry. Pushing his knob harder against my bumhole, he let out a rush of breath as he entered me. I could feel the sensitive brown tissue of my bottom hole hugging the rim of his purple crown as he grabbed my hips. He'd stripped me of my anal virginity, and introduced me to an amazingly deviant sexual act.

Driving the entire length of his veined shaft deep into my tight arse, his heavy balls coming to rest against my puffy pussy lips, he'd fully impaled me on his beautiful organ. I'll never forget the feel of his solid rod shafting my rectum, his bulbous knob repeatedly sinking deep into the dank heat of my bowels. Grabbing my hips, he fucked my arse with a frenzied vengeance as I flopped back and forth over the table like a rag doll.

His spunk finally jetted from his orgasming knob, lubricating our illicit union as he fucked me over the table, as he told me that I was a dirty little girl-slut. I loved his crude words, his dirty talk. Filthy, tight-arsed little whore; common slag; cumslut; vulgar little cock lover . . . I could hear his spunk squishing deep inside my arse as he repeatedly rammed his cock head into me and drained his balls. Dirty little schoolgirl; arse-fucking tart . . .

That afternoon as I sat in class, I could feel his creamy spunk oozing from my inflamed bumhole, wetting my knickers. From that day on, I craved anal sex. My lecturer came back for more, meeting me in the stock room regularly. He'd fuck me long and hard, until his spunk flooded my bowels. Using his fingers, his cock, a wax crayon . . . He'd use anything and everything to shaft my tight rectum. He'd tongue my anus, licking and tasting my bumhole before ramming his huge knob deep into the fiery core of my young body. He'd fuck my arse daily. Some weeks later, I heard that he'd also fucked his marriage . . .

Richard's swollen knob finally slipped past my relaxing sphincter muscles, his shaft driving deep. The filling sensation was exquisite. My pelvic cavity bloated, my anal tube stretched tautly around his granite-hard cock, lovingly hugging his beautiful organ, I clung to the sides of the dining-room table as he began his fucking motions. Again and again, his ballooning knob journeyed along my tight rectal duct to the hot depths of my bowels. I could feel my anal ring dragging back and forth along his shaft, his heavy balls battering the fleshy swell of my pussy lips. This was real sex.

'Coming,' he announced all too soon. His creamy spunk spurted deep into my quivering body, lubricating his crude rectal pistoning, cooling the cavern of my burning bowels. He grabbed my hips and fucked me with a vengeance. Although an old man, Richard was able to come two or three times during his visits to my house. He seemed to have a never-ending supply of spunk and an everlasting erection. Unlike y husband.

I listened to the squelching sound of spunk, the slapping of his lower belly against my naked buttocks, as I rocked my hips to meet his thrusts. I was in my element with my rectum crudely shafted, pumped full of spunk. I knew that I could never relinquish my life of adultery. The very concept of monogamy left me cold. One man, one cock . . . No, that wasn't for me. I couldn't survive without a string of sexual relationships, a variety of cocks.

'You're good, Cindy,' Richard gasped, stilling his knob deep within the heat of my bowels. 'I don't know what I'd do without you.'

'And I don't know what I'd do without you,' I lied. He believed that he was my only lover. 'I mean it, Richard. You're my salvation.'

'And you're a sweet girl.' As his deflating cock left my rectum with a loud sucking sound, he slapped my buttocks. 'So, do you want some more? Or are you still troubled by something?'

After hauling my trembling body off the table, I turned and smiled at him. I *was* troubled, deeply troubled. I had everything to lose and nothing to gain. A beautiful home, money, a loving, caring husband . . . If Rod discovered my adulterous ways, I'd lose everything. After pulling my navy-blue knickers up my long legs to conceal my spunk-dripping anus, I lowered my gymslip and told Richard that I was feeling tired. A kindly, considerate man, he understood. Adjusting his trousers, he brushed back his silvery hair and moved to the door.

'Until the next time,' he said with a warm smile.

'I'll look forward to it,' I murmured. 'And I'll make up for –'

'You don't have to make up for anything,' he interrupted me. 'You take care, Cindy.'

'Yes, yes I will.'

I waited until I heard the front door close, then climbed the stairs and slipped out of my school uniform. My knickers were wet with spunk, the sopping material clinging to me. I loved the feel of the cold, wet material against my naked skin, and decided to leave them on for a while. My time with Richard had been ruined, but I at least had his spunk in my knickers to comfort me. Taking the photograph from behind the wardrobe, I gazed at my leather-bound body and sighed. I needed comforting now more than ever. Who was trying to destroy me, and why?

Recalling my many lovers, I wondered whether I'd annoyed one of them and they were trying to get back at me. I'd left a few broken marriages in my wake, but I could hardly take all the blame. If a man was going to cheat on his wife, and get caught, then he should understand and accept the consequences. If Rod caught me, I'd have no one to blame other than myself. I could hardly point the finger of blame at Ian or Richard.

The phone beside the bed rang, and I was surprised to hear Rod's voice. He never rang or called in during the day. He never made any contact when he was working. What did he want? Was he suspicious? Had the blackmailer been in touch with him? He said that he hoped to leave the office early and be home by three. I didn't want him home early. I liked my days, my time with my lovers, my time alone. Had he given me too much space, too much freedom? Trying to sound enthusiastic, I said that I was looking forward to seeing him. I replaced the receiver and grabbed a summer dress from my wardrobe.

Strolling around the garden, enjoying the summer sun, I again recalled my lovers. There was David, a young man of eighteen who'd told me that he loved me. Love? Huh, he didn't know the meaning of the word. There again, neither did I. He'd been upset when he'd discovered that he was one of many who'd shared my naked body. But he wouldn't resort to blackmail, I was sure. Besides, that was a year previously. I couldn't imagine who would blackmail me. But, I again reminded myself, I wasn't being blackmailed. Yet.

Two

I couldn't believe it when Rod turned up at 3.30 – with Alan Johnson. What the hell did the slimy little man want? I despised him. And I decided that he was the blackmailer. My reckoning was based on his demeanour and the way he grinned at me as he sat on the sofa and eyed my naked legs. He focused on my nipples, which pressed through the flimsy material of my summer dress, licking his narrow lips. But my decision was based on more than his lecherous gaze. As Rod left the lounge to fill the kettle, Alan asked me how I spent my days. Did I get bored or lonely? Did I entertain visitors?

'I keep myself busy,' I returned, sitting in the armchair opposite him. 'I don't have time for boredom or loneliness.'

'Stuck in the house all day?' he sighed. 'I couldn't do it. Rod's stuck in the office all day every day. At least I get out and meet clients.'

'Each to their own,' I said coldly.

'I'm often round this way, Cindy. I'll have to call in and have a coffee with you.'

'I'm out a lot of the time,' I stated firmly. 'And when I'm in, I'm busy.'

'Don't you ever have friends call?'

'Friends, yes. But *only* friends.'

I was coming across as rude, but couldn't help that. He wasn't Rod's boss, but they worked closely together. It was best not to cause waves. Call in for coffee? Sure now that he was the blackmailer, I wondered whether I should invite him round. What did he want? What was he after? He'd make his move at some stage, so it might as well be sooner rather than later. He was on a good salary, so he wouldn't want money in return for his silence. Sex? By the way he ogled me, that was more than likely.

'I might be in tomorrow morning,' I finally conceded.

'Oh, right. Shall I . . . If I'm in the area –'

'Yes, why not?' I said as cups rattled in the kitchen. 'Just for a cup of coffee.'

'And a chat,' he breathed, grinning at me.

'Alan and I have some papers to go through,' Rod said, carrying a tray of coffee into the lounge. 'Is it all right if we stay in here? Or would you rather we went up to the study?'

'Stay in here, if you wish,' I replied, rising to my feet. 'I'll go and sit in the garden.'

Taking my coffee out to the patio, I pondered on Alan's visit the following morning. Having seen me in my bondage gear, he'd no doubt make his demands – his demands for crude sex. I was going to have to plan ahead, decide how to deal with him. Blackmailers always come back for more. The last thing I wanted was Alan bloody Johnson threatening to brandish the photograph to all and sundry and call round for sex every five minutes. Even if he gave me the original photograph, he was bound to keep a copy. But, if I gave into his demands, I'd never be free of him.

'Isn't that strange?' Rod said as he joined me on the patio half an hour later.

'Very strange,' I replied, having no idea what he was talking about. 'Has Alan gone?'

'No, no. He's in the loo. We went through the papers in the office this morning. I don't know why he wanted to come here and go through them again.'

'Didn't you ask him why?'

'No, I didn't. Sweetheart, would you mind awfully if Alan stayed to dinner?'

'I don't mind at all,' I breathed, dreading the thought. 'I was going to suggest we have a barbeque.'

'That's a good idea. How about inviting Jilly over?'

'Er . . . yes, I might give her a ring. By the way, we're rather low on beers.'

'No problem. I'll nip out and get some. Is there anything else we need?'

'Another bottle of vodka wouldn't go amiss.'

'Right you are. I'll tell Alan what we're doing and then I'll nip out.'

As he walked back into the house, I let out a sigh. The last thing I'd wanted was Rod coming home early, let alone Alan bloody Johnson staying for dinner. I was still wearing my spunked navy-blue knickers, so I decided to change before the barbeque. Jeans and a T-shirt would be appropriate, and ensure that Alan had nothing to stare at. Silently fuming as my unwanted guest joined me on the patio, I wondered whose idea it had been that he should eat with us. Had he suggested it? Or had Rod asked him without consulting me first?

'Rod's gone to buy some booze,' Alan said, sitting on a patio chair opposite me. 'It'll be a nice change to have a barbeque. Living alone in a flat, I usually end up with a take-away.'

'Why don't you just get down to business?' I asked him coldly.

He frowned and cocked his head to one side. 'Business?' he echoed.

'You know what I'm talking about, Alan.'

'Do I?'

'Yes, you do. Let's not wait until tomorrow. Just tell me what it is that you want.'

'I thought you'd never ask.' He chuckled, raising his eyebrows and gazing at my naked legs.

'You drove past here the other day. Why?'

'I often drive past, Cindy. You must know that I've always fancied you. I've never said anything because . . . Rod's my friend.'

'So, this is what you do to a friend? You come sneaking round here, creeping up the drive and spying on me . . .'

'Cindy, I —'

'I want the photograph, Alan. What do you want in exchange?'

He frowned again, and then grinned. 'Now, there's a leading question,' he whispered.

'Don't play games with me. How many photographs are there? Is it just the one?'

'Yes, yes,' he murmured pensively. 'Just the one.'

'You want sex with me, and you thought that blackmail was the best way to go about it?'

'As I said, I've always fancied you. Yes, I drive past and look at the house. Yes, I —'

'Sneak up the drive and take photographs of me through the lounge window. Did you see the man I was with?'

'The man? Oh, yes, I did.'

'He's just a friend, Alan. He likes me to dress up for him, that's all there is to it. It's not adultery, if that's what you're thinking.'

'What is it, then?' he asked me accusingly.

'It's . . . It doesn't matter what it is. I want the photograph.'

'And I want sex, Cindy.'

'And I don't want sex with you. So, where do we go from here?'

'You tell me. The ball is in your court.'

Looking around the garden, I wondered what to do. Would a quick blowjob behind the bushes satisfy him? I'd sucked enough cocks and swallowed enough spunk during my marriage. One more wouldn't make any difference. But he'd come back again and again, and I couldn't let that happen. There was no way I was going to be beholden to Alan bloody Johnson. He must have driven past the house a dozen times and noticed men arriving or leaving. He may even have spied through the lounge window on several occasions, and finally decided to bring his camera along with a view to blackmailing me. I had to put a stop to this before it got out of hand.

'What else do you know about me?' I asked him. 'What has your poking your nose into my business unearthed?'

'I know enough,' he replied confidently, brushing his blond hair away from his grinning face. 'Enough to destroy your marriage. You used the word "adultery". You also mentioned "blackmail". They're ugly words, Cindy.'

'You're the blackmailer,' I returned.

'And you're the adulteress. This is an interesting situation. We're both guilty. Different crimes, but we're both guilty. As I said, the ball is in your court.'

'The photograph . . . how will I know that you've not kept a copy? You've already proved that you're a despicable, blackmailing bastard who thinks nothing of attempting to screw his friend's wife.'

'And what have you proved, Cindy?'

'One photograph of me in bondage gear is hardly proof of adultery. Look, this is getting us nowhere. Rod will be back soon. We'd better finalise this.'

'Finalise it, then,' he quipped.

Finalise it? Again wondering whether a blowjob would satisfy him, shut him up, I knew that I'd have no problem in sucking the spunk out of his knob. The notion excited me, dampened my spunk-wet schoolgirl knickers. But I didn't want to bow to pressure, to blackmail. There was nothing I liked more than a damned good mouth fucking, a crude throat spunking, but not with a gun pointed at my head.

'Finalise it,' he repeated, gazing into my blue eyes.

'How? By allowing you to fuck me and then hoping that you'll keep your side of the bargain? No, I don't think so.'

'It's up to you, Cindy. That's the offer: that's the deal. What have you done with the photograph?'

'Hidden it, of course.'

'Is that wise? What if Rod finds it?'

'He won't.'

'You should have destroyed it. Go and get it.'

'What?'

'I want to burn it, Cindy. I'll bring the original round in the morning, and you can destroy it. If you have a copy floating around and Rod finds it . . . we could both end up in the shit.'

'Both?'

'Don't you see? Your marriage will be over and . . . Rod will discover that I took the photograph. He's not going to think much of me, is he?'

'No doubt you'd lie your way out of it.'

'Neither of us wants to end up in the shit, Cindy. Go and get the photograph.'

Leaving him on the patio with a smug grin across his face, I slipped up to the bedroom and took the photograph from behind the wardrobe. He was right: I should have destroyed it. The chance of Rod discovering it was small, but it was a chance, all the same. after grabbing a box of matches from the kitchen drawer, I returned to the patio to my blackmailer.

Alan held his hand out to take the photograph, but I backed away. I said that I didn't want him gloating over the picture. He laughed and said that he'd already wanked as he'd stared at the photograph and pictured my sweet cunt. He then reassured me that there was only one copy and he'd bring the original round in the morning. But he wanted my sweet cunt in exchange. He wanted to fuck my sweet little cunt. I didn't like him, but I loved the way he talked dirty.

'Just the once,' he said. 'Just one good cunt fucking.'

'You don't have to tell me that it'll only be once,' I returned, clutching the photograph to my breast. 'And, when this is over, I never want you to come here again.'

'It's a deal, Cindy.'

'Right, I'm going to burn this,' I stated firmly. Hearing the front door shut, I froze.

'Rod's back,' Alan said. 'Give me the bloody photograph before . . .' He snatched the photograph and he stuffed it into his jacket pocket. 'You can burn them both in the morning,' he whispered.

'I don't trust you, Alan.'

'And Rod obviously can't trust you.' He chuckled. 'Talk of the devil,' he trilled as Rod emerged from the house. 'I was just saying how well you've done in the garden.'

'It is looking nice,' Rod said proudly. 'It's been a lot of work, but well worth the effort. Right, I'll fire up the barbeque.'

'And I'll pour the drinks,' I said, leaving my seat. 'The matches are on the table.'

Alan and Rod chatted and laughed as they messed about with the barbeque. I was in no mood for socialising. And I certainly wasn't going to have sex with Alan Johnson. I'd doublecross him, I decided. If I could get my hands on the photographs and burn them before . . . But he was sure to keep a copy. He was a horrible little man, but he wasn't stupid. This was a nightmare, and I could see no way out of it. But I now knew who the blackmailer was, and what he wanted. That was a start.

I kept a low profile for the next couple of hours. Not wanting to eat, I took a shower and then hovered in the lounge until Alan had gone. I couldn't believe that I'd been caught red handed. After five years of screwing around behind Rod's back, Alan Johnson, of all people, was threatening to destroy me. What made matters worse was that Alan not only worked with Rod, but was also a friend. How many more barbeques would he invite himself to? How many times would he happen to be passing the house and call in?

'You all right, love?' Rod asked, peering round the lounge door.

'Yes, I'm fine,' I replied.

'You seem quiet. I've hardly seen you all evening.'

'I'm sorry. I'm just a little tired, that's all. I'm pleased that Alan enjoyed the barbeque.'

'We'll have to invite him round again. Living alone can't be much fun.'

'Hasn't he got a lady friend?' I asked hopefully.

'No, no. Are you all right with him, Cindy?'

'What do you mean?'

'Oh, I don't know. I get the impression that you don't like him.'

'Whatever gave you that idea? I was feeling tired, that's why I came in here.'

'You haven't eaten. Shall I make you a sandwich or –'

'Rod, I'm fine,' I snapped unintentionally. 'I'm just tired, all right?'

Not wanting to chat with Rod, I went to bed early. My mind was in turmoil, my thoughts continually dragged back to Alan Johnson and the photograph. If I wasn't careful, Rod would realise that something was wrong, and I didn't want to have to endure his searching questions. I lay awake half the night thinking, scheming. But I planned nothing. Every idea I came up with, every time I thought that I'd got the answer, I realised that there were flaws. I was going to have to play this by ear. There was no other way.

Alan turned up at ten o'clock. Clutching a plain brown envelope, he followed me into the kitchen and suggested we have coffee. I felt beholden to him. I didn't have to be nice, friendly, but I did have to go along with him. Play the game? That's all it was to him, a game. He tossed the envelope on to the kitchen table as I poured the coffee. It was strange to think that the envelope held the key to my marriage, my future. A plain brown envelope, a photograph . . . That was all it would take to destroy my life. Alan was going to gloat, I knew as I passed him his coffee and pulled out the photographs. He was going to gloat, snigger . . .

'Not a bad shot,' he said smugly. 'What do you think?'

'I think many things, Alan,' I sighed. 'I think you're a bastard, I think –'

'Do you ever give Rod a thought?' he cut in, obviously twisting the knife. 'Do you ever think about your husband when you take other men's cocks into your dirty little cunt?'

'If you're going to be offensive –'

29

'Yes? If I'm going to be offensive, what will you do?'

'Shall we look upon this as a business arrangement? There's no necessity for rudeness or pleasantries. We have business to conduct, so let's get it over with.'

'As you wish,' he chortled. 'Why not begin by taking your clothes off?'

'No, Alan. I'll begin by burning the photographs.'

'I'd rather you –'

'What's the matter? Don't you trust me?'

'We're going to have to trust each other, Cindy. You go and burn the photographs, and I'll wait here for you.'

I grabbed the matches and left by the back door. I went to the end of the garden and set fire to the photographs. I watched the flames creeping over the pictures, destroying the evidence of my adultery. How the hell had I got myself into this predicament? I reflected as the flames died down. I'd never come anywhere close to a situation like this. Blackmail was the stuff of the movies; it couldn't be happening to me. Complacency had been my downfall.

Whether or not Alan had made copies of the photograph, I had no idea. Trust each other? I didn't know what to think as I made my way back to the house. I'd been looking forward to the summer, wearing miniskirts with no panties and having plenty of sex . . . Now? Alan had given me the evidence, and I now had to give him what he wanted in return.

'All done?' Alan asked me as I stepped into the kitchen.

'Yes,' I breathed. 'And now I'd like you to go.'

'Go?' he echoed. 'Oh no, Cindy. Not until I've had –'

'You're having nothing. What will you do if I don't keep my side of the deal? What will you do now that

I've destroyed the photographs? Or have you kept copies?'

'No, I haven't kept copies. Unlike you, I kept my word.'

'In that case, you have nothing on me.'

'I know that you're an adulterous whore, Cindy. But I didn't think that you'd do this.'

'You have a lot to learn, Alan. You dare to cross me, and you'll find yourself –'

'Talking to Rod?'

'What do you mean?'

'I mean, talking to Rod about your dirty secrets. I know far more about you than you realise. I was willing to accept sex in way of payment but –'

'Rod won't listen to you,' I cut in. 'Rod and I are the perfect couple. Everyone says how well matched we are, how happy we are. Do you really think that your sleaze attempt will sway Rod?'

'Do you want me for ever lurking, for ever spying? Do you want to have to look over your shoulder every time you entertain another man? I'll drop hints to Rod. I'll say that I've seen men at your door, different men coming and going. I'll mention in passing that I saw you walking into a bar with a young man and . . . Think about it, Cindy. I could cause a hell of a lot of problems for you.'

He was right, I knew. Dropping hints to Rod would cause problems; problems I could do without. Just one quick fuck, I decided. One quick fuck and . . . There was no point in trying to kid myself. Alan would be back for more. Once he'd driven his hard cock into my tight pussy and fucked me, he'd be round every day for more. I couldn't see that I had a choice, I mused. I either allowed Alan to fuck me, or faced huge problems with Rod.

'Come on, Cindy. What's it to be?' Alan asked me impatiently.

'All right,' I conceded. 'You win. Come into the dining room.'

'I knew you'd see sense,' he said and chortled triumphantly.

'I'm warning you, Alan. You play about with me, you try to come back for more, and you'll be very sorry.'

'You might want me to come back for more. After you've enjoyed a good length, you might beg me to come back.'

'Don't be ridiculous. I don't even like you, let alone fancy you. Shall we get this over with?'

'Why don't you begin by showing me your panties?'

'I'm not going to begin anything. The deal is that I allow you to fuck me. No foreplay, no messing about.'

After slipping my panties off, I stood with my feet wide apart and leaned over the table. I didn't want to see his face as he fucked me. I didn't want to see the satisfaction depicted in his expression as he pumped me full of his spunk. He had won, which riled me. He'd beaten me. Although he no longer had the photographs, he could plant seeds of doubt in Rod's mind. Things were fine with Rod. He worked hard and earned good money; I kept the house pristine . . . Alan could easily destroy everything I had, and I couldn't allow that to happen.

'Get it over with,' I ordered him, tugging my skirt up over my back.

'You have a beautiful little bum,' he remarked. 'You're a good-looking tart, Cindy.'

'Just do it,' I breathed, resting my head on the table and squeezing my eyes shut.

'I'll bet you're hot and tight. I'll bet –'

'I don't want to discuss it,' I snapped. 'Just get it over with.'

As he kneeled behind me and kissed the rounded cheeks of my bottom, I felt a quiver run through my pelvis. His fingertips running up and down my inner thighs, I knew that he was gazing at the swollen lips of my pussy rising alluringly either side of my opening sex crack. I was very wet. My juices oozed between my inner labia, and I wondered whether he'd lick me there. Would he lap up my pussy milk and drink from my adulterous cunt? The notion sent shudders through my womb, and my stomach somersaulted as his tongue ran up and down the deep gully of my firm buttocks.

Parting my buttocks wide, exposing my anus, he ran his tongue over the delicate brown tissue surrounding my anal whorl. I quivered, stifling my gasp of pleasure as he tongued me. I couldn't let him know what he was doing to me; the immense satisfaction his tongue was bringing me. He was a blackmailer, and I was the victim. But he was good; he knew exactly what to do. The tip of his wet tongue entered my tightly closed anal hole. He teased me there, tasting inside me.

Listening to the sound of his zip as he stood behind me, I wondered how many men had tugged their zips down in my house during my five-year marriage? How many cocks had I had shafting my tight pussy, ramming deep into my hot rectum? I'd always been careful to steer well clear of Rod's friends. I met my lovers in bars, shops, the park, anywhere and everywhere. But now? This was just another cock, I consoled myself. It was no big deal. Another man, another cock, another load of spunk pumped deep into my yearning pussy . . . How many cocks had I had?

Was Alan big? I wondered. Would he come quickly? Although I loved having sex with many different men, I shuddered as I felt his bulbous knob slip between the puffy lips of my pussy. My eyes squeezed shut, I gripped the sides of the table as his rock-hard shaft entered me, his solid knob journeying along the hugging sheath of my pussy until he'd impaled me completely. He *was* big, surprisingly big. For some reason, I'd imagined him to have a small cock. A horrible little man with a small cock. How wrong I was.

'You're tight,' he breathed, grabbing my hips as he withdrew slowly. 'And very wet. How many men have fucked you since you married Rod?'

'Shut up,' I spat. 'Just fuck me and then get out of my life. For good.'

'You love it, don't you?' he asked me, ramming his knob deep into the tight sheath of my pussy. 'You love a damned good fucking.'

Remaining silent as he repeatedly drove his huge cock deep into my wet pussy, I wondered why I'd never given a thought to Rod. He was happy, I mused. He knew nothing about my sexual exploits, so why give him a thought while I was fucking other men? None the wiser, he had no worries. It wasn't as if I was going to leave him for another man. Far from it, in fact. I had the best of both worlds. Not only did I have my cake, but I was scoffing it. I'd never leave Rod.

Listening to the squelching of my pussy juices as Alan fucked me with his massive organ, I felt my clitoris swell in response to his massaging shaft. My juices flowing freely from my pistoned pussy, I again consoled myself with the thought that a cock was a cock, no matter who the owner. But this was blackmail. In the past, I'd invited men to my house to fuck me. Now, I was being forced.

I stifled my gasps of pleasure as my inner lips slid back and forth along his huge shaft. Alan was big, his

34

massive organ stretching my pussy taut as he repeatedly rammed into me. I could feel his swinging balls battering the gentle rise of my mons, his lower stomach meeting my naked buttocks. My clitoris emerged fully from its pinken hide, and again I stifled a gasp of pleasure. I wasn't going to give Alan the satisfaction of knowing that my arousal was rocketing. My pussy muscles rhythmically contracting, lovingly hugging his huge shaft, I tried to think of anything and everything other than sex.

As Alan grunted and informed me that he was coming, I hoped that this was the end of the nightmare. I could feel his spunk filling me, lubricating our fucking. Never again, I mused, deciding to take a shower the minute he'd gone. Would he come back? Would he turn up on the doorstep clutching yet another copy of the incriminating photograph? *We're going to have to trust each other.* Could he be trusted? Did I want him to come back and fuck me again? I didn't know what I wanted as he drained his balls into my pussy.

'Now, get out of here,' I hissed as he slowed his thrusting motions. I'd have liked him to lick my clitoris to orgasm. 'And don't come back.' I'd never had the pleasure of such a huge cock.

'God, you're a tight-cunted little whore.' He chuckled, finally slipping his deflating cock out of my violated pussy. 'At last, I've fucked your dirty little –'

'Please leave, Alan,' I cut in, hauling my body upright. I loved his dirty talk. 'Go now, and never come back.'

'All right, all right.' He laughed.

I gazed at his flaccid cock, amazed by the sheer size of his organ. As I watched a cocktail of spunk and girl juice drip from his purple knob and land on the carpet, I'd have loved to have kneeled before him and sucked him clean, sucked him to orgasm. This was supposed to be a business arrangement, I reminded myself as a long strand of spunk left his knob slit and finally dropped to the floor. To suck the remnants of his spunk out of his cock would have been heavenly. But no.

'I enjoyed that,' he enlightened me, zipping his trousers. 'By the way, Rod suggested I join you for another barbeque.'

'No, Alan. You'll decline his offer and never come to this house again. Do you understand?'

'It'll be strange working with Rod knowing that I've fucked his wife. Whenever he mentions you, I'll picture my cock fucking your tight little cunt.'

'You're a vile man,' I hissed.

'You liked me tonguing your bumhole, didn't you?'

I loved it. 'No, I didn't. You're crude, you're disgusting . . .'

'You taste wonderful, Cindy. Would you like me to lick you there again?'

Yes . . . 'No.'

'I'll tell you what I'd really like to do. I'd like to push my cock deep into your sweet little arse and fuck you rotten.'

'Get out,' I yelled, trying not to lose control and beg him to mouth fuck me and throat spunk me and arse fuck me . . . 'Just get out.'

He sniggered as he walked to the front door. I could feel his spunk running down my inner thighs. A stark reminder of my side of the bargain: the payoff. But was it a payoff? Would he be back for more? It wasn't allowing Alan to use me for sex that bothered me. It was the sheer satisfaction in his expression, the thought that he had something on me, that pissed me off. He'd won, and was gloating. But his cock was so big and . . . I was drowning in my own confusion.

I ran my finger through the pool of spunk on the carpet. Creamy, lubricious ... Alan was a bastard, I reminded myself as my clitoris swelled. My pussy draining, a blend of spunk and pussy juice dripping on to the carpet, I recalled Rod once asking me what the white stain was on the dining room floor. I'd lied, said that I'd spilled some milk. He'd had no idea that it was a teenage boy's spunk. The lad had called at the house asking whether I'd like him to wash my car. He'd said that he'd wash the car for five pounds. He'd leaped at the chance when I'd suggested that he wash me for five pounds – with his tongue.

Climbing the stairs, I smiled as I recalled taking the lad into the dining-room and tugging his trousers down. His cock had stiffened quickly as I'd stroked the tight sac of his scrotum. Wanking his cock, fondling his teenage balls, I'd taken his purple knob into my thirsty mouth and sucked hard. He'd gasped as he looked down at me in amazement. A virgin, he'd never had the pleasure of mouth fucking a girl. He'd shaken uncontrollably as I'd taken his bulbous glans to the back of my throat and kneaded his young balls.

Slipping his cock out of my hot mouth, I'd licked his scrotum as I'd wanked his solid shaft. His spunk shot all over my face, dripped from my chin and pooled on the floor. Before his flow had stemmed, I'd taken his orgasming cock into my mouth and had sucked him dry before ordering him to leave. What must he have thought? Had he told his friends? They'd never have believed his story of a frustrated housewife sucking his cock.

My thoughts turning to Alan, all I could do was hope that I'd never see him again. But instinct told me that I'd not heard or seen the last of the bastard. Would I end up sucking his cock?

The phone rang while I was watching television with Rod that evening. My heart raced and my hands trembled as he answered it. Was it Alan Johnson? I hated feeling like this. Nervous, twitchy, tense ... Thankfully, it was Neil, Rod's brother. He wanted to call in on his way home from the tennis club. I wasn't in the mood for visitors, but Rod invited him round and I had no say in the matter.

There was tension between Rod and me, and I knew that it was coming from my side. Alan had been playing on my mind, and I'd let the housework go. Alan's tongue had been playing on my mind. The way he'd licked my bottom hole and tongued my rectal sheath ... And his cock was so big. I'd thought that I'd split open as he'd rammed his magnificent organ deep into my adulterous cunt. I had to stop thinking about Alan bloody Johnson.

Rod didn't comment, but he'd obviously noticed that the kitchen wasn't pristine as usual. There were magazines strewn across the sofa and I'd not taken out the empty coffee cups. Did he suspect anything? I wondered, trying to push all thoughts of Alan's massive cock out of my mind. Shit, everything was going wrong. It was most unlike me to have to clear up because we were expecting a visitor.

'Are you all right?' Rod asked me as I gathered up the magazines.

'Yes, I'm fine,' I lied. 'How was Alan today?'

'How was he? Well, er ... his usual self, I suppose. I told him that we'd invite him to our next barbeque. Living alone, he must –'

'He won't be coming to all our barbeques, will he?'

'No, of course not. As he's out on the road all day, it'll be handy having him round now and then. We'll be able to discuss business and –'

'I hope this isn't going to become a regular thing. I enjoy our time together, Rod. To have Alan here . . .'

'Cindy, I won't be inviting him round every evening. He's a friend, and we work together. You don't like him, do you?'

'It's not that I don't like him. I enjoy our time together, that's all.'

Again, I could feel tension between us. I knew that Alan Johnson would try to wheedle his way into our lives, and it riled me. What really annoyed me was that Alan had discovered my secret life. He'd always eyed me with a lecherous gaze, but that had never bothered me. Now, he was a serious threat. And that *did* bother me. I was losing control of the situation. Throughout my marriage, I'd been playing dangerous games. But I'd always won the games. I couldn't allow Alan to win.

When Neil arrived, I thought he seemed different towards me. He repeatedly looked at me, as if he was keeping an eye on me. I put it down to my imagination; I knew that I was wound up. What with Alan Johnson and the bloody photographs, I wasn't my usual bubbly self. I was going to have to put an end to this nightmare before it drove me crazy. There was no way I could live like this. Could I carry on seeing my secret lovers knowing that Alan was lurking, watching, spying? I certainly couldn't live without them, without their beautiful cocks.

Neil was older than Rod. He was happily married to Sue, an attractive woman of his own age. He wasn't bad looking. With dark hair and deep-set eyes, he was actually better looking than Rod. He was usually smiling and joking, having fun and enjoying life to the full. But something was bothering him. He knew nothing about me, I was sure. But I detected that something was wrong. Like me, he wasn't his usual bubbly self. What was it? Had he rowed with Sue? If he had, then it would be a first.

'How are things?' I asked him as Rod left the lounge to make the coffee.

'Keeping pretty busy,' he replied, his dark eyes locked to mine. 'And you?'

'I'm fine. How's Sue? We'll have to get together one evening.'

'Cindy, I need to talk to you,' he whispered mysteriously.

'Oh? What's the problem? Is Sue all right?'

'Yes, yes, she's fine. Is Rod working tomorrow?'

'Rod? Yes, of course he is. He works all day every day.'

'Will you be in tomorrow morning?'

'Er . . . yes, I think so. What is it, Neil? What's wrong?'

'I'll talk to you tomorrow.'

As Rod brought in the coffee, I felt that Neil knew something about me. I was becoming paranoid. Of course he didn't know anything. He'd never met Alan Johnson; he couldn't have known about my lovers or the photograph . . . So, why did he want to come round and talk to me when Rod was out? If he'd had a problem with Sue, he'd have talked to Rod as well as me. Intrigued, and worried, I didn't know what to think.

Things were going wrong for me. I'd thought that my lifestyle, albeit adulterous and deviant, was safe and secure. What with the Alan and his bloody photograph and now Neil's mysterious words, I felt that I was losing my grip. Even though I'd given Alan Johnson what he'd wanted, I still felt threatened by him. But there was no way I could give up my life of adulterous sex. Every time I met a man, I thought about his cock. It was almost an obsession. I'd look at men's trousers, picture their cocks, their heavy balls, and imagine sucking their knobs and swallowing their spunk.

Leaving Rod and Neil chatting in the lounge, I went up to my bedroom. I flopped on to the bed and closed my eyes. My life was fast becoming a mess. At least I'd destroyed the photographs. Were there more? Would Alan turn up again for coffee, and sex? I tried to forget about Alan bloody Johnson, and decided to visit Jilly in the morning.

But could I forget his beautiful cock?

Three

Rod had left for work; I'd cleared the breakfast things, and I felt good. I wasn't worried about Alan bloody Johnson. This was going to be a good day, I was sure. Neil's problems were probably to do with Sue, I'd decided. I'd been reading things into his words that weren't there. He wanted to have a chat with me. What was wrong or suspicious about that? He'd probably thought that it was best to talk to me, a woman, about his marital problems. Or he might have been worrying about Rod working too hard. Whatever it was, I was sure that it had nothing to do with my secret life.

He seemed jittery, uneasy, when he finally arrived. I made him a cup of coffee and chatted about the beautiful weather and the garden. But he wasn't listening. He paced the kitchen floor and wouldn't sit down and relax. He repeatedly looked at me as if he was about to say something. The suspense finally becoming too much to bear, I asked him what the problem was.

'Sex,' he said.

'Sex?' I echoed, cocking my head to one side in surprise. 'What about it?'

'I'll let you into a secret, Cindy,' he said, finally

settling at the table and sipping his coffee. 'I've been seeing someone else for over a year.'

'God,' I breathed, sitting opposite him. This was an incredible revelation. 'But, I thought that you and Sue were –'

'That's what everyone thinks. It's the same with you and Rod, isn't it?'

'What is?'

'Everyone believes that you're the perfect couple.'

'Well, we are. We couldn't be happier. Does Sue know about this other woman?'

'No, no.'

'Another woman?' I breathed incredulously. 'But, why? Why see another woman when you have Sue?'

'Sex. It's as simple as that. Sue is . . . I should say, Sue *isn't* particularly adventurous in bed. Don't get me wrong, we do have sex. Once a week, the same old position, the same old thing. She won't try anything out of the ordinary.'

'Such as?' I ventured, amazed by his frank disclosure.

'Such as oral sex. Such as anal sex. Such as –'

'Anal sex?' I gasped. 'That's not just out of the ordinary, Neil. Anal sex is –'

'What? What is it?'

'Well, it's . . .'

'Don't you have anal sex?'

Stunned by his question, I couldn't believe that this was my brother-in-law. Why tell me about his other woman? Why talk to me about anal sex? We'd always got on well together, but not to the point where we discussed anal sex. Toying with my coffee cup, I realised that I'd lost count of the cocks I'd had fucking my bum. The stretching sensations, the feel of my anal ring rolling back and forth along a solid shaft, the spunk cooling my bowels . . . Unlike his

43

brother, Neil was obviously into anything and everything. But, why tell me?

'I don't know what to say,' I finally murmured. 'You're going to have to sort this out, Neil. If Sue discovers –'

'You haven't answered my question,' he interrupted me. 'Don't you have anal sex?'

'Well, I . . . I don't want to discuss my sex life. What Rod and I do is private; it's our business.'

'Do you have oral sex?' he persisted. 'I'm only asking because Sue reckons that I'm abnormal. She can't bear the idea of taking my cock into her mouth.'

'Neil,' I gasped, holding my hand to my mouth. 'I really don't think –'

'It's a simple enough question, Cindy.'

'I suppose sex with Rod is . . . It's not all it could be.'

'It's not all you *want* it to be?'

'I didn't say that.'

'But, that's what you meant.'

His dark eyes locked on to mine. I wondered what he was thinking. Was he making moves towards me? I couldn't imagine him sneaking off to have sex with another woman. And I certainly couldn't imagine him pushing his cock into a girl's arse. He wasn't like that. There again, it seemed that he was. Oral sex, anal sex . . . Perhaps I should have married Neil instead of Rod. We thought along the same lines, enjoyed the same things . . . No, I couldn't allow Neil to become another of my sexual conquests. As much as I liked him, as good looking as he was, as tempting the thought, it would be a fatal mistake to embark on a sexual relationship with my brother-in-law. Besides, he already had another woman.

'You and I are two of a kind,' he said.

'How do you make that out?'

'I've always known that Rod isn't exactly over-sexed. And I've always had the notion that you are.'

'I'm not oversexed,' I returned indignantly. 'I enjoy sex, but I'm certainly not *over*sexed.'

'Aren't you?'

'No. For God's sake, Neil, I –'

'Cindy, I have a proposition.'

'If it's what I think it is, the answer is no. Neil, you're my brother-in-law.'

'So? We're not blood related. Besides, you haven't heard my proposition yet.'

'Go on, then. What is it?'

'The woman I'm seeing, I want to put an end to it.'

'That's probably a good idea.'

'But, if I do that, I won't have a decent sex life.'

'And? Where do I come into this? As if I can't guess.'

'I've always liked you, Cindy. You're young, attractive, sexual, sensual . . .'

'Cut the compliments and get to the point.'

'You and me. We'd be good together.'

'Neil, I can't believe that you're saying this. I'm your brother's wife. Your wife is my sister-in-law. God, talk about keeping it in the family.'

'Forget the ties for a minute. We both enjoy sex, real sex.'

'You don't know what I enjoy. You've talked about oral and anal sex. What makes you think that I want anal sex? With my brother-in-law, of all people.'

'Don't you?'

'Well, I . . . No, no, I don't. Look, I think we'd better forget that this conversation ever took place. Dump this woman you've got on the side and think of Sue and your marriage.'

'Haven't you ever been unfaithful to Rod? Haven't you ever been tempted, Cindy?'

45

'No, I . . . Of course I've looked at other men. We all have our private thoughts, Neil. But acting on them is another thing. It's adultery, for starters.'

'Have you ever been unfaithful to Rod?'

'No, no, I haven't.'

'Just give it a try, Cindy.'

'What?'

'Just this once.'

Although I was severely tempted, I couldn't allow myself to succumb to my feminine desires. Leaving the table, I gazed out of the window at the garden. We'd enjoyed many barbeques, many lovely evenings. Neil and Sue had often come round and we'd laughed and joked until the sun had gone down behind the trees. I'd destroy that if I allowed myself the pleasure of Neil's cock. We'd for ever be snatching chances to grope or fuck. It wouldn't work.

'I'm hard,' Neil said, standing next to me and pressing the solid bulge of his crotch against my hip. 'Hard and desperate for the feel of your hand.'

'Neil, what the hell's come over you?' I breathed, fighting my inner yearning.

'Feel me,' he whispered huskily.

'Neil, I –'

'Just feel me.'

Pressing the back of my hand against his bulge, I felt my stomach somersault. I couldn't believe that I was doing this. Groping my brother-in-law in the kitchen. I must have been mad. I'd had other men in the kitchen. Or, I should say, they'd had me. Over the table, up against the cooker . . . But this was Neil, my husband's brother. I had to fight, I had to win the battle raging in my tormented mind. If I pulled his cock out, if I wanked him or took his purple knob into my mouth and . . . As usual, I was weak in my arousal. As usual, I was a slut.

Tracing the outline of his solid cock, I squeezed his swollen knob. This was wrong, very wrong, but . . . I was already having trouble with Alan Johnson. To succumb to my brother-in-law would be a fatal mistake, only adding to my mounting problems. I could hear him breathing deeply as I kneaded his cock through his trousers. And I could feel my clitoris stiffening and my juices seeping between my swelling pussy lips. I had to fight; I had to fight myself.

Saying nothing, I tugged his zip down and hauled out his rock-hard cock. He let out a long sigh of pleasure as I wrapped my fingers around his fleshy shaft and squeezed gently. His cock was warm, long, hard, thick . . . Unable to control myself, I pulled his foreskin back and ran my thumb over his silky-smooth knob. The temptation to kneel before him and suck on his solid cock was overwhelming me, but I fought desperately to control my base instincts.

For the umpteenth time, I reminded myself that this was my brother-in-law; I shouldn't be doing this. Why was he allowing me to do this? Why had he asked me to do this? Had he no control over his sexual urges? Had his marriage gone so terribly wrong that he not only had another woman but was also coming to me for sex? What the hell had given him the idea that I'd be game for an affair? I wasn't game, I reflected. I had Ian and Richard and . . .

'Suck it,' he breathed shakily.

'Neil,' I murmured. 'I can't.'

'Please, Cindy. You've taken me this far. Why not –'

'Because it's wrong,' I cut in.

Wanking his shaft, massaging his ballooning knob through the fleshy hood of his foreskin, I felt my tight panties flooding with milky nectar. My nipples ripening, my young body trembling, I prayed for him to come quickly. Once he'd reached his orgasm, once my hand had filled with his creamy spunk, he'd zip his trousers and I'd be free of temptation. Or would I? Even after he'd come, I could easily kneel before him and taste his cream; suck the remnants of spunk out of his cock.

Wanking him faster, I finally brought out his spunk. I could feel his cream filling my hand, running over my fingers. I'd have loved to have sucked his cock and swallowed his spunk. He was my brother-in-law, my husband's brother, my ... Shit, I was wanking my brother-in-law's cock, splattering the kitchen floor with his spunk.

Squelching sounds echoed around the marital kitchen as I continued to move my hand up and down the solid shaft of his erect cock. His spunk running in rivers over my hand, his legs sagging, he leaned against the sink to steady himself as I retracted his foreskin fully and massaged his spunk into his orgasming knob. I'd done it, I thought happily, remorsefully. I'd actually wanked off my brother-in-law.

'God, I needed that,' he finally breathed.

'Neil, I want you to forget that this happened,' I said, releasing his cock and washing my hand in the sink. 'It was wrong. We shouldn't have –'

'Wrong? Why?'

'You know damned well why it was wrong. What would you think if Sue wanked off Rod?'

'I wouldn't know about it, would I? And no one knows about us.'

'Us?' I echoed, fearing the worst. There was no way I was going to strike up a relationship with him. 'We're not an item, Neil. We're not having an affair, OK?'

'If you say so. But, you must admit that you enjoyed wanking me.'

'No, I . . . I don't know why I did it.'

'You did it because you wanted to.'

'I didn't want to,' I returned angrily. 'You caught me at a time when –'

'When you were feeling horny?'

'No.'

'Don't mess me about, Cindy. You've had other men, so why not have me?'

Paralysed by his words, I felt my heart race, my hands tremble. *You've had other men* . . . What the hell did he mean by that? What did he know about me, about my secret life? No one knew of my secret sex life, my many male lovers. He was guessing, I was sure as I filled the kettle. Making out that I'd not heard what he'd said, I offered him another cup of coffee. But he wasn't going to drop the subject.

'You've had other men,' he repeated.

'Other men?' I echoed, forcing a laugh. 'What *are* you talking about?'

'Cindy, all I'm asking is that we meet now and then for sex. I could come here or you could come to my place.'

'All you're asking is that we meet now and then for sex? Neil, it's adultery. And, to make matters worse, I'm your sister-in-law.'

'We've already been through that. So, you're my sister-in-law? What of it?'

'You're talking as if you're planning to call in for a cup of coffee.'

'Cindy, don't make me . . . I don't see what your problem is.'

'Don't make you what?'

'You've already committed adultery.'

Sure that he knew something about me, I poured the coffee and tried to come across as calm. *You've already committed adultery*. What did he mean by that? Was he talking about my wanking him? Or was he talking about something else? I was going to have to play this very carefully. Wishing that I'd not succumbed to my inner craving and touched his knob, wanked his beautiful cock to orgasm, I decided to turn the situation round.

'Unless you stop this, I'll talk to Sue,' I threatened him.

'And I'll talk to Rod,' he countered.

'What about? Surely you're not planning to tell him that I wanked you?'

'No, not that.'

'What, then?'

'I'll leave you with this thought, Cindy. I know that you're into bondage.'

'What?'

'I don't want another coffee. I'll be seeing you.'

'Neil, wait a minute,' I called as he headed for the front door. 'Neil . . .'

As he left, I leaned on the table to steady myself. My legs like jelly, my hands trembling, my heart banging hard against my chest, I went over his words again and again. *I know that you're into bondage.* How the hell did he know about that? As far as I was aware, he'd never met Alan Johnson. He knew nothing about my private life. Was he guessing? No, he couldn't have been. He knew something about my secret life, there was no doubt about it.

I paced the kitchen floor, my chest tight with anxiety. I bit my lip as I wondered what to do. It was pretty obvious that Neil wasn't going to give up. He wanted sex, and reckoned that he was going to get it. My mind in turmoil, I again wished that I'd not touched his cock. I also wished that I'd not allowed Alan to blackmail me. I should have . . . Hindsight was useless. I had to turn my thoughts to the future and make my plans.

The phone rand and, on answering it, I was horrified to hear Alan's voice. He said that he needed to talk to me and that he'd be round in ten minutes. I told him where to go, said that I didn't want anything to do with him, but he took no notice. Did he have copies of the photograph? Had he talked to Neil and shared my dirty secret with him? Banging the phone down, I decided not to answer the door when he called. But I had to discover what it was that he wanted.

I reckoned that this was the worst day of my life. I couldn't understand how I'd got myself into this situation within such a short time. Five years of playing around, five years of deceiving, lying, cheating, screwing, spunk swallowing ... And then threatened with ruination within a matter of days. When the doorbell rang out, I dashed through the hall and let Alan in. This was my chance to deal with him once and for all, I decided, leading him into the lounge. This was going to end, immediately.

'What the hell do you want?' I snapped.

'There's no need to be like that, Cindy,' he returned. 'I was in the area so –'

'I told you that I never wanted to see you again.'

'I had a chat with Rod this morning,' he said mysteriously.

'Oh?'

'Quite a long chat.'

'And?'

'He's suspicious, Cindy. Very suspicious.'

'What do you mean?' Suspicious? 'What the hell are you talking about?'

'He reckons that you're up to something.'

'What have you told him? If you've said anything about us –'

'I haven't said a word about us. In fact, Rod did

all the talking. He said that he's going to start keeping an eye on you.'

'What? Why on earth would he do that? And why tell you?'

'We're friends, Cindy. He opened up and . . . It's all right, you don't have anything to worry about.'

'Don't I? What makes you think that?'

'Because I said that I'd keep an eye on you.'

'*You?*'

'Cindy, he reckons that you're playing around. I said that the idea was ridiculous, but he's got it into his head that you're cheating on him.'

'But . . .'

'I said that I'd keep an eye on the house and even go to the trouble of calling in now and then.'

'I don't want you calling in now and bloody then.'

'It's either that, or Rod will drop in on the odd occasion. Unannounced.'

'Shit. This is your doing, Alan. Had you kept your nose out of my business –'

'And my cock out of your pussy?' He sniggered. 'It's no good blaming me, Cindy.'

'Why are you telling me all this?'

'I thought you ought to know. As I said, you have nothing to worry about. I'll tell Rod that I've called round when I've been passing and everything has been fine. Of course, your future all depends on what I say to Rod. If I say that I've seen a man –'

'Do you know Rod's brother? His name's Neil.'

'I've met him at the office a couple of times. Why?'

'Have you said anything to him about me?'

'Why would I say anything to Neil?'

'You tell me.'

'I've not said anything to anyone. I'll keep Rod happy, so you'll have no worries.'

'And what do you want in return? As if I don't know.'

'In return for saving you from divorce? The odd blowjob would suffice.'

'Don't be vulgar.'

'I'll rephrase that. Oral sex would suffice.'

'If you think that I'm going to –'

'I'm a man of my word. I haven't kept copies of the photograph, and I'm willing to lie to Rod to save your marriage. The choice is yours, Cindy.'

'And if I tell you to go to hell?'

'Let's not be negative. Rather than look on the black side, look on the bright side. You'll be free to cheat on your husband. Rod always lets me know what's going on at the office. If he has to go out, he rings me. Should he decide to come home early or call home during the day, he'll let me know and I'll be able to warn you. It's a good deal, Cindy. You think about it.'

He was right, it *was* a good deal. To be warned when Rod was leaving the office during the day or when he was coming home early would be a great advantage. I'd have time to get rid of my lover, time to pull my panties up and veil my spunk-oozing sex crack. But I'd be for ever beholden to Alan, and I didn't want that. Did I have a choice? What was the alternative? To have Alan fire Rod's suspicion? Weighing up the pros and cons, I tried not to take the size of Alan's cock into consideration. But I have to admit that I was swayed by his massive organ.

'All right,' I finally conceded. 'You have a deal.'

'Good. As I'm here, we might as well start now.'

'Now? But I –'

'Now, Cindy.'

As he slipped his trousers and shorts off, I gazed in awe at the sheer size of his erect cock. The shaft was long, solid, broad, topped with a beautifully swollen knob, which glistened invitingly in the light. His balls were huge, heavy, fully laden. Settling on the sofa with his thighs wide apart, his balls hanging invitingly off the edge of the cushion and his cock standing to attention, he grinned at me. He knew that I wanted his cock, he knew that I wouldn't hesitate to suck his knob into my wet mouth and drink his spunk. But I wasn't going to show my eagerness. Kneeling before him, watching his balls heave and roll within their fleshy sac, I told him that I didn't want to do this.

'Of course you do,' he returned with a chuckle. 'You can't resist such a fine specimen, and you know it.'

'I'm only doing this because –'

'Come on, Cindy. You don't have to lie to me. You want my cock, so take it.'

'I'm not a slut, Alan.'

'I didn't say you were.'

I grabbed his firm shaft by the base and leaned forwards, running my tongue over the velveteen surface of his swollen glans and tasting his salt. He was right, I couldn't resist such a fine specimen. But I wanted to suck a cock to bring mutual pleasure, not in way of a blackmail payoff. How many times did he intend to call round for a blowjob? I wondered, as I took his purple plum to the back of my throat and sank my teeth gently into the warm flesh of his veined shaft. How many times did he plan to mouth fuck me each week?

Slipping his knob out of my mouth, I ran my wet tongue up and down his shaft. I moved down, nibbling and licking his scrotum. His balls heaved, rolled as I snaked my tongue over his fleshy sac. Breathing deeply, he let out a moan of pleasure as I sucked a ball into my hot mouth. I breathed in the male scent of his pubic curls as I mouthed on his testicle. I felt my clitoris stiffen, my juices of desire seeping between the swelling lips of my cock-hungry pussy. How many times each week did I want him to mouth fuck me?

Again taking his knob into my mouth and allowing my saliva to run down his fleshy shaft, I bobbed my head up and down. He let out gasps of pleasure, his cock twitching, his knob swelling, as I deftly performed the illicit oral act. I'd sucked a hundred or more cocks, swallowed copious quantities of fresh spunk. And yet, every time I took a swollen knob into my thirsty mouth, it was as exciting and satisfying as the first. I was a slut, and I couldn't deny it. A cum-slut?

Alan talked to me as I sucked and mouthed on his beautiful knob. He said that I was a good cock sucker, that I knew how to please a man. He asked me whether my cunt was wet, whether I'd had Rod's cock spunking up my cunt recently. I liked the way he talked to me, his dirty words, his crude comments, his decadence. He said that he'd like to give me a breast job, spunk all over my hard tits. My womb contracting as I listened to his dirty talk, I ran my wet tongue up and down his shaft, licked beneath the rim of his crown. I wanted him in my pussy, my bum, fucking me, spunking me ... But I couldn't come across as a dirty, filthy slut.

Again I took his knob to the back of my throat. I kneaded his heavy balls and moaned softly through my nose. I wanted his fresh creamy spunk flooding my mouth. Sliding his cock out, taking his glans between my full lips, I tongued his spunk slit. He said that he'd spank my bottom if I didn't swallow every last drop of his spunk. Was he into spanking? Did he know how much I enjoyed playing the role of a naughty little virgin schoolgirl and having my naked buttocks smacked?

'I'm going to enjoy my visits,' he breathed, clutching my head as his body became rigid. 'Fucking your pretty mouth, spunking down your throat . . . Rod's wife sucking my cock, desperate to drink my spunk . . . Who would have believed it?'

His body trembling, he gasped and gripped my head tighter as his spunk gushed from his throbbing glans and bathed my snaking tongue. Sucking hard and repeatedly swallowing his cream, I drank from his beautiful knob as he writhed and gasped in his illicit orgasm. I gripped the shaft of his huge cock, and bobbed my head up and down, mouth fucking myself with his solid organ as I drank the fruits of his loins. He was man, all man. And I was a cum-slut.

I thought about Rod as I committed oral adultery in the marital lounge. He'd be at the office, working hard, oblivious to my lewd behaviour. With Alan keeping an eye on me, calling in now and then to make sure that I wasn't being unfaithful, Rod would have no worries. But I was going to have to be careful, play my dirty sex games safely. Turning my thoughts to Neil, I wondered where that road would take me. He knew something about me, but what? Bondage? Why had he mentioned that? Swallowing the last of Alan's spunk, I slipped his deflating cock out of my mouth and locked my eyes to his. Had Alan spoken to Neil?

'You're good,' he breathed shakily.

'I know I am,' I replied. 'I think you'd better go now.'

'If I'm around tomorrow morning . . .'

'I'm not in tomorrow, Alan. It would be best if you rang first. I can't have you turning up as and when it takes your fancy.'

'No problem,' he agreed, standing and tugging his trousers up. 'Our little arrangement is going to work very well.'

'I hope so.'

'You enjoyed that, didn't you?' he asked me, flashing me a knowing smile.

'Yes,' I murmured. There was no point in lying.

'I liked the way you sucked my ball into your pretty little mouth. Licking my cock, sucking my knob . . . You're damned good, Cindy.'

'You've already told me that. Please go now, Alan.'

'I'll be in touch, OK?'

'OK.'

As he left the house, I licked my spunk-glossed lips and gazed out of the lounge window. Alan walked down the drive with a spring in his step. He was obviously a very happy man, I reflected. And so he should be. After all, he had an extremely good deal. Was I happy? Did I have a good deal? Wandering off the familiar path I'd followed for many years, I felt that I was entering unchartered waters. Had I lost my bearings? Where was I heading?

I spent the rest of the day moping about, mooching around the house. My mind was unsettled, and I didn't like it. I felt as if I'd lost control of my life. Neil's mention of bondage had unnerved me; Alan's deal worried me; and Rod's suspicion hung over me like a heavy rain cloud. When Rod came home and dumped his briefcase on the hall table, I tried to come across as normal. But it wasn't easy. Offering him a scotch, I realised that I'd not prepared the evening meal. So much for normality.

'Sorry,' I breathed softly as he wandered into the kitchen and stared at the barren cooker. 'I've not been feeling very well.'

'Are you all right?' he asked me, his dark eyes showing concern.

'Yes, yes. I've just been feeling a little tired,

drained. I can't think why. What would you like to eat?'

'Don't worry, love. I'll ring for a take-away. By the way, Neil came into the office this afternoon.'

'Oh?' I tried not to show my shock. 'What did he want?'

'I think he was hoping to see Alan.'

'Alan? Why would he want to see him?'

'I don't know. I think he's got something on his mind.'

'Neil or Alan?'

'Neil. He seemed worried. Mind you, Alan was in a funny mood today. He was asking me what you do all day, whether you have many visitors.'

'How odd. I wonder why he wants to know about me?'

'He might be coming round later to drop off some paperwork, so you can ask him.'

This was all I needed. Bloody Alan Johnson stirring things up, asking Rod questions . . . And why the hell did he want to come round? He was obviously trying to get his foot in the door, and I didn't like it. Drop off some paperwork? He was going to gloat, I knew. He'd grin at me, wink and make odd facial expressions behind Rod's back. We'd come to an arrangement, and I wasn't going to put up with any nonsense.

'What time is Alan coming round?' I asked Rod.

'I don't know. He just said that he'd call in later.'

'I think I'll go out for a walk. The fresh air might do me some good.'

'What, now?'

'I have a terrible headache, Rod. You order yourself a curry and I'll see you later.'

'Aren't you going to eat?'

'No, no. I might have something when I get back.'

'All right. love. I'll see you later.'

I grabbed my bag and left the house, with no idea of where I was going. But I had to get out, get away from Rod – and Alan. Walking down the street with the early evening sun warming me, I made my way to a local pub. Rod didn't like pubs. He was all for going to a restaurant, but pubs were out of the question as far as he was concerned. He didn't like the atmosphere, the smell of beer, the loud talk and laughter . . . Unlike me.

I ordered a vodka and orange, sat on a bar stool and looked around the pub. There were half a dozen men chatting and joking. They'd probably called in for a quick one on their way home from work. Their wives would be preparing dinner, trying to keep the kids under control. They'd have been shopping, doing housework . . . That wasn't for me, I mused, returning a young man's smile. I did shopping and housework, of course. But there was far more to my day than mundane tasks. I also entertained men.

Sipping my drink, I lowered my eyes and focused on the crotch of the young man's trousers. Was he big? Were his balls full? I was wearing my short summer dress, my naked thighs exposed to his gaze. What was he thinking? What images were looming in his male mind? My naked body? My bared pussy? Did he want to fuck me? I prided myself on knowing what the majority of men liked. A glimpse of panties, the triangular patch of material bulging with my full sex lips, my braless nipples pressing through my flimsy blouse, my deep cleavage exposed . . . Was this young man in the majority?

He couldn't take his eyes off me. Staring at my thighs, he was oblivious to the conversation going on around him. In his mid-thirties with dark hair cascading over his forehead, he wasn't bad looking. Was he married? I wondered, again eyeing the

59

inviting bulge of his crotch. What would it take to shatter his marriage vows? How easily would he fall prey to his base male instincts and slip into the alluring pit of adultery?

I'd pulled many young men in pubs, I reflected. Rod and I once went to a friend's birthday do in a pub. After a few vodkas, I was game for anything, and more than ready for adulterous sex. Rod got talking to someone so I responded to a young man's winking eye and followed him through the side door into the beer garden. In the bushes, I kneeled before him and pulled out his cock. The taste of salty spunk blended with vodka was heavenly.

During that eventful evening, while Rod was busy chatting, I sucked off a total of three men. I didn't know them, and they weren't part of the birthday group. I'd never lure our male friends into crude sexual acts. That would be far too risky. Strangers who were giving me the eye, gazing at my naked thighs, focusing on my ripe nipples pressing through the thin material of my blouse . . . They were the men lucky enough to mouth fuck and throat spunk me.

I wondered whether Alan had arrived, what he was saying to Rod. I grinned at the young man. I was about to make my move, lick my lips provocatively and entice my victim over, when the door swung open. Turning, I was horrified to see Neil walking towards me. What the hell did he want? How did he know where to find me? Composing myself, I smiled at him, trying to appear nonchalant, innocent. He eyed my naked thighs and asked me what I was doing in the pub.

'Having a drink,' I replied nonchalantly.

'Without Rod?' he asked me.

'Rod's waiting in for someone. I was out for a walk and decided that a vodka and orange would go down well. What are you doing here?'

'I was passing and –'

'Without Sue?'

'I saw you come in here, Cindy.'

'And you thought you'd join me?'

'We need to talk.'

'Again?' I asked as he ordered a beer. 'What are we going to talk about this time? Bondage?'

'Yes, amongst other things.'

'Neil, I don't want to talk about bondage, anal sex, oral sex –'

'Cindy, I suggest you listen to me. Keep that pretty little mouth of yours shut for a few minutes and listen.'

'OK, I'm listening.'

'What we did this morning . . . I want more.'

'But –'

'And you're going to give me more. We're going to come to a nice little arrangement.'

'No, we're not,' I cut in angrily. 'As I said this morning, I'm your sister-in-law and –'

'I told you to keep your pretty little mouth shut.'

'Neil, if you're going to be rude to me –'

'I know things about you,' he whispered, glancing at the group of young men.

'Such as?'

'You'd do well to keep on the right side of me. Look, I don't want to cause trouble. We've always got on well, so let's not spoil it.'

'I'm not spoiling anything,' I returned. 'I was sitting here enjoying a quiet drink . . .'

'And eyeing up those men?'

'Neil, I think you'd better tell me what this is all about. What do you know about me? And what's all this nonsense about bondage?'

'As I said, I don't want to cause trouble. But, unless you give me more, I'll have no choice.'

'Cause trouble? What are you talking about?'

'That's just it, I don't want to have to talk about it. You're an attractive girl, Cindy. Far better looking than Sue. You enjoyed what we did this morning, didn't you?'

'It was a mistake. You caught me at a bad time.'

'I caught you at a good time, I'd say. I'll call in tomorrow morning, OK?'

'No, it's not OK. Neil, I don't want to have an affair with you. Can't you get that into your head?'

'Don't force me to –'

'To what? I do wish you'd stop talking in riddles. Are you threatening me?'

'Yes, I am.'

'With what?'

'That's just it, Cindy. I don't want to have to tell you. I'll be round to see you tomorrow morning.'

As he downed his beer and walked out of the pub, I felt anger welling in the pit of my stomach. What the hell did he know about me? Why wouldn't he come out with it? He'd threatened me, but with what? I instinctively knew that, unless I had sex with him, I'd be in trouble. It was obvious that he wasn't bluffing. He knew something about me, my private life, and would probably talk to Rod unless I agreed to his demands.

After finishing my drink and leaving the pub, I walked to the park and sat by the pond. I had some serious thinking to do. My life was becoming a mess; confusion was beginning to reign. Reckoning that Alan had shown Neil the photograph, I was sure that it wouldn't be long before Rod was told about my illicit double life. The choice was mine: I either had sex with my brother-in-law, and kept Alan bloody Johnson happy, or I could say goodbye to my marriage. For five years, I'd played around, enjoyed man after man, cock after cock . . . What the hell had gone wrong?

Four

Rod had enjoyed his breakfast and kissed my cheek before going to work. He'd seemed fine, far from suspicious. He'd not minded my taking a walk the previous evening and had even fussed over me when I'd got home. I'd been fortunate enough to have missed Alan Johnson. But I knew that he'd be in touch before long. He'd want to come round, pull his cock out and mouth fuck me. I wasn't too bothered about Alan, and Rod was behaving normally. It was Neil I was concerned about.

I'd thought about wearing jeans and a T-shirt for Neil's visit. I'd not wanted to look tartish and have him think that I was giving him the come-on. But I changed my mind. It was a beautiful summer day, so why the hell shouldn't I wear what I liked? I decided to be myself and wear what I'd normally wear on such a warm day, dressing in a red miniskirt and loose-fitting blouse. But I couldn't help myself as I eyed my reflection in the dressing-table mirror. I couldn't resist the temptation to take my bra off.

I had a beautiful pair of firm tits topped with elongated nipples. As I leaned forwards, my blouse fell open, leaving the brown teats of my breasts clearly visible. Why hide beauty? I mused. Besides, I enjoyed the feeling of my blouse brushing against my nipples. I also enjoyed watching men watching me. They'd stare, trying to glimpse my tits as I moved about. I was an expert at flashing my tits, leaning forwards and *inadvertently* displaying my ripe milk teats. There again, I was supposed to be trying to put Neil off the idea of having sex with me. But the excitement, the danger, my soaring arousal . . . I was powerless in my weakness.

Neil turned up at ten o'clock and made himself comfortable in the lounge. What was on his mind? I pondered. What was he up to? Again, I asked him what he knew about me. He seemed awkward, embarrassed, and wouldn't talk about it. I didn't pursue the matter as there seemed little point. Besides, I didn't like playing mind games. He could keep his secret, whatever it was.

It seemed strange to think that this was my brother-in-law threatening me. Sitting on the sofa, looking me up and down, this was the man I'd known for over five years. He'd come to our barbeques, birthday celebrations, Christmas dinners . . . After focusing on the sensitive teats of my erect nipples clearly defined by the silk material of my blouse, he lowered his eyes to my miniskirt and gazed at my naked thighs. He was part of the family, and yet he was becoming part of my private life, my secret life. He was no longer like a brother-in-law. Changes were taking place.

'What did Alan Johnson say about me when you went to the office yesterday?' I finally asked him.

'Alan wasn't there,' he replied, his dark eyes locked to the deep ravine of my cleavage.

'You went to see him. Why?'

His eyes left my cleavage and looked up at me as I stood before him. 'Cindy, I called into the office to see Rod. Why are you worried about Alan?'

'I'm not worried about him. How well do you know him?'

'Not very well. Look, I haven't come here to talk about Alan.'

'Then, why have you come here?'

'I'm not going to beat about the bush, Cindy.'

'That'll make a change.'

'We're going to enjoy a sexual relationship. Before you say anything –'

'I wasn't going to say a word.' I had to appear confident. 'Carry on.'

'You and I are two of a kind, Cindy. We both enjoy sex to the full. As I told you, I have someone on the side. And you've had flings, haven't you?'

'I'm not saying anything.'

Sitting in the armchair opposite him, I knew that I was coming across as relaxed and confident. My short skirt and naked thighs gave me a sense of power. Whatever Neil knew about me, whatever he'd thought that he'd unearthed, I didn't care. There was no way he could have discovered my male lovers. He might have guessed that I was up to something behind Rod's back, but he had no proof. He might have mentioned the word 'bondage' to gauge my reaction. He was testing the water, probing, searching.

'You wore a short skirt at Christmas,' he said, eyeing my naked thighs as I reclined in the armchair. 'I remember glimpsing your panties.'

'Really?' I murmured. 'How fascinating.'

'You were giving me the eye, Cindy. I would have made a move, but . . .'

'But what?'

'I had nothing on you then. Now I know things about you, now that I've discovered –'

'Neil, I don't have a great deal of time,' I sighed. 'I have to go to the bank and do some shopping. I'd love to stay and chat with you, but I've a pretty busy day ahead.'

'I'm sure you can make time to repeat yesterday's performance,' he said, standing and moving towards me.

I felt my womb contract as he unzipped his trousers and hauled out his erect cock. He had such a beautiful cock. Long, hard, thick, suckable ... Cocks had been my downfall, I reminded myself. Downfall? Cocks had never got me into trouble before, I reflected, wondering once more how many I'd sucked. To outsiders, I was a happily married woman. To family and friends, I was a faithful, loyal and very loving wife. In truth, I was a dirty little tart.

Standing before me, Neil jutted his hips forwards and presented his organ to me. Hauling out his full balls, he looked down at me with expectation reflected in his dark eyes. He was desperate to feel the wet heat of my mouth encompassing his swollen knob, my tongue exploring his spunk slit. And I was desperate to drink from his fountain head, desperate to swallow his spunk. My clitoris stirring, I knew that I had to fight my inner desires. To embark on a sexual relationship with my husband's brother would lead to trouble, I kept reminding myself.

'As I said,' I began, checking my watch, 'I really don't have a great deal of time.'

'Time enough,' he breathed. 'Besides, you can't resist a hard cock.'

'You're right, Neil, I can't resist a hard cock.'

'So, what are you waiting for?'

'I can't resist my husband's hard cock. He's far bigger than you. Did you know that?'

'Suck it, Cindy. If you don't –'

'Yes? What will happen if I don't suck it?'

'If you don't, then I'll be forced to talk to Rod.'

'Don't start that again, Neil,' I sighed. 'You repeatedly make idle threats, but you won't say exactly what it is you're threatening me with. Now, if you'll excuse me?'

'How's this for an idle threat? If you don't suck my cock, I'll tell Rod about the photograph.'

'Photograph?' I echoed, my heart banging hard against my chest. I had to appear unnerved. 'What photograph?'

'The one I have in my possession. The one of you in bondage gear.'

I couldn't believe that Alan had given Neil a copy of the incriminating evidence. How could he have doublecrossed me like that? We'd made a deal, come to an arrangement – and the bastard had betrayed me. This was fast becoming a nightmare. I now had two men threatening me, blackmailing me to have sex with them. This was Neil, my brother-in-law. What sort of man was he? Unscrupulous, cheating, two-timing . . . Were we two of a kind? Unsure what to say, I thought it best to play innocent.

'Bondage gear?' I breathed, frowning at him. 'I don't know what you're talking about.'

'You know very well, Cindy,' he said and chuckled triumphantly, running his hand up and down the veined shaft of his solid cock. 'I didn't want to have to mention it. It's not a nice subject.'

'What isn't?' I asked him, persisting futilely with my innocence.

'Do you want me to show Rod the photograph?'

'Neil . . .'

'Or are you going to suck my cock?'

Gazing at his rock-hard organ, I didn't know what to say. Unable to believe that my brother-in-law was blackmailing me, I wondered whether Alan had more photographs of me with other men. How many times had he lurked outside the house when I'd been entertaining my male visitors? How many times had he gazed through the lounge window? How many bloody photographs had he taken? He might have been compiling a dossier of evidence against me over several months. How many photographs had he given to Neil? Until I came up with a plan, until I found a way to sort this out, I had to play along with Neil.

'I'll be honest with you,' I said softly, focusing on his swollen knob, 'I have no idea what you're talking about, but I can't deny that I've always fancied you. At Christmas, I deliberately exposed my panties hoping that you'd make a move. Yesterday, when I held your cock in my hand ... You know that I want you, don't you?'

'Yes, I do.'

'I've always wanted you.'

I wrapped my fingers around his hard shaft, and ran my hand up and down his cock. He had a copy of the photograph, and he was blackmailing me, but I didn't want him to think that I'd submitted to his threat. I had to keep in with him, keep him on side. But I didn't want him to believe that I felt beholden to him. My thinking was going crazy. Of course I was beholden to him, and he knew it. He knew damned well that I had no choice. I suck his cock, or say goodbye to my marriage.

Wanking his rock-hard cock, watching his purple knob appear and disappear as I moved his foreskin back and forth, I wondered whether he'd carry out his threat. Would he tell Rod about me? Would he ruin my marriage by showing Rod the photograph? Although I'd known Neil for over five years, I realised that I didn't know him at all. I'd never dreamed that he'd blackmail me, that he'd stand in my lounge demanding that I suck his cock. I didn't know Neil at all, and had to be very careful. Did his wife know him? No, she didn't.

Sue, my sister-in-law, was a lovely person, good company, fun to be with . . . and she had a lying, cheating husband. I was a lying, cheating wife but, in my mind, my infidelity was different. I had sex with other men because I enjoyed sharing my body. To me, my playing around wasn't betrayal or adultery. I was enjoying my individuality, my young body, my life. And I'd never leave my husband. Neil simply wanted to use me to deposit his spunk. Would he leave Sue?

'So, you remember Christmas?' I said, wrapping both hands around his cock shaft. 'I hope Sue didn't realise that I was flashing my panties at you.'

'Had I made a move . . . Would you have –'

'I went out into the garden twice hoping that you'd follow me.'

'I didn't know.'

'Then, it was your loss. I was ready for you, Neil. I wanted you, and you ignored me.'

My mouth watered as I wanked my brother-in-law's cock. I leaned forwards and sucked his purple knob into my spunk-thirsty mouth. Running my wet tongue around the rim of his crown, savouring the salty taste, I thought it strange that this was the very cock that had fucked Sue. Had she sucked Neil's knob? Had she mouthed and gobbled on his ripe plum and swallowed his spunk? Sue and I had never discussed sex. And I'd never dreamed that we'd be sharing the same cock. The notion excited me, wetted my panties.

Neil gasped and trembled, but said nothing as I moved my head back and forth, repeatedly taking his bulbous glans to the back of my throat. What was he thinking? Had he imagined fucking my mouth since the day he'd met me? Had he pictured the full lips of my pussy when he'd glimpsed my panties? Had he thought about my naked body when he'd fucked Sue? More to the point, had he spied through the window and watched me performing my cock sucking with other men?

Kneading his heavy balls as I wanked his shaft and mouthed on his ballooning knob, I wondered how the atmosphere would be the next time he called round with Sue; the four of us chatting as we enjoyed a barbeque, laughing and joking . . . Neil and I would flash knowing glances at each other while our partners were left in the dark. Ignorant, naïve, oblivious to our adultery. Neil and I would keep our dirty little secret under wraps, our partners never discovering the shocking truth. Would he try to grope me whenever he had the chance? Would I grab the bulging crotch of his trousers when no one was around?

The thought of slipping into the lounge and sucking his cock and swallowing his spunk excited me. We'd make some excuse or other to leave Rod and Sue on the patio, and then sneak away to enjoy an illicit mouth fucking. I was a tart, and I couldn't deny it. But was I so terrible? I mused, gobbling on his purple plum. As long as Rod didn't know about my secret life, my dirty life, then we'd remain the happy couple. But my secret life was under threat.

The phone rang as Neil's spunk flowed into my mouth and bathed my tongue. Bobbing my head up and down, wanking his granite-hard shaft and kneading his rolling balls, I wondered who the caller was. Rod hardly ever rang during the day. It might be Jilly, I mused, as I swallowed down my brother-in-law's spunk. It was about time we got together for a chat over coffee.

'That was amazing,' Neil gasped as I sucked the last of his orgasm and swallowed hard. 'We should have got together years ago. I didn't ignore you at Christmas. I just didn't realise that you wanted me. I didn't even know that you went into the garden.'

'Be quiet,' I whispered, grabbing the phone.

'Cindy, it's me,' Alan said as I pressed the receiver to my ear. 'Rod's on his way home.'

'What, now?'

'Yes.'

'Shit. OK, thanks.'

'Cindy, I need to talk to you.'

'And I need to talk to you. How dare you . . . I'll speak to you later.'

'What was that about?' Neil asked, zipping his trousers as I hung up.

'Er . . . nothing. Just a friend of mine. Look, you'd better go.'

'Which friend?' he persisted. 'A man?'

'It was Jilly, if you must know. She's coming round for coffee.'

'I wouldn't mind a cup of coffee. I haven't seen Jilly for ages, so –'

'Neil, please go now.'

'All right, all right, I'm going. When I'm next here, will you flash your panties for me?'

'No, I won't. You had your chance at Christmas, and you blew it.'

'But –'

'You're blackmailing me, Neil. Do you honestly think that I –'

'Flash your wet panties, Cindy. Or else. In fact, it would be better if you didn't wear panties. When I'm next here, I want to look up your skirt and see your sweet cunt smiling at me.'

I gazed out of the window, and was horrified to see

71

Rod's car pull up in the drive. Trying to calm myself, I realised that Neil calling round wouldn't appear suspicious. He was Rod's brother, so why shouldn't he come round? There again, if Rod was keeping an eye on me, if he was checking up on me . . . Hearing the front door open, I took a deep breath and informed Neil that Rod had arrived. Neil seemed pleased, no doubt because he wanted to wink at me and gloat. He was a bastard.

'Hi, Neil,' Rod said, walking into the lounge. 'What are you doing here?'

'Wondering when your next barbeque is,' Neil replied. 'I was passing so I thought I'd call in.'

'Did you forget something?' I asked Rod, smiling sweetly at him. Was the smell of sex hanging in the air?

'I left some important papers in the study. Have you had coffee or . . .'

'I can't stay,' Neil said. 'It was only a quick call. I'll be in touch.'

'Surely you have time for a cup of coffee?' Rod whined.

'I've got to go. I'll see you both soon.'

'OK,' I said, ignoring his winking eye. Was his spunk glistening on my lips? 'We'll let you know when the next barbeque is.'

'This weekend, if the weather holds out,' Rod said, seeing his brother to the front door.

'Great, I'll look forward to it.'

The taste of Neil's spunk lingered on my tongue. I brushed my long blonde hair back with my fingers and let out a sigh of relief. Had Alan not phoned and warned me about Rod coming home, I might have been caught in a compromising position. Had Richard or Ian been with me . . . In the past, I'd been complacent, stupid. Now, I was going to have to be very careful. If Alan wasn't able to warn me for some reason, Rod might come walking into the lounge and discover me with another man's cock in my mouth. With his brother's cock pumping spunk into my mouth . . .

'Why aren't you wearing a bra?' Rod asked me accusingly, clutching his precious papers as he returned to the lounge.

'I was about to take a shower when Neil called,' I lied. 'I had to throw something on quickly.'

'I'd have thought you'd have found something less revealing than an open blouse. And you should have put a bra on.'

'It was all I had at the time. I just grabbed the nearest thing and . . . Anyway, Neil's my brother-in-law. He's family, isn't he?'

'He's still a man, Cindy.'

'What do you mean by that? For goodness sake, you surely don't think that he'd make a pass at me?'

'All I'm saying is –'

'Hadn't you better get back to the office?'

'Yes, I suppose so. Has he been round before during the day?'

'Neil's often been round, you know that.'

'During the day, while I've been at the office?'

'I don't know. I suppose he must have done. Over five years, he must have called round when you've been out.'

'Recently, I mean.'

'I don't know, Rod. I don't think he's been round recently. I . . . I really can't remember. I would have told you had he called.'

'Would you?'

'Of course I would. You seem to be forgetting that he's your brother. Don't you trust him?'

'Yes, but –'

'You don't trust me? Is that it?'

'No, of course not. I'll see you this evening, love.'

'Before you go, I want to ask you something.'

'What's that?'

'I want an honest answer, Rod. Do you trust me?'

'You know I do.'

'Are you sure?'

'Of course I'm sure. What's brought this on?'

'You tell me. The other day, you were going on about Alan Johnson noticing a man at the front door. And then you went on about Jilly not ringing my mobile. Are you suspicious of me? Is that it?'

'No, Cindy. Why should I be?'

'I suppose I have the opportunity to play around behind your back. I'm here alone all day, aren't I? If I was that kind of woman, I could have several men visit me every day.'

'That's true. But you're not that kind of woman. Look, I'd better get back to the office. I'll see you this evening, OK?'

'OK.'

I didn't feel at all easy as he left the house. He *was* suspicious of me, that was certain. But, why? Why, after all these years, did he think that I was playing around behind his back? And to suspect his own brother . . . Rod hadn't actually said that, but I knew that he didn't trust Neil – or me, for that matter. He must have trusted Alan Johnson, I reflected. After all, to have Alan call into check up on me . . . Had Alan lied to me? Had he said that Rod was suspicious so that he could call round to see me?

This was getting worse by the day. Alan, Neil, the photograph, Rod's suspicious mind . . . I felt that there was a conspiracy against me. Was I becoming paranoid? I wondered. Was I reading things into the situation that weren't there? The photograph was there, I'd seen it. And Neil had seen it. No, I wasn't becoming paranoid. The incriminating photograph, blackmailed for sex . . . I had every reason to worry. Answering the phone, I raised my eyes to the ceiling as Alan asked me how I was.

'I couldn't be better,' I snapped sarcastically. 'Seeing as you gave Neil a copy of that bloody photograph, I'm over the moon with joy.'

'What?'

'You heard.'

'Cindy, I . . . I haven't got copies of the photograph. And, if I had, I certainly wouldn't pass them around.'

'Lying bastard.'

'Cindy, I haven't got copies of the bloody photograph,' he repeated firmly. 'And there's no way I'd give Neil a copy. What the hell would I gain by doing that?'

'I don't know, Alan. But you've destroyed what you had with me. Don't think that you'll be welcome here again. Blackmail or not, our deal's off.'

'Wait a minute. Did Neil tell you that he had a copy?'

'Yes, he did.'

'And he said that I'd given it to him?'

'Well, no. He wouldn't, would he?'

'I think we need to talk. I'll be round as soon as I can.'

'Alan, I don't want you here.'

'This isn't as simple as you think, Cindy. In fact, it's a bloody mess. I'll be with you soon.'

More mysteries, more mind games. What the hell did he want to talk to me about? He was going to try to wriggle his way out of this, I was sure. How the hell would he explain how Neil had come by a copy of the photograph? There was no explanation. Other than the fact that he had given Neil a copy. Fuming, I paced the lounge floor. This had become a dangerous situation. Alan and Neil had damning evidence of my whoredom. How long before Rod set eyes on me in my bondage gear?

'What's this all about?' I asked, opening the front door to Alan.

'Sit down and I'll tell you,' he replied, walking into the lounge. 'The photograph . . .' he began, standing with his back to the window. 'I didn't take it.'

'What?'

'I wasn't the one who took that photograph.'

'But you had a copy of it. You had the original. You brought it round here and –'

'Cindy, when we were on the patio and you were going on about my taking photographs . . . I knew nothing about it. I had no knowledge of any photograph.'

'But, you said –'

'No, *you* said that there was a photograph. I was intrigued, and played along with you to learn more. Then, you told me all I needed to know.'

'I didn't say anything.'

'You gave me the photograph, Cindy. That told me everything. I'd never seen it before. I had no idea that you were cheating on Rod. I had no idea that you were being blackmailed.'

'You bastard. You tricked me.'

'Yes, I did trick you. For some reason, you blamed me, accused me of taking the photograph. All I did was allow you to ramble on, and you revealed all. All I did was take advantage of your unwitting revelation.'

'If you didn't take the photograph . . . Shit. Neil must have taken it.'

'It looks that way.'

'You're a bastard, Alan. You knew that I was being blackmailed, and yet you thought nothing of using my predicament to use me for sex.'

'All's fair in love and sex,' he quipped, eyeing my deep cleavage. 'No bra. Very nice.'

'Bastard.'

'Swearing at me won't get you anywhere. What demands has Neil made? What has he said?'

'He wants sex, Alan. Like you, he wants to use me to satisfy his lust.'

'What man wouldn't? You're a horny little angel, Cindy. What man wouldn't want to use your beautiful young body to –'

'Shut up, I'm trying to think.'

'So, you've been a naughty little girl. Your brother-in-law caught you with your knickers down and now –'

'Shut the fuck up, Alan,' I snapped.

'And now he wants what's inside your knickers.'

'I hope you realise that you're in serious trouble?'

'Me?' He laughed. 'How the hell do you work that out?'

'If Rod discovers that you've been here, blackmailing me to have sex . . .'

'Hey, now hold on. This has nothing to do with me.'

'No, *you* hold on. This has everything to do with you, Alan. You blackmailed me. You forced me to have sex with you. You work with Rod; you're his friend . . . and you forced me to have sex with you.'

'You're not going to tell Rod that, surely?'

'If the shit hits the fan, of course I'll tell him.'

'Well, at least some good has come out of this.'

'What's that?'

'Us, you and me.'

'*Us?*' I echoed, frowning at him. 'You think that we have something between us after the way you've –'

'Come on, Cindy. You love a length of hard cock.'

'Yes, I do. But not yours. I cannot believe that, after all you've done, you have the audacity to suggest that we have something between us.'

'Don't forget that Rod has asked me to keep an eye on you.'

'That's rubbish.'

'Is it? When I phoned to warn you that he was on his way here, who were you with?'

'No one.'

'Neil was here, wasn't he?'

'No, he wasn't.'

'I might have to have a word with Rod. Tell him that I've been here to see you, to check up on you and ... How about saying that I looked through the lounge window and saw you with another man.'

'You really are stupid, aren't you? For years, you've leched over me. You then attempt to blackmail me when you know damned well that someone else is trying the same thing. You then threaten to tell Rod a load of rubbish about other men visiting me. For God's sake, Alan.'

'All right, all right,' he sighed. 'I'm sorry, OK?'

'No, it's not OK.'

'How can I help you? Neil is blackmailing you, so . . .'

'How can you help me? By keeping Rod sweet, for a start. As for Neil, there's nothing you can do. Only I can deal with my brother-in-law.'

'How do you intend to do that?'

'I don't know yet.'

That was a good question. How the hell could I deal with Neil? I'd been a fool, I reflected. I'd not only told Alan about the photograph, but given him

78

a copy. I'd got the wrong man, as good as told him everything, and submitted to his threat by allowing him to fuck me. But I wasn't bothered about Alan. He was an opportunist, and I couldn't blame him for that. A thousand thoughts battering my tormented mind; I wondered whether to ring Sue and tell her about Neil's other woman. But I had no proof, nothing to substantiate my claim. I was at a complete loss as to what to do.

'How many men are there?' Alan asked me. 'How many lovers do you have?'

'None,' I returned firmly.

'Come on, you can tell me. I know about your bondage gear; I know that you're having sex with your brother-in-law . . . and I've had your hot little pussy hugging my cock.'

'If all you're going to do is quip about –'

'Do you take money in return for sex?' he persisted.

'Alan, I am *not* a prostitute. I have sex with other men because –'

'So, you admit it?'

'I can hardly deny it, can I?'

'Have you ever fucked another man while Rod's been in the house?'

'Of course not. I'm not totally bloody stupid.'

'No, no. I mean, for the hell of it, for the excitement.'

'No, I haven't.'

'You should try it, Cindy. Sucking another man's cock while your husband is lurking –'

'I wish you'd shut up. You don't seem to realise the gravity of the situation.'

'Gravity? I wouldn't worry, if I were you. Neil wants your body, so what's the problem?'

'The problem is that he's blackmailing me. And he's my brother-in-law.'

'So? Just think of him as another of your many lovers. Look, I'd better be going. Don't worry, it'll be all right on the night.'

'I hope so,' I sighed, seeing him to the front door. 'Keep Rod happy, OK?'

'OK. I'll be seeing you, Cindy.'

Alan wasn't so bad, I decided as I returned to the lounge. Neil had said that we were two of a kind. If anything, Alan and I were two of a kind. At least I now knew who had taken the photograph. At least I now knew that my brother-in-law was an unscrupulous bastard. But what was I going to do about him? Allow him to use me for sex whenever he needed to drain his balls? If I could get my hands on the photograph ... But Neil wouldn't have left it lying around. He'd have hidden it well, and there'd be copies. *Just think of him as another of your many lovers.* Was that the way to deal with the problem?

Wondering whether I could take a photograph of Neil in a compromising position, I made myself a cup of coffee and sat in the garden. I had to relax my mind, I decided, placing my coffee on the patio table and reclining in the chair. The threats, the confusion, the worry ... I had to calm my mind and relax. Wishing that I'd sucked Alan's cock to orgasm and swallowed his spunk, I felt my clitoris stir, my juices seeping between my swelling pussy lips. Having taken Neil's cock into my wet mouth and tasted his fresh spunk, my arousal had soared to frightening heights. I needed the relief of orgasm.

Tugging my wet panties off, I parted my legs and slipped my hand between my thighs. Toying with the fleshy cushions of my outer labia, pulling and twisting the pinken wings of my inner lips, I felt a quiver run through my contracting womb. Where were my lovers? What was young James doing? Was he wanking, thinking about my naked body as he brought out his spunk? Perhaps he was in his garden, I mused. Watching me, lurking, spying, wanking. I needed a man; a solid cock shafting the tight sheath of my yearning pussy. But my fingers would have to suffice.

I massaged the erect nub of my sensitive clitoris, encircling the base of my sex button, then closed my eyes and let out a sigh of pleasure. Sitting on the patio beneath the sun, my young body trembling uncontrollably, I parted my thighs further and moved down in the chair until my naked buttocks were over the edge of the cushion. I imagined James kneeling before me with his huge cock stretching my pussy to capacity, his knob battering my cervix as he fucked me senseless.

Fantasising had always played a major role in my sex life. Very often when I lay in my bed masturbating, I'd imagine half a dozen young men all standing around my naked body, their hard cocks in their hands, their spunk raining down over me. I'd picture three hard cocks fucking me: my mouth, my pussy, my bum . . . On the odd occasion when Rod fucked me, I'd think of other men. My lovers, complete strangers, it didn't matter. A huge purple knob pumping my mouth full of spunk or a naked buttock-spanking session, my fantasies were like a tonic to me.

My clitoris responded to my intimate massaging. I reached beneath my thigh and drove two fingers deep into the drenched sheath of my tightening pussy. Working on my pussy with two hands, fingering and massaging, I again let out a gasp of pleasure as my juices flowed in torrents from my gaping sex hole. My erect nipples caressed the thin material of my blouse as I masturbated vigorously. I imagined young James sucking me there, mouthing on my milk bud as he fucked me. I'd often masturbate when Rod was sleeping beside me; take myself to massive multiple orgasm while he dreamed his dreams of his work, the office. He didn't know me at all.

'Yes,' I breathed as my clitoris exploded in orgasm. The squelching of my pussy juices mingling with my whimpers, disturbing the still summer air, I repeatedly rammed my fingers deep into my cunt and massaged my pulsating clitoris faster. Sustaining my incredible pleasure, I imagined two solid cocks forced into the tight sheath of my rectum, fucking me there, pumping creamy spunk deep into my hot bowels. Again and again, shockwaves of pure sexual bliss crashed through my young body, shaking me to the core as my juices of lust gushed forth.

Riding the crest of my orgasm, I recalled the time I'd masturbated knowing that I was being watched. I'd been playing in the wooded area on the common when I saw a teenage boy climbing a tree. Making out that I didn't know that he was there, I lay on the ground beneath the tree and pulled my knickers down. My eyes closed, my skirt up over my stomach, my slender legs spread, I fingered and frigged my pink pussy. Watching him through my eyelashes as he gazed down at me, I pulled my T-shirt up and exposed the ripening mounds of my young breasts to his wide eyes.

Knowing that my indecent act of self-abuse was being witnessed, I'd reached the most fantastic orgasm ever. My pussy milk had spilled from the tight sheath of my pussy, splattered my inner thighs as I'd finger fucked myself beneath the trees. Finally slowing my masturbating rhythm, recovering from my self-induced pleasure, I'd grinned as spunk had rained down from the tree and splattered the grass beside me.

The thrill and excitement of being watched had planted ideas in my young and extremely fertile mind. Ideas, fantasies, plans ... On that fateful day, I'd discovered the power of my pussy. I often went to the common on my way home from school. The boy was usually there, peering down from the tree, watching as I lay on the ground with my legs spread and my fingers buried deep within my pussy. Where was the boy now? I wondered ...

My orgasm finally beginning to wane, I opened my eyes and gazed across the lawn at the bushes. Was James there? Although satisfied after my mind-blowing climax, I still needed a solid cock. Was I a nymphomaniac? I pondered, my fingers stirring the warm cream within my gaping sex crack. I enjoyed sex to the full, all aspects of sex. Would Neil return and demand that I allow him to fuck me? Neil, my brother-in-law, blackmailing me, using and abusing me ...

What had gone wrong? I wondered as my fingertip caressed the sensitive tip of my clitoris. My private life exposed, my dirty little secret out. What did Neil know about me? How much did he know? He was a real threat, a danger. Unless I put an end to his blackmail ... A photograph of Neil completely naked with his erect cock in full view would be more than enough evidence of his adultery. My face out of frame to protect my identity, Neil's cock buried deep within my tight pussy ... If I threatened to show Sue ... But I'd probably end up dropping myself in the crap. Shit, I was already deep in the crap.

Five

Neil turned up the following morning clutching a photograph. To my horror, it wasn't the infamous one of me in my bondage gear. This one showed me kneeling before Richard with his huge cock bloating my mouth. I was in my school uniform, white ankle socks, gymslip, blouse . . . There could be nothing more incriminating, I mused, as Neil tossed the photograph on to the kitchen table. He had me just where he wanted me, and there was nothing I could do.

'I've been thinking,' he said, looking me up and down. 'I've never seen you naked.'

'And you're not going to,' I returned coldly, walking into the garden.

He followed me and looked up at the sun. 'It's hot, Cindy. Why don't you take your clothes off?'

'Neil, I –'

'Take your clothes off, or I'll take the photograph to Rod's office.'

'Neil, we've known each other for years. Why are you doing this to me? I thought that we were good friends?'

'We are, Cindy. Good, intimate friends.'

'So, why are you treating me like this?'

'Why are you treating my brother like this? What's he ever done to deserve a slut like you?'

'I am not a slut,' I returned, knowing full well that I was a filthy little tart. 'I don't want you blackmailing me and –'

'And I don't want to have to blackmail you. Forget about the photographs. Forget about blackmail and enjoy sex with me.'

'Neil, I don't want to have sex with you.'

'In that case, the photographs will see an end to your marriage. Rod's my brother, and I don't like the way you've cheated him. Clothes off, Cindy. Or I end your farcical marriage.'

Unbuttoning my blouse, I knew that he wasn't joking. He was a bastard, and would think nothing of ruining my marriage. Portraying me as a cheating slut, he'd watch me squirm and no doubt revel in my plight. Take the photograph to Rod's office? What would he say to his brother? How would he explain how he had such a photograph in his possession? Surely, he wouldn't tell Rod that he'd been lurking at the lounge window with a camera?

I allowed my blouse to fall off my shoulders and stood on the patio before my blackmailer with my naked breasts in full view. He knew what he wanted, and he knew that he was going to get it. Trying to think of him as just another of my many lovers, as Alan had suggested, I unzipped my miniskirt and allowed it to fall down my legs and crumple around my ankles. Neil grinned as he gazed at the bulging triangular patch of my tight panties. What was he thinking? Was he picturing the full lips of my vulva? Were my sex lips wet with my juices? Whatever he was thinking, I knew that I had to do as he'd asked. I had no choice.

I lowered my panties, revealing the tightly closed crack of my pussy to his wide eyes. My blonde fleece doing little to conceal my intimacy, I stepped out of my skirt and panties and stood before Neil. The choice was sex with my brother-in-law or a ruined marriage. I didn't want to lose Rod. But there was more to it than that – I didn't want to lose my way of life. I had money, a nice home, holidays . . . and as many cocks and as much fresh spunk as I could handle. I'd not only be losing Rod, but also my very existence.

'You have a good body,' Neil remarked, sitting on a patio chair.

'I don't need you to tell me that,' I said. 'Shall we get it over with?'

'Get what over with?'

'Sex, Neil. That is what you want, isn't it?'

'Yes, yes, of course. But, as you know only too well, there's far more to sex than a quick fuck. I want you to be my sex slave.'

'Now, wait a minute –'

'I hold the key to your marriage, Cindy,' he cut in. 'Don't ever forget that.'

'How long have you known?'

'About your secret life?'

'Yes.'

'For three years.'

'And you've never said anything? Why wait until now?'

'I've often thought about fucking you. I suppose I was waiting until I needed you. I've had Jackie, my tart on the side, to play around with. But I get bored, Cindy. Bored with the same old fanny. I now have a new fanny to enjoy.'

'If Rod ever discovered what sort of brother –'

'Rod will never discover anything about me. Neither will Sue. What they don't know won't hurt them. Besides, you've been fucking around for years. All I'm doing is grabbing a piece of the action.'

'You have no qualms about fucking your brother's wife?' I asked him.

'You have no qualms about cheating on your husband?' he returned. 'Let's not talk about morals, loyalty, scruples . . . You're my sex slave, Cindy. As I said, I hold the key to your marriage.'

'What do you want me to do?'

'Place one foot on the table. I want to see your sweet little girl slit gaping wide open.'

Following his instruction, I looked down at my sex crack as I managed to place my foot on the table. The wings of my inner lips protruding invitingly from my vulval gully, I felt my stomach somersault as my arousal rocketed. I'd never been blackmailed before; I'd never been forced to have sex. The idea of being forced to commit crude sexual acts excited me. But I wasn't going to tell Neil that. Breathing deeply as he ran his fingertip up and down the yawning valley of my pussy, I felt my clitoris swell, juices seeping from my sex slit.

As Neil murmured crude comments about my naked body and talked about my tight little cunt, I couldn't believe that he was like this. Neil told me that I had lickable pussy lips. I'd thought that I knew Neil, but I was very wrong. So what was Rod really like? As Neil's finger entered the tight sheath of my pussy, I trembled with desire. I might not have known Neil, but I knew Rod. He was quiet, reserved, unadventurous in bed . . . I knew my husband only too well.

'Bend over the table,' Neil ordered me, withdrawing his wet finger from my hot pussy. 'I want to take a look at your sweet little bottom hole.'

'Neil, I don't want this,' I said meekly, trying to come across as humiliated and anxious as I slipped my foot off the table.

'What you want or don't want is not my concern,' he returned. 'It's what I want that's important. Now, stand with your feet wide apart and bend over the table.'

Complying, I took my position and rested my head on the table. After moving his chair behind me, he parted the firm cheeks of my bottom and peered at the brown ring of my anus. I could almost feel his gaze burning into the delicate tissue surrounding my tight bottom hole. Would he fuck me there? I wondered, as his fingertip teased the entrance to my rectum. Would he force his solid cock deep into my bum and flood my bowels with his spunk? Was that what I wanted him to do?

His wet tongue teased my anal iris, licking and tasting me. I let out a rush of breath. I'd always been rather partial to having my bottom hole licked and tongued. My first experience of anal oral sex had been at school with a young lad in my class. We'd gone into the trees on the common and I'd allowed him to pull my knickers down. We'd experimented together, learned and discovered. Leaning over a fallen tree, I'd shown him my bottom, asked him to examine me there, tickle me there.

Parting my naked buttocks, he'd prodded and poked my bottom hole with his fingertip, sending quivers throughout my young body. As he licked me I'd gasped. I couldn't believe what he was doing to me. Licking my bottom hole? Tasting my brown hole? Amazed, and aroused as never before, I'd writhed and squirmed over the tree as he pushed his wet tongue deep into my bum. Little did I know then that anal oral sex would become a passion of mine.

'You're a filthy little slut, Cindy,' Neil breathed, kissing each firm buttock in turn and bringing me back from my schooldays. 'A dirty, filthy, cheating little whore.'

'You can talk,' I countered. 'The way you've cheated on Sue and –'

'I've had a couple of flings,' he confessed. 'But you've given your cunt to a thousand men.'

'Don't be ridiculous.'

'I'll bet you've lost count of the cocks you've had. As I said, you're a dirty, filthy, cheating little whore. And you know it.'

I said nothing as he encircled my anus with his fingertip. What could I say? After all, he was right. The sensations driving me wild as he teased my brown ring, I quivered and stifled my gasps. I couldn't reveal my arousal. If he thought that I was deriving pleasure from his intimate attention, his crude violation of my young body . . . Letting out a rush of breath as he pushed his finger into the tight sheath of my rectum, I knew that I couldn't conceal my pleasure. My naked body trembling uncontrollably, my breathing fast and shallow, there was no way I could veil my arousal.

He pushed his finger deeper into my bum, holding my buttocks wide apart with his free hand. There was no love, no affection – only cold sex. But wasn't that what I was used to? I could feel his finger deep inside my bum, massaging the fleshy walls of my rectum, waking the sleeping nerve endings there. Cold, crude sex. My womb contracting, my juices of desire streaming between my puffy pussy lips, I clung to the sides of the table as my libido soared. I couldn't deny his expertise. He was good; he knew exactly what to do.

Managing to force a second finger past my defeated anal sphincter muscle, stretching my anus wide open, he again murmured his crude words of lust. *Tight-arsed bitch, vulgar little whore, cock-sucking slag . . .* I loved the way he talked to me; I loved the feel of his fingers exploring deep within me. But, more, I loved the notion of blackmail, being forced to submit and endure his obscene act of anal abuse.

Why had Rod never paid attention to my bum? I pondered, as my heart raced. Why had he never pleasured me there? The sun beating down on my naked body, my brother-in-law sexually abusing me, I couldn't understand why Rod was so staid and strait-laced. Didn't he like sex? How could brothers be so very different? Neil was a pervert who obviously loved all aspects of sex. Whereas Rod . . . There was no point in thinking about Rod, I decided, as a third finger opened my anal ring to capacity and drove deep into the dank heat of my arse.

'Have you ever had a cock shafting your tight little arse?' Neil asked me.

'No,' I lied, hoping that he'd force his beautiful cock deep into my yearning rectal duct.

'What a waste,' he said, chuckling. 'You're so tight and hot.'

'If you dare to –'

'Shut up, bitch,' he snapped. 'You're my slave, and you'll do as you're told.'

Gasping as he slipped his fingers out of my gaping bottom hole, I listened to the sound of his zip. He was standing behind me, the purple head of his solid cock slipping between the dripping lips of my pussy. After lubricating his swollen glans, running his cock head up and down my sex-drenched crack, he suddenly rammed the entire length of his organ deep into my spasming pussy. I whimpered and writhed as he withdrew slowly before again propelling his knob deep into me.

I imagined Rod walking into the garden and catching us as Neil clutched my hips and repeatedly fucked me. What would he say? Would he blame

Neil, or me? Or both of us? What would I say? If I heard the front door open, I'd not have time to dress. This was risky, I knew. But I was loving every second of the enforced arse fucking. My husband could have easily caught me committing debauched acts over the years, but he'd never suspected me before. Poor Rod, naïve in his stupidity, his trust. He'd married a common slut, a two-timing little tart. Why was I such a tart?

I pondered on the almost frightening height of my libido, and recalled spying on a boy at school. He'd gone into the bushes edging the playing field and had pulled out his cock. I'd watched as he'd wanked and shot his spunk over the grass. I'd never seen a cock before, let alone witnessed spunk jetting from a purple knob. The experience had left me wondering, pondering, wanting.

The next time the boy had slipped into the bushes, I'd not only followed him but also offered to do it for him. My heart had raced as I'd wrapped my fingers around his warm shaft and wanked him. His balls had jerked, bounced, as I'd run my hand up and down his fleshy shaft. His purple knob appearing and disappearing, I'd waited excitedly for his white cream to come. Bringing out his spunk, the slimy liquid flowing over my hand, hanging in long strands from my fingers, I knew then that I was hooked on wanking cocks.

After going through virtually every boy in my class, wanking their hard cocks, I accepted a dare and moved on to knob sucking and spunk swallowing. I was young, naïve and virginal. But I'd quickly become a tart. By the time I'd left school, I don't think there was one boy who'd not enjoyed shoving his cock into my mouth and throat spunking me. I'd always been a dirty little slut. But I'd loved every minute of my schooldays . . .

'And now for your tight little arse,' Neil said, chortling, sliding his pussy-wet cock out of my drenched pussy and stabbing at my brown hole. I could feel his plum opening me there, slipping into my contracting rectum as he pushed hard against me. Filling, stretching, opening . . . His knob journeyed along my tight duct to my bowels, his full balls coming to rest against my juice-smeared pussy lips, and he fully impaled me on his cock. Another cock, I reflected. How many men had entered me there? Neil was right: I'd lost count.

'God, no,' I cried, feigning horror as I clung to the patio table. 'Neil, please . . .'

'Please, what? Please, give me more?'

'No. For God's sake, I can't take it.'

'Take it you can, and take it you will. Surely, you're not going to tell me that you've never had your arse fucked?'

'Of course I haven't,' I gasped, making a perfunctory struggle to break free. 'What the hell do you think I am?'

'A filthy slag, Cindy. A filthy, arse-fucking little slag.'

My body rocked with the enforced anal fucking. I again did my best to stifle my gasps of sheer sexual bliss. Blackmailed, forced to endure anal sex, used and abused . . . If only Neil knew how much I enjoyed his cruelty. I could feel my anal ring dragging back and forth along his slimed shaft as he fucked me, his bulbous knob repeatedly driving deep into my hot bowels, his balls smacking the swollen lips of my sex-dripping pussy as he increased his pistoning rhythm.

As Neil gasped, his spunk flowing from his throbbing knob and lubricating the enforced union, I was reminded of the time when Rod had come home and asked me why I was half-naked. My face flushed from an anal fucking only minutes earlier, I'd said that I was about to take a shower. Fortunately, my teenage lover had left by the back door and made his escape over the garden fence. My near downfall wasn't due to Rod coming home early. I'd spent longer than usual enjoying a hard cock and had been oblivious to the time. With spunk bubbling from my bottom hole and running down my naked legs, I'd thought it amazing that Rod believed me. I'd felt sure that he'd have realised what I'd been up to, what with my panties on the floor and my blouse open.

'Tight-arsed bitch,' Neil breathed, repeatedly ramming his spunk-jetting knob deep into the very core of my young body. 'Dirty little arse fucker.'

'Please, stop now,' I gasped, clinging to the sides of the patio table. 'I hate you, and I never want to see you again.'

'You'll not only be seeing me again, but enjoying my cock again.' He laughed, finally sliding his deflating cock out of my rectum.

'I hate you,' I sobbed. 'You're an animal.'

'And you're a slut. Look at the state of you. Get off the table and stand up.'

'Bastard,' I hissed, hauling my body up and facing him. 'When I next see Sue, I'll –'

'Say nothing to her. Keep your pretty little mouth shut, and you'll be all right. You'd do well to play the game, Cindy. If you don't ... There's no need to remind you of the consequences. You're my slave, Cindy. You'll jump to attention when I snap my fingers; you'll pull your knickers down when you hear my zip; you'll open your mouth and your legs at the sight of my cock ...'

'One day, Neil. One day, you'll be sorry for this.'

'I doubt that very much. I don't know why you keep kidding yourself.'

93

'What do you mean?'

'Making out that you're a prim and proper loving wife when you're nothing but a dirty slut. You're a lump of female meat, Cindy. You're a lump of meat with three holes. Three eminently fuckable holes.'

'Go now,' I cried, covering my face with my hands and sobbing.

'Don't turn on the tears,' he said, laughing at me. 'You've had your arse fucked rotten, and you loved it. Don't make out that you're shocked and horrified. I know how much you enjoy a length of cock up your tight arse. You're nothing but a lump of female meat with three fuckable little spunk holes.'

'Get out,' I yelled, still turning on the tears.

'I will. But I'll be round in the morning to fuck your tight little arse.'

As he left, I cupped my firm breasts and grinned. He liked my naked body, my pussy, my arse. And I loved his crude words, the way he treated me. Lowering my head and kissing each nipple in turn, I felt my womb contracting again, my juices flowing once more. I'd wanted more sex, more crude fucking. As he'd said, he'd be back. I knew that I wouldn't have to wait too long for the feel of his cock inside me. Walking down the garden with the sun warming my naked body, I felt Neil's spunk oozing from the inflamed eye of my anus. A stark reminder of a beautiful experience, I mused. If only he knew how I felt. If only he realised how much I'd enjoyed his illicit act. But he didn't, and never would.

Wandering past the bushes by the shed, the prickly leaves scraping my naked skin, I felt a shiver run up my spine. To me, everything was a sexual experience. Even the feel of the bushes sent my arousal soaring. Turning and allowing the rough leaves to caress my naked buttocks, I was about to massage my clitoris to orgasm when I thought I heard the front door close. Staring at the house, I froze as Rod stepped on to the patio and frowned at me.

'What on earth are you doing?' he asked, walking across the lawn towards me. 'Cindy, what the hell . . .'

'I'm looking around the garden,' I said cheerily.

'Naked?'

'Why not?'

'But . . . I hope the neighbours can't see you.'

'No one overlooks the garden, Rod,' I sighed. 'It's such a lovely day that I thought I'd enjoy the sun. Get a tan, perhaps.'

'Your clothes are strewn across the patio. What did you do? Strip off and –'

'I've been sunbathing, Rod. Anyway, what are you doing here?'

'I had to go out to a client and thought I'd call in to see you. Do you often walk around the garden naked?'

'If the sun's hot, yes.'

'I don't understand you, Cindy.'

'What do you mean? There's nothing *to* understand. Apart from the fact that I'm trying to get an all-over suntan.'

'I thought I saw Neil's car leave as I turned into the road. Has he been here?'

'Neil? No, no, he hasn't. Rod, I'd hardly answer the front door like this.'

'I'm sure it was his car.'

'If he called, then I didn't hear the bell. Had I heard the bell, I'd have put something on before opening the door. I don't know why you're making such a fuss. Good God, I'm only enjoying the sun.'

'I'm sorry, love. I just didn't expect to find you naked in the garden. It's a good job I didn't have Alan with me.'

'Imagine that,' I said with a giggle. 'Alan finding me naked in the garden.'

'Cindy, it's not funny.'

'I think I'll get dressed,' I breathed. 'It's suddenly turned chilly.'

As we walked back to the house, I imagined him arriving a few minutes earlier and catching me with his brother's cock shafting my bum. Again, I'd come close to disaster. Why had he come home? I wondered, grabbing my clothes from the patio. It was so unlike him to call in during the day that I became extremely suspicious. Watching him fill the kettle for coffee as I dressed, I again realised that I was going to have to be extremely careful in the future. If Rod was going to drop in like this . . .

'I've got to work late this evening,' he announced.

'How late?' I asked him, trying not to come across as relieved.

'There's a meeting with a client. I won't be home until at least ten. Will you be OK?'

'Yes, of course. I'll probably watch TV.'

I had the feeling that this was a trap. What did he plan to do? Come home a few hours early in the hope of catching me with my knickers down? I was becoming paranoid again. Rod knew nothing about my secret life, my lovers. He had to go to a meeting, that was all. But my suspicion had been roused. Boring though the notion was, I'd have to spend the evening alone, fully dressed, watching the bloody television.

The rest of the day passed uneventfully, and I wondered why Ian hadn't been in touch. I'd heard nothing from Richard and began to think that my male friends had been frightened off by Rod. No, that wasn't the case. I had to stop worrying about Rod, I knew, as I paced the lounge floor. I had nothing to worry about. He was at a meeting and wouldn't be home until ten o'clock.

There was nothing worth watching on television, and boredom quickly set in. I listened to music, knocked back a couple of large vodkas and finally wandered out into the garden. It was a lovely evening, but a wasted evening. The sun hovered above the trees; the air was warm and still . . . and my panties were wet with my desire. What a waste, I again mused, walking across the lawn. I was hot, wet and ready for crude sex. But alone with my yearning.

I almost jumped out of my skin as a football flew over the bushes and landed a few feet away. I was about to grab the ball and throw it back when I heard a rustling noise in the bushes. I slipped behind the shed as the lad from next door emerged from the undergrowth; I'd not realised that there was a way into our garden. Had I been naked . . . Grinning, I saw an opportunity for sex. The lad was in his teens, muscular, fresh . . . and no doubt in need of draining his young balls.

'What do you think you're doing, James?' I asked him.

'Oh, er . . . sorry, I was just getting the ball,' he replied awkwardly.

'Do you often come into my garden?'

'Well, no.'

'Don't worry about it,' I said with a chuckle. 'It's just that you gave me a fright.'

'I am sorry. I should have gone to your front door and asked you.'

'No matter. Actually, it's rather nice to see you. How are your parents?'

'Oh, they're fine.'

'I can't believe how you've grown. When we moved here five years ago, you were a little schoolboy. Just look at you now.'

'Yes, well . . . I'd better get back.'

'Why don't you stay for a while?' I breathed, eyeing the bulge in his jeans. 'I could do with some company.'

'Well, I don't know.'

'It's all right, my husband's not around.'

I couldn't help picturing his young cock as he gazed at the deep ravine of my cleavage. Was he a virgin? I wondered. Had he felt the wet heat of a girl's mouth encompassing his swollen knob? Had he pistoned a young girl's tight little pussy and filled her with his fresh spunk? My libido rocketing, I knew that I had to have him. I imagined him wanking his firm cock, bringing out his spunk as he thought about girls' naked bodies. In his teenage years, his hormones would be running wild, his thoughts perpetually centred around sex. My panties became wet with my juices of lust, my clitoris stiffening expectantly . . . This was an opportunity I couldn't miss.

'You're a good-looking young man, James,' I said, licking my full lips as I felt the muscles of my spunk-thirsty pussy tighten. 'Have you got a girlfriend?'

'Er . . . no, no I haven't,' he replied sheepishly.

'So, what do you do?'

'What do I do?' he echoed, frowning at me.

'For sex, James. What do you do seeing as you haven't got a girlfriend?'

'Well . . . nothing.'

'Surely you masturbate?' I giggled unashamedly.

'No, no,' he replied, obviously shocked by my brazen question.

'You're a virgin, aren't you?'

'Yes.'

'Would you like me to change that?'

Staring at me with his mouth gaping, his dark eyes wide, he fiddled nervously with his fingers. He obviously couldn't believe that the woman next door had offered to have sex with him. And I couldn't believe the risk I was taking. Seducing my neighbours' son? This was playing too close to home, I knew, as he grabbed his football. But he was so young, muscular, firm, fresh . . . and a virgin in dire need of a hot, wet pussy.

'Don't go,' I said as he moved towards the bushes.

'I think I'd better,' he breathed.

'Are you frightened?'

'No, it's just that –'

'You don't fancy me?'

'It's not that I –'

'What is it, James? What's the matter?'

'Nothing.'

'Look at my miniskirt. Are you wondering what's beneath my skirt?'

'I know what you have there.'

'Do you? Have you ever seen a girl's pussy?'

'Yes. Well . . . only in pictures.'

Lifting my skirt, I displayed the triangular patch of my white panties to his disbelieving eyes. Could he resist me? I wondered, jutting my hips forwards and blatantly displaying the bulge of my tight panties. Could he resist the temptation of my intimate attention. I had a good body, even though I say it myself. Firm tits, long blonde hair framing my pretty face – and a cock-hungry pussy. No man could resist my beautiful pussy, I reflected.

'Are you stiff?' I asked him.

'Yes, very,' he breathed softly, unable to take his eyes of my wetting panties.

'We'd better do something about that.' I giggled, pulling the front of my panties down. 'So, you've only seen pictures of this?' I said huskily.

'Yes, only pictures.'

'Well, what do you think? What do you think of my cunt crack?'

'I . . . You're . . .'

'Horny?'

'Yes, very.'

His eyes almost popped out of his head as he gazed longingly at my sex crack. I felt a quiver run through my womb. The idea of exposing myself to a teenage lad sent my arousal to frightening heights. I felt my clitoris swell between the puffy lips of my pussy. James was like a breath of fresh air; a much needed tonic. Rod wouldn't be home until ten o'clock, giving me more than enough time to seduce the teenage hulk.

'Follow me,' I ordered him, lowering my skirt and walking to the end of the garden. 'I'll see what I can do for you.'

'But . . . what about your husband?' he asked.

'What about him? He's not here, James.'

'You're married,' he breathed.

'That figures, seeing as I have a husband. Do you want me to relieve the hardness of your cock?'

'Yes, very much.'

Having led him behind the bushes by the shed, I instructed him to strip me naked. He began by unbuttoning my blouse, opening the garment to reveal my straining bra. His dark eyes wide with excitement, as my blouse slipped off my shoulders and fell to the ground, he lifted the silk cups clear of my firm breasts. My nipples ripening, rising in the cool air, standing proud from the darkening discs of my areolae, I unhooked my bra and tossed it over the bushes. Following his gaze, I looked down at my suckable nipples. Elongated, sensitive . . . and in dire need of a hot, wet mouth.

James squeezed each mammary globe in turn, pinching and twisting my erect nipples. Young, inexperienced, virginal, hungry to learn . . . Lowering his head, he instinctively sucked my milk teat into his wet mouth. He slurped and mouthed at my breast, his tongue exploring the brown protrusion of my nipple. I let out a gasp of pleasure as he moved to my other nipple and sucked hard.

I allowed him to suckle for a while, and then ordered him to remove my skirt. Obediently dropping to his knees, he unzipped the garment and tugged it down my long legs. He was almost there, I mused, as he looked up and locked his questioning eyes on to mine. I smiled and nodded, indicating for him to slip my panties down. My stomach somersaulting, my womb rhythmically contracting, I watched as he pulled the garment down to my knees and gazed longingly at my juice-dripping sex slit.

'Kiss me there,' I ordered him. Wasting no time, he buried his face between my legs, pushing his mouth hard against the soft flesh of my vulva. I could feel his hot breath against the puffy lips of my pussy, and then the wetness of his tongue probing my valley. He licked me fervently, lapping at my inner flesh like a thirsty dog. My sex cream flowed in torrents from my hot pussy, and I threw my head back to look up at the darkening sky. Another sexual conquest, another young man attending to my most intimate needs. I was in my element.

His tongue swept over my clitoris. He moved down and lapped up the cream flowing from my hot pussy hole. Drinking from my tight cunt, losing himself in his teenage arousal, he clutched my naked buttocks and forced his mouth hard against the pink flesh surrounding my pussy. His cock would be solid, straining against the zip of his jeans, I knew, as he repeatedly swallowed my pussy milk. Young, horny, he might cream himself before I'd had a chance to suck his knob.

'Stand up,' I said, kneeling on the soft grass. He gazed at me as I unbuckled his belt and tugged his zip down. 'I'm going to suck your cock, James. You'd like me to suck your cock, wouldn't you?'

'God, yes,' he gasped.

'You'd like to give me a good mouth fucking and a throat spunking, would you?'

His jeans were around his ankles. I pulled his shorts down and grinned as his beautifully hard cock catapulted to attention. His balls heaving and rolling, his cock twitching expectantly, I retracted his foreskin and gazed longingly at the purple plum of his swollen glans. Mine for the taking, I mused, squeezing his silky globe between my finger and thumb. Mine for the sucking.

'Shall I lick your balls, James?'

'Yes, please, yes.'

'You have a wonderful cock, beautiful balls. Tell me, how often do you wank?'

'Well . . .'

'Once a day? Twice a day?'

'Once, I suppose.'

'And what do you think about? Girls' wet cunts?'

'Yes.'

'In future, you'll think about my wet cunt.'

'Yes, yes, I will.'

I licked his scrotum, breathing in his aphrodisiacal male scent. He gasped, his cock twitching as I salivated over his heaving ball sac. after running my wet tongue up his shaft, teasing him, I moved back to his balls. He was obviously desperate for the feel of my mouth around his cock, desperate for my tongue to explore his purple plum. Nibbling on his hairy ball sac, I jumped as he let out a gasp and his spunk jetted from his knob. The white cream splattered my long blonde hair, raining over my face. I sucked his glans into my mouth and drank from his fountain head.

He was too young and horny to hold back, I reflected, as I sucked the salty spunk from his throbbing knob. But I knew teenage boys only too well. After all, I'd sucked many a teenage cock at school. I knew that he'd be able come again and again before I'd finished with him and sent him home. Snaking my tongue over his orgasming knob, his spunk jetting to the back of my throat, I repeatedly swallowed hard. He tasted heavenly. Fresh cream, warm, lubricious ... He was to become another of my regulars, I decided. Living next door, he'd slip through the bushes and offer me his cock every day.

'Sorry,' he breathed as his spunk flow ceased. 'I didn't mean to come so quickly.'

'Don't apologise,' I said, slipping his deflating cock out of my spunk-bubbling mouth. 'You'll come again before you go, James. I can promise you that.'

'But, your face, your hair ...'

'You've given me a facial, James. Don't worry about it. There's nothing I like more than receiving a facial.'

'You're amazing,' he gasped as I lapped up a thread of spunk hanging from his glistening knob.

'I get better.' I giggled. 'Now, would you like me to strip you of your virginity?'

'Yes, I would,' he said eagerly, his cock shaft rising to attention.

'All right, but you'll have to promise me something first.'

'Anything.'

'In future, when you need to wank, you'll come to me. I'll wank you, James. I'll wank you with my mouth and drink your spunk, all right?'

'God, yes.'

I suddenly heard a noise coming from the house. I grabbed my clothes and leaped to my feet. Surely

Rod wasn't back already? I wondered anxiously, as James tugged his jeans up. Just when I was about to enjoy a virgin cock shafting my sex-drenched pussy, I thought angrily, ordering James to grab his football and get back to his garden. Finally dressed, I waited for James to go before emerging from the bushes and wandering back to the house.

Strangely, Rod wasn't there. I searched for him, called out, but he wasn't there. I'd definitely heard someone in the house, heard a thud like the front door closing. I must have been mistaken, I finally concluded. I'd sent James home for no reason at all. I'd so wanted to feel the solid shaft of his virgin cock entering me, fucking my tight pussy, shafting the hot duct of my rectum . . . There was always tomorrow, I thought dolefully, switching the television on and flopping on to the sofa. I'd seduce young James tomorrow. And the next day, and the next . . .

Six

'I'm afraid I'll be late again this evening,' Rod said after breakfast. Having grabbed his briefcase, he walked to the front door. 'Sorry, love, but it can't be helped.'

'Don't worry about it,' I replied, planning to lure young James into my garden. 'If you have to work late, then you carry on.'

'Will you be all right?'

'Of course I will.'

'It's this damned client. There are problems with . . . I won't bore you with the details. Why don't you invite Jilly over for the evening?'

'Yes, I might do that.'

'OK, I'll see you later.'

The minute he'd closed the front door, I went into the back garden and slipped into the bushes where James had emerged. I was desperate for his teenage cock, the taste of his fresh spunk, but he was nowhere to be seen. I wasn't sure whether he was at college or had a job. Having had little contact with his parents, I knew nothing about him. Yearning for crude sex, I hoped that Richard or Ian might call. Maybe one of my other lovers would ring me. I couldn't survive the day without a hard cock; it just wouldn't be possible.

Squatting in the bushes, keeping watch on the open back door, I could hear voices. It was definitely

James's voice, and another male. Perhaps he was talking to his father, I mused, again thinking that I was playing too close to home. There again, what was I worrying about? James would hardly tell his parents that I'd sucked his cock. And he'd never talk to Rod about my infidelity. Initiating young James into the fine art of decadent sex, I knew that I was safe enough.

'I'm, not lying,' James said, leaving the house with another young man in tow. 'If her husband hadn't come home, I'd have fucked her.'

'Yeah, yeah.' His friend laughed.

'She lifted her skirt up and pulled her panties down.'

'Of course she did, James. It's the sort of thing all married women do – in your dreams.'

'I don't care whether you believe me or not,' James returned. 'She's a damned attractive woman. And she fancies me rotten.'

'James, she's married. What the hell would she want with you?'

'My cock,' James announced proudly. 'She sucked me off.'

A damned attractive woman? I liked that comment. Watching from my hide as the lads chatted, I felt a wave of excitement roll through me. A teenager telling his friend how attractive I am, how I'd pulled my panties down, how I'd sucked him off . . . With fresh meat around like young James, there was no way I could remain faithful to my husband. Richard was hardly a spring chicken, but he had a big cock and amazing staying power. Old, young . . . I had the best of all worlds.

'I'll show you her garden,' James said, walking towards the bushes. 'With any luck, you'll get a look at her.'

Leaving the bushes, I dashed to the patio and slipped my panties off. Time for a little exhibitionism, I decided, sitting on a chair with my legs parted wide. My eyes closed as if I was relaxing beneath the summer sun, I watched the bushes through my eyelashes. James's face peered through the foliage, followed by his friend's. They stared at me, whispering and stifling their gasps as I allowed my thighs to part further. Did James's friend believe him now? I wondered as my juices seeped between the engorged lips of my naked pussy. Two young men, two solid cocks in dire need of female attention ... This was going to be a good day, I was sure.

Fanning my face as if I was hot, I slipped my blouse off and unhooked my bra. Tossing the garments on to the patio table before again closing my eyes and relaxing, I could feel the heat of the sun warming my firm breasts. My nipples rising proud from my areolae, my womb contracting, my clitoris swelling in expectation, my excitement heightened as the lads ogled my young breasts. There were two teenage cocks only yards away from my half-naked body, two pairs of heavy balls waiting to be drained ... I had to have them.

I wondered whether to slip my hand between my parted thighs and masturbate for the benefit of my voyeurs. I tugged my short skirt up to allow the sun to tan my thighs. The boys were watching, gazing at my pussy, and no doubt hoping to get their hands on my young body. Unable to resist temptation, I slipped my fingers between my pouting lips and massaged the solid nub of my clitoris.

I could hear whispers, the bushes rustling, as their excitement grew. Would James emerge from his hide? I wondered, moving my fingers in a circular motion around the bulb of my clit. Would he ask me to carry on where we'd left off the previous day and strip him of his virginity? The thought of showing off my young body turned me on no end. Why had I never done this before? I reflected. There again, I'd never had the opportunity to display my feminine intimacy to a couple of teenage lads.

'Hi,' James said, finally leaving the bushes.

'Oh, James,' I breathed surprisedly, sitting upright and closing my thighs. 'I didn't see your football come over.'

'No, I . . . I just thought I'd say hello.'

'Oh, right. Er . . . I was sunbathing. That's why I'm half-naked. You don't mind, do you?'

'Mind?' he echoed, his eyes locked on to my tits.

'My being half-naked.'

'Oh, er . . . no, of course not.'

'Did you enjoy your visit to my garden last night?'

'Yes, very much.'

'You've been thinking about me, haven't you? Thinking about my body.'

'Yes, I have. I was wondering . . . Well, I just thought that –'

'I know what your thoughts are, James,' I cut in, smiling at him as I parted my thighs wide. 'Why don't you kneel down and kiss me again? Kiss me like you did yesterday.'

Without a word, he kneeled between my feet and gazed longingly at the yawning valley of my pussy. I was wet, my creamy juices oozing from my open love hole and trickling down between my buttocks. Breathing deeply as James moved in and buried his face between my legs, I felt as horny as hell. If only Rod had appeased my yearning pussy, I mused dreamily, toying with the teats of my breasts. If only he'd attended to my feminine needs, then, perhaps . . . I'd still not remain faithful. It wasn't that Rod didn't satisfy me, I mused. No one man could satisfy me, only a string of men.

I gasped as James's tongue lapped up my flowing pussy milk. I noticed his young friend gazing through the bush at the incredible scene. Proof enough of James's sexual exploits, I mused. Would the lad wank himself to orgasm and spurt his spunk in the bushes? Or would he rather I allowed him to mouth fuck me? Reckoning that he, too, was a virgin, I relished the thought of breaking in two young lads. Their first time, their first pussy spunking. They'd remember me for the rest of their days.

The time had come to enjoy two teenage cocks, I decided. As much as I loved the feel of James's wet tongue sweeping eagerly over the sensitive tip of my erect clitoris, I was desperate to enjoy a double mouth fucking. Would his friend join us? I mused, gazing at the bushes. Or had he already wanked and wasted his fresh spunk? He'd be able to come again, I thought happily. I was sure that the lads would be able to spurt their spunk several times and, hopefully, Rod wouldn't come home and ruin my dirty sex games.

'Call your friend over,' I said, pushing James away from my sex-wet pussy.

'My friend?' he echoed, looking up and frowning at me. 'What friend?'

'The lad hiding in the bushes,' I replied with an impish giggle. 'I'm sure he'd like a piece of the action.'

'Oh, er . . .' he stammered, turning and facing the bushes. 'Simon, she wants you to join us.'

The lad emerged and walked across the lawn with the crotch of his jeans bulging with his obvious arousal. Reckoning that I'd caught him just in time, before he'd wanked and wasted his spunk, I ordered both young men to strip naked. Obediently following my instruction, they tugged their clothes off with an urgency that sent quivers through my young womb. Two cocks, I thought happily, focusing on each solid member in turn. Two pairs of spunk-laden balls desperate to be drained.

Their young balls were rolling within their fleshy sacs, heavy laden with their teenage cream. The boys had good bodies, muscular, firm. James had the larger cock, I observed, my mouth watering. But his friend's cock wasn't exactly small. Ordering my innocent lovers to stand before me, I leaned forwards and retracted their foreskins. Kissing each purple glans in turn, gasps of male pleasure disturbing the still air, I reached out and cupped both pairs of heaving balls in my hands. Their cocks twitched; their naked bodies trembled. They were lucky lads, I mused, meeting a horny slut like me. They couldn't have wished for more.

I grabbed each rock-hard shaft and pulled them together. I licked first one swollen knob and then the other. Savouring the taste of their salt, I ran my tongue up and down their veined sex rods, breathing in the male scent of their black pubes as I worked on their beautiful cocks. Wetting their hard shafts, savouring the taste of sex, I managed to suck both knobs into my spunk-thirsty mouth. The boys obviously couldn't believe their luck as I swept my tongue over the silky-smooth surfaces of their beautiful plums. Gasping, swaying on their sagging legs, they weren't going to take long to pump out their spunk and flood my gobbling mouth.

I fondled their heavy balls as I performed my double plum sucking, recalling the time at school when I'd sucked two cocks into my wet mouth. The lads were brothers, and they'd been teasing me all day because I'd spilled something down my skirt. After school, I followed them across the common. They were stunned when I stopped them and said that the stain on my skirt was spunk. I said that I'd sucked off a boy's cock in the lunch hour and he'd come all over my skirt. They didn't hesitate when I suggested that they double mouth fuck me.

We'd slipped behind some bushes and I'd kneeled on the ground before them as they'd pulled out their stiff cocks. Gobbling on their knobs, wanking their shafts, I'd fondled their balls as they'd gasped and trembled. They'd come very quickly, both pumping my mouth full of fresh spunk, bathing my darting tongue and filling my cheeks with their teenage spunk. From then on, I met them every day after school and allowed them to double mouth fuck me, double throat spunk me. Sheer sexual bliss.

'You're incredible,' Simon breathed, breaking my reverie. 'I wish you were *my* next-door neighbour.'

'I wasn't lying,' James said triumphantly. 'I told you that she was good.'

I decided to drink their spunk before allowing them to fuck me. My exhilaration rising fast, my red lips stretched tautly around their shafts, I kneaded their heavy balls. They were close to spunking, I knew, as their naked bodies shook uncontrollably. Breathing heavily, swaying on their trembling legs, they let out low moans of pleasure as I snaked my tongue around their swollen knobs. The sound of my slurping mouth filled my ears. I wanked their rock-hard shafts in my desperation to bring out their teenage cream. Heavy breathing, gasping, moaning . . . They were almost there.

My mouth finally flooded with spunk as they reached their goals, and I repeatedly swallowed hard. Unable to keep up with the flow, I could feel the male cream streaming down my chin and splattering my breasts. I was in my sexual heaven. Two cocks, a double mouth spunking . . . What better way could I have spent the morning? Sucking and swallowing, I again hoped that Rod would keep away. If he arrived home now . . . Was he suspicious? I mused. Had Neil hinted at my infidelity? Neil didn't know the half of it.

Trying not to think about Neil, his blackmailing, I sucked out the last of the lads' spunk and slipped their knobs out of my mouth. Licking my sex-glossed lips, I ran my tongue up and down their deflating shafts and lapped up the spilled cream. They looked down at me in amazement, gazed in awe at my spunked mouth, my lapping tongue. They obviously couldn't believe their luck as I cleansed their shafts and knobs. And I couldn't believe *my* luck.

Leaving my chair, I slipped my skirt off and lay on my back on the lawn beneath the summer sun. Spreading my limbs, my well-juiced cunt crack gaping wide open, I grinned as the boys scrutinised my naked body. They were obviously wondering who was to fuck me first, but I had other plans. Ordering James to kneel astride my head, I told Simon to lick my cunt crack and suck out my girl juice. They took their positions without question, Simon's tongue delving into my juice-dripping slit and James kneeling with his full balls hovering above my gasping mouth.

I licked James's scrotum, and gazed at his cock-shaft rising above my face, his purple knob pointing skywards. A monument to teenage males. With Simon's tongue working on my swollen clitoris and James's cock twitching above my wide eyes, I knew that I'd found my niche. The sun warmed my naked body as I licked and nibbled on James's ball sac. My juices flowed freely from my yawning sex hole as his friend licked me. I closed my eyes and lost myself in my sexual delirium.

Taking one of James's balls into my mouth, I sucked gently. He let out a rush of breath, his naked body trembling again as his cock swelled to an incredible size. Simon's tongue delved into the sex-drenched sheath of my pussy, lapping up my flowing pussy milk. I spread my legs to the extreme to allow him deeper access to the sexual centre of my young body. I could hear him slurping as he drank from my hot cunt. The sound of sheer sexual bliss, I mused dreamily, slipping James's rolling ball out of my mouth.

Ordering James to wank his magnificent cock, I said that I wanted him to give me a facial. Readily complying, he grabbed his shaft and began moving his hand up and down. I again licked his scrotum, nibbling and biting his fleshy ball sac as he wanked faster. Young and virile, he came quickly. His white spunk jetted from his orgasming knob and rained over my blonde hair. He moved back to allow his spunk to splatter my face. My mouth open wide, I felt his orgasmic liquid splashing on to my tongue as he towered above me gasping in orgasm.

Simon was obviously unable to hold back any longer and stabbed hard at my pink sex hole. I'd wanted to keep the young virgins waiting a little longer for full-blown sex, but it didn't matter. His granite-hard shaft entering me, stretching my pussy wide open, he rammed his cock fully home and let out a triumphant cry of male satisfaction. He was a man now, I mused, swallowing the spunk raining into my mouth. After withdrawing, he again rammed his cock into me, finally finding his rhythm and enjoying his first fuck.

My naked body jolted as spunk rained over my flushed face. I knew that I now had two more lovers to add to my list. My brother-in-law wasn't a lover,

I reflected dolefully. He was blackmailing me. But I'd deal with him at some stage. Neil wasn't going to cross me and get away with it. He was threatening me, my very way of life, and I wasn't prepared to allow that to continue. Neil would have his comeuppance, I swore.

'Yes,' Simon gasped as his spunk flooded my spasming pussy. He'd done it, I thought happily, as James brought out the last of his come. Simon was a fully fledged man. I could feel his teenage spunk oozing from the cock-bloated entrance to my pussy and running down between my firm buttocks. Again and again, he rammed himself deep into my cunt, fucking me hard, spunking my cervix. He might have achieved his goal, I mused, but I'd nowhere near finished with him.

'You like spunk, don't you?' James asked me, moving to my side and gazing at the white liquid covering my face.

'Whatever gave you that idea?' I giggled as Simon made his last penile thrusts and drained his swinging balls.

'You're so hot and tight,' Simon breathed, finally stilling his manhood deep within my spunk-flooded pussy. 'That was incredible.'

'You were very good,' I praised him. 'Now, James, are you ready to become a man?'

'In a minute,' he replied, looking down at his flaccid cock.

'To rouse your cocks, why don't you both examine me?' Rolling on to my front, I parted my legs wide. 'I love having my bottom hole examined,' I said with an impish giggle. 'Play with me, play with my bumhole.'

Settling either side of my naked body, the teenagers parted the firm cheeks of my buttocks and exposed the delicate brown tissue surrounding the inlet to my rectal duct. Toying with my anus, teasing me with their fingertips, examining me, they were obviously in their element. I doubted that they could believe that this was happening as they stroked my anus. A horny housewife demanding crude sex? This was the stuff of dirty magazines. It didn't happen in real life.

I gasped as my pussy lips were parted wide by fumbling fingers. They needed to learn, I mused dreamily as fingers entered my spunk-flooded pussy. They needed to examine me fully, and experience crude sex, to prepare them for the world. This was a good start. A double mouth fucking, examining my bottom hole, exploring the hot depths of my pussy sheath ... This was the best initiation any teenage boy could have.

'Finger my bottom,' I breathed shakily. 'I want fingers deep inside my bottom and my cunt.'

One lad eased a finger deep into the tightening duct of my rectum as the other pushed several fingers into my cunt. My thighs parted to the extreme, my sex holes crudely and eagerly attended to by two young men, I closed my eyes and revelled in the intimate attention. The amazing sensations building, a second finger entering the constricted sheath of my rectum, I lay trembling on the soft grass beneath the summer sun as the boys stretched my bared sex holes wide open.

I could have stayed there all day and revelled in my incredible pleasure. My pussy juices squelching, my rectum gripping two thrusting fingers, I imagined half a dozen young men attending to my most intimate feminine needs. Fingers, hands, mouths, tongues, cocks, spunk ... Perhaps James would round up a few friends and bring them to my garden, bring them to my naked body.

Ordering the boys to push as many fingers into my holes as they could, I recalled the first time I'd had my pussy fisted. While on honeymoon in Tenerife, I'd left Rod sleeping in the hotel room early one morning and had gone for a walk along the beach. Desperate for sex, I'd met a young man and offered him my bikini-clad body. I'd led him to a patch of grass beneath a palm tree, and allowed him to yank my bikini off and spread my thighs wide.

I'll never forget the incredible experience. I was wet with desire as his fingers slipped with ease into my tight little pussy. As he'd managed to force his entire fist into my pussy cavern, I'd gazed in amazement at the inner lips of my pussy wrapped tautly around his wrist. I'd never known anything like it as he'd flexed his fingers, stretching my young cunt to capacity. The heavenly sensations driving me wild, I'd come like I'd never come before as he'd fist fucked my sweet cunt. Rod asked me whether I'd enjoyed my walk when I'd got back to the hotel. My walk had been most exhilarating.

'I'm ready now,' James said bringing me back to the present.

'Your cock's hard?' I asked him.

'Yes, very.'

'You'd better fuck me then,' I breathed. 'Fuck me hard, James.'

'Oh, I will,' he assured me as the fingers left my burning sex holes.

'Fuck my tight cunt hard and fill me with your spunk.'

My face resting on the grass, I waited in anticipation as James positioned himself between my spread thighs. The second virgin was about to become a man, I mused, as he pressed his bulbous glans between the dripping lips of my cock-hungry pussy. I

116

breathed heavily as his knob entered me and began its pioneering journey along my tight sheath to my ripe cervix. Already brimming with Simon's spunk, my pussy spasmed, gripping James's hard cock as he impaled me fully.

'God,' he breathed as his knob kissed my cervix and my inner lips gripped the root of his organ. After withdrawing, he drove into me with a vengeance as I lay gasping on the grass. This was real sex, I mused, ordering Simon to finger fuck my bottom hole as James found his pistoning rhythm. Complying with my crude instruction, Simon drove two fingers into my rectal canal as James repeatedly drove his knob deep into the very core of my abused body.

I had a lot to teach my young pupils, I thought dreamily. The fine art of bondage and spanking, the decadent act of double cock fucking my tight pussy ... They were eager to learn, and I was keen to teach them all I knew. Before I'd finished with them, they would have experienced every possible sexual act, discovered the true meaning of decadence. Having reached manhood, they'd now pursue other girls, hunger for their firm tits, thirst for their sweet little virgin cunts. Would they crave anal sex?

I decided to teach the lads the crude act of anal sex before allowing them to leave. I let out a rush of breath as James's spunk flooded my burning pussy. He gasped and grunted as he discovered manhood, repeatedly ramming his throbbing knob deep into my tight cunt. The second stripping of male virginity, I thought happily, as he drained himself. They'd both mouth fucked me and pumped their spunk down my throat; they'd fucked and spunked my pussy ... All they had to do now was give me a hard anal fucking.

'Bloody hell,' James gasped, finally collapsing over my naked body. 'That was fantastic.'

'You're both doing very well,' I praised my young pupils as James withdrew his deflating cock from my spunk-bubbling pussy. 'But the lesson's not over yet.'

'You want more?' Simon asked incredulously as James lay on the grass by my side.

'Of course I want more,' I replied with a giggle. 'You've must have realised by now that I'm a nymphomaniac? Before you both leave, you're going to . . .' My words tailed off as I heard cups rattling in the kitchen. I froze. 'Get out of here,' I whispered to the boys. 'Grab your clothes and run.'

As they scurried into the bushes like frightened rabbits, I couldn't believe that Rod had come home. Surely, he must have seen me through the window? The back door was wide open; I was naked on the lawn, brimming with teenage spunk . . . He must have heard me talking to the lads. My stomach churning, I decided to relax and make out that I was sunbathing. Had Rod seen or heard me, he'd have come out into the garden. I was safe, I was sure. I'd got away with fucking two teenage lads under Rod's nose.

'So, you're the slut?' a young woman asked as she stepped out on to the patio.

'Who the hell are you?' I breathed, folding my arms to conceal my breasts.

'My lady friend,' Neil said, joining the woman. 'Jackie, this is Cindy.'

'What the hell . . .' I began as the girl grinned at me. 'How dare you come into my house and –'

'Calm down,' Neil sighed. 'We thought we'd call in for a cup of coffee.'

'A cup of coffee? How did you get in?'

'Rod gave me a key when you went on holiday, remember?'

'Get out, for fuck's sake. I'm not having you walk

into my house with your bit of rough whenever you feel like it.'

'She's a fiery little bitch,' the girl said.

'And she's a slut,' Neil rejoined, looking down at me huddling on the lawn.

'Unless you both get out of here, I'll –'

'You'll what?' Neil asked me. 'Tell Rod that you fucked two young lads on the lawn?'

'What do you want, Neil? What the hell do you want?'

'It's not so much what I want. It's what Jackie wants.'

'What are you talking about?'

'Jackie is . . . How shall I put it? She's bisexual.'

'What?'

'She likes both sexes, Cindy. We seem to have called at the right time. I must say that I wasn't expecting you to be naked and ready for lesbian sex.'

'Lesbian sex? Fuck off,' I spat, shocked by my brother-in-law's words. 'If you think that I'm going to –'

'I don't think, Cindy. I know.'

'There's no way I'm going to allow that slut to touch me. What the hell do you think I am?'

'In serious trouble,' he returned as the girl gazed longingly at my naked body. 'The photographs I took just now . . . I really don't think that Rod will understand, do you? His naked wife getting fucked on the lawn by two young lads? I really can't see that he will –'

'This has gone too far,' I cut in angrily. 'You can't expect me to –'

'I expect you to do exactly as I say, Cindy. Now, why don't you lie back and relax and allow Jackie to love you?'

'Love me? If you think –'

119

'The choice, as always, is yours.'

As Neil's slag sat beside me on the grass and pulled her T-shirt over her head, I thought that I must be dreaming. This wasn't happening; it couldn't be happening. The fact that I didn't know Neil at all hit me like a ton of bricks. Rod's brother, the man I'd known for over five years, was trying to force me to have lesbian sex. This was like something out of a horror movie. Why was Neil doing this? He'd always been like a brother to me, but now . . .

The girl, his tart, was no more than eighteen years old. Although she was extremely attractive, her jet-black hair cascading over the firm mounds of her naked breasts as she removed her bra, there was no way I was going to have sex with her. Neil wasn't only a bastard, he was evil. It was one thing allowing him to fuck me, but to have sex with his bit of filth on the side . . .

'Relax and enjoy yourself,' Neil said.

'Neil, I –'

'Would you like me to phone Rod? I'll call him and invite him to watch, if you wish?'

'For fuck's sake, Neil. Why are you doing this to me?'

'Doing what? Jackie wants to make love to you. You like sex, don't you?'

'With men, yes.'

'Try it, Cindy. You never know, you might enjoy it. Now, lie on the grass and relax.'

My heart racing, my stomach churning, I lay back and closed my eyes. Never had I been so humiliated in all my life. As the girl's fingers toyed with my erect nipples, I shuddered. I'd had plenty of sex over the years, tried anything and everything with a hundred men. But never had I dreamed about lesbian sex. Tweaking my teats, the girl leaned over my naked body and licked the firm mounds of my tits. I shuddered as her fingers slid down over the smooth plateau of my stomach and stroked the fleshy cushions of my outer labia. Blackmailed, humiliated, degraded . . . But I had no choice.

As the girl massaged the sensitive nub of my clitoris, I instinctively knew that this was only the beginning of a horrendous nightmare. Neil had me exactly where he wanted me, squirming on a hook with no possible way of escape. Recalling the previous evening when I'd sucked James's cock and thought I'd heard a noise in the house, I reckoned that it was Neil. He'd obviously been lurking, spying, taking photographs to build his dossier of evidence against me. And he now had photographic evidence of my whoredom, pictures of two teenage lads fucking me on the lawn. He'd caught me. I was well and truly hooked.

'Give her a good licking,' Neil ordered the lesbian slut.

'She's bubbling over with spunk,' the girl said, easing a finger deep into my pussy.

'Even better. You can suck out a blend of spunk and girlie juice.'

Settling between my splayed thighs, the slut peeled my outer lips wide apart and licked the wet folds nestling within my gaping valley. Her tongue repeatedly sweeping over the tip of my erect clitoris, I tried to forget that this was a female between my legs. This was Ian, Richard, James, any man . . . But, with her long hair tickling my lower stomach, caressing my inner thighs, there was no way I could forget. This was a crude act of lesbian sex. Her finger slipping out of my tight pussy, she moved down and pushed her tongue deep into my spunk-brimming sex duct.

My mind was awash with a thousand confusing thoughts. I wondered whether I'd have to reciprocate and lick the slut's pussy. No, I decided. There was no way I was going to lick out another woman's pussy. My clitoris swelling, my womb contracting, I tried to deny the building pleasure. I couldn't allow a female to turn me on. A tongue was a tongue, I tried to convince myself. Male or female, what was the difference? The difference was lesbianism, and I wasn't a lesbian.

Neil took several photographs as the slut tongue fucked the tightening sheath of my pussy. Naked on the lawn, my limbs spread, a girl licking between the wet lips of my vulva ... If Rod ever got to see the photographs ... Why hadn't I ever had a clue, an inkling, as to the darker side of my brother-in-law? This was a well-kept secret, I reflected. The times he'd been round with Sue and enjoyed a drink with Rod and me, the times we'd got together and ... Not once had I ever dreamed that he was a pervert.

'Our little secret,' he said, and chuckled as the girl slurped and sucked between my thighs. 'Rod and Sue will never discover our relationship. You'll have all the sex you want, I'll fuck you as and when I feel like it, and Jackie –'

'No,' I interrupted him. 'This won't work.'

'Won't work? Why ever not?'

'Because Rod will realise that something's wrong.'

'He's never realised before, Cindy. Good God, you must have fucked a thousand men, and he's never been suspicious.'

'That's different. The men I know ... Rod has never met them; he knows nothing about them. You're his brother, for fuck's sake. Don't you think that Sue will be suspicious the next time you're both here?'

'Why should she be?'

'Because you'll wink at me, grin at me, try to grope me at every opportunity and –'

'Don't be ridiculous. Of course I wouldn't jeopard-
ise our relationship by slipping my hand into your
wet panties. We all get on very well together, and
that's the way it'll stay.'

'No, it won't.'

'You're forgetting something, Cindy.'

'Oh?'

'You're the one who's been playing around behind
Rod's back. You're the one who's spent the last five
years cheating and lying and fucking other men. If
the shit hits the fan, you're the one who will pay
dearly for your adultery. Sue and I will continue to
be the loving, faithful couple. Whereas you'll end up
with nothing.'

He was right, I knew, as I listened to the girl's
slurping tongue. If anyone was going to lose, it would
be me. I was going to have to get rid of my lovers.
Richard, Ian, James . . . They'd all have to go before I
could begin to formulate my plans. Get my own house
in order, and then work on Neil's downfall. I'd have
to get my hands on the photographs, the evidence.
But I didn't think that would be too difficult. I had a
key to his house. All I'd have to do would be to sneak
round when he was at work and Sue was out . . .

'You taste heavenly,' the slut breathed as she drank
from my pussy. 'Would you like to taste me?'

'No, I would not,' I returned firmly.

'You don't seem to have grasped the situation,'
Neil said. 'You'll do exactly as you're told, other-
wise . . .'

'OK, go ahead and ruin my marriage,' I hissed. 'I'd
rather lose Rod than lick out some filthy slut's cunt.'

'If that's the way you want it, that's fine by me.
Come on, Jackie. Let's be going.'

As the girl grabbed her bra and blouse and dressed,
I wondered whether Neil would ruin me. What would

he gain by ending my marriage? Nothing. Watching the evil pair step into the house, I hauled myself to my feet and gathered up my clothes. My life was a mess, a complete and utter mess. After only a few days, years of playing around had come to an end. All I had to look forward to now was Neil's cock and his slut's tongue and pussy.

'Is everything all right?' James asked, emerging from the bushes.

'Yes,' I replied, smiling at him. 'Where's your friend?'

'Gone home. That girl . . . I was watching you. Is she forcing you to have sex?'

'Yes, she is,' I sighed. 'And the man. James, I think it best that you don't come here again.'

'But . . . I thought . . .'

'Things are getting out of hand. As much as I like you, as much as I want you, I don't think it's a good idea.'

'Please,' he breathed, holding my naked shoulders and gazing at my firm breasts. 'Please, let me come and see you again.'

'All right,' I conceded, again falling prey to my inner desires. 'But this must be a well-kept secret. We'll have our fun, but no one must know about it.'

'What about Simon?'

'You can bring Simon here, but tell no one else.'

'Shall I stay now? I have plenty of time.'

'No, James. I'd like you to, but . . . they might come back. I don't want you to get caught up in this.'

'In what? Tell me what's going on.'

'Go now. Go back to your garden. I'll call you when . . . when I need you.'

'OK. But you're sure that you're OK?'

'Yes, I'm fine.'

Watching him slip into the bushes, I was about to call him back and have him spank my naked buttocks. I'd have given anything to have spent the rest of the morning with him, loving him, lusting him. Anything? Would I have given my marriage? What was my marriage worth? I pondered. Rod, and my beautiful house, plenty of money ... My pussy muscles tightened as I imagined young James fucking me, his cock repeatedly ramming deep into my sex-starved pussy. I wandered into the house and closed the back door. God, how I wanted James, his solid cock, his wet tongue, his thrusting fingers ... What was my marriage worth?

Seven

'Neil and Sue are coming round,' Rod told me as he replaced the phone. 'I'm glad I didn't have to work late.'

'I was glad too,' I sighed. 'I was hoping to spend the evening with you.'

'They're only calling in for a while, love. It'll be nice to see them. I haven't seen Sue for ages.'

'I suppose so.'

'Are you all right?'

'Yes, yes. As I said, I was hoping to ... Oh well, not to worry.'

'When they've gone, we'll sit down and watch a film together. I'm sure they won't stay for long.'

'Yes, I'd like that.'

'By the way, I spoke to old Saunders from next door.'

'Oh?'

'He came over as I parked the car and apologised for James getting into our garden through the bushes.'

'I ... I didn't know he had.'

'To retrieve his football, apparently. It might be an idea to stop walking around the garden naked. I said that the neighbours might see you.'

'James didn't see me, did he?'

'His father didn't mention it. There again, I don't suppose James would have told him if he'd seen you naked. You must be careful, Cindy. You know what lads of that age are like.'

'Do I?'

'Hormones, love. Their hormones go wild during their teens. One glimpse of your naked body and . . .'

'And what?'

'Well, you know.'

'No, I don't know. What are you suggesting?'

'I'm not suggesting anything. I just think that it's best that young James doesn't see you naked. You seem very tetchy, Cindy. You haven't been your old self for several days. Is everything all right?'

'Yes, yes, of course.'

'Something's on your mind, I know it.'

'It's just that . . . we've had Alan round for a barbeque; Neil's been round and now he's coming here with Sue; you had to work late last night . . . I just wish things would calm down a little.'

'They will, I promise. I won't be working late again for a while and . . . Oh, that'll be them.'

As Rod answered the front door, I felt my chest tighten, my stomach churn. I hadn't seen Sue since all this began, and I wasn't sure whether I could face her. Her husband had fucked me; his tart had licked my pussy . . . God, what a bloody mess, I thought, as I heard Neil's voice in the hall. What a fucking mess.

'Hi,' Sue said, beaming as she walked into the lounge and flung her arms around my neck. 'How are you?'

'Fine,' I replied. 'It's great to see you.'

'I don't know where the time goes. I've been meaning to ring you, but never got round to it. It was Neil's idea to come over.'

'Oh, right,' I breathed, frowning at Neil as he followed Rod into the lounge.

127

'Hi, Cindy,' he said, winking at me. 'How are things?'

'Fine,' I replied. 'And I hope they stay that way.'

'Drink, anyone?' Rod asked.

The situation was unbearable. Neil kept looking at me; Sue rambled on about this and that, and Rod was trying to play the host by offering everyone sandwiches. I knew that Neil would try to get me alone at some stage, and I was right. As I went into the kitchen to make Sue a cup of tea, he followed me. Squeezing my breasts, he said that he had something for Rod. It was an envelope containing the photographs.

'When I leave, I'll make out that I found it on the ground by the front door,' he said and chuckled softly. 'I'll pass it to Rod and –'

'And ruin my marriage.'

'It's up to you, Cindy. You won't play the game, so what choice do I have? I'm not bluffing.'

'I know you're not bluffing, Neil. You're the sort of bastard who'd delight in ruining people's lives. Whether it be my life or your brother's . . .'

'There'll be a massive row this evening. After I've gone, Rod will open the envelope and that'll be the end of your marriage. That doesn't have to happen, Cindy. All you have to do is play the game.'

'All right,' I finally conceded. 'I don't want to see Rod hurt so –'

'You don't want to see him hurt? That's a laugh. After all you've done behind his back . . .'

'OK, I've said that I'd go along with you. Just shut up now.'

'How about a quick hand job while we're waiting for the kettle to boil?'

'Don't be ridiculous,' I snapped.

'When you've made the tea, tell Rod that you're going to show me around the garden.'

'Neil . . .'

'Tell him, Cindy.'

Taking the tea into Sue, I hovered for a while before mentioning the garden to Neil. He talked about the good weather we'd been having and how the weeds were getting out of hand. He then suggested that I show him around the garden. Rod was so busy telling Sue about his job that he was totally oblivious as I left the lounge with Neil in tow. I didn't want this, I reflected, walking across the lawn to the end of the garden. A quick hand job? This was a crazy situation, and a very dangerous one.

'This'll do nicely,' Neil said, slipping behind the bushes by the shed. 'Pull your knickers down.'

'Neil, we can't . . .' I began as I joined him.

'I'll pull them down for you,' he whispered, lifting my short skirt up over my stomach and yanking my panties down. 'Nice and wet,' he breathed, his finger slipping between the puffy lips of my pussy.

As he pushed his finger deep into my contracting pussy, I felt a ripple of pleasure run through my pelvis. A second finger entered me, stretching the walls of my sex sheath and inducing my pussy milk to flow. I knew that I was becoming weak in my arousal. My panties stretched between my knees as I stood with my feet apart. I felt my legs sagging as my pussy muscles tightened around his pistoning fingers. My clitoris swelled expectantly. I hoped that he'd unzip his trousers and drive his cock deep into me.

Slipping his fingers out of my pussy, he dropped to his knees and pulled my outer labia wide apart. His wet tongue ran up and down my sex crack, sweeping over the sensitive tip of my sex button. He again thrust two fingers deep into my hole and massaged my inner flesh. I shuddered and let out a rush of breath as I clung to his head to steady myself. The sensations driving me wild, I hoped that Rod or Sue wouldn't decide to look for us just yet. I needed to come, desperately.

His free hand moving behind me, his finger flipping between my firm buttocks, he teased the delicate brown tissue surrounding my anus. Again, I gasped and whimpered as he took me ever closer to my orgasm. His finger entered my rectum, driving deep into the very core of my trembling body. He sucked my clitoris into his mouth and finger fucked my pussy until I cried out in the grip of my climax.

Tossing my head back, I shuddered as my orgasm peaked and shook my very soul. There was something highly arousing about being licked and sucked to orgasm by my blackmailing brother-in-law in the garden. Dangerous, exciting, I loved the notion of the clandestine act of adultery. My juices squelched as Neil increased his finger-thrusting rhythm. My clitoris pulsated wildly within his hot mouth. I thought that I was going to pass out with pleasure. My rectal duct gripping his pistoning finger, I lost myself in my sexual delirium. Dizzy, gasping for breath, shaking violently, I finally began to drift down from my amazing climax.

'God, no more,' I gasped, my long blonde hair cascading over my sex-flushed face as he slowed his double finger fucking.

'You're something else,' he whispered, slipping his fingers out of my burning sex holes. 'Kneel down and you can give me a blowjob.'

'It's too risky,' I complained, glancing at the house as he stood before me. 'If they come out here . . .'

'They won't. And, if they do, we'll have plenty of time to sort ourselves out.'

'Neil, I –'

'Just get on with it.'

Pulling my panties up and kneeling as he hauled out his hard cock, I retracted his fleshy foreskin and took his ripe plum into my wet mouth. I'd never done anything like this when Rod was around. I'd sucked a hundred cocks during my five-year marriage, but only when he'd been at work. This was risky, bloody stupid. But I supposed that Neil was right. We'd have plenty of time to sort ourselves out before Rod and Sue reached the end of the garden.

'Jackie enjoyed licking your cunt,' Neil breathed, obviously trying to disgust me. 'She's taken quite a fancy to you.' Ignoring him, I bobbed my head up and down, repeatedly taking his bulbous knob to the back of my throat in an effort to bring out his spunk before the others came looking for us. Neil called me a slut as I ran my tongue over his silky-smooth glans and wanked his rock-hard shaft. A cock-sucking slut, a spunk-gobbling whore. I might have been a slut, but he was a bastard.

Again thinking that there was no way out of my predicament, I wondered whether I could turn the situation round. Perhaps, the next time I was at Neil's place, I could wink at him, keep giving him the eye until he responded and roused Sue's suspicion. Alone with Neil in the kitchen, I could let out a sexy giggle. Perhaps I might tell him, rather too loudly, to keep his hands to himself. Sue would believe that he was trying to get off with me. And, of course, I'd fuel her fire of suspicion.

But would that really do any good? I wondered as Neil came closer to his orgasm. What would I gain? Neil would retaliate, simply fire Rod's suspicion and I'd probably be worse off. There was only one thing I could do, and that was get my hands on the incriminating photographs. Once I'd destroyed the evidence . . . Easier said than done, I mused. There was no way I could search his house. Even if I had the chance, I'd never find the photographs. He'd probably taken them to work, hidden them somewhere in his office. I was going to have to do something about my predicament, but what?

Taking his cock to the back of my throat, sinking my teeth gently into his solid shaft, I was desperate for him to come. Was I addicted to spunk? I mused. How much spunk had I swallowed since discovering cocks during my schooldays? Pints? Gallons? Moving my head back and holding Neil's purple knob between my full lips, I wanked his shaft and tongued his spunk slit. The taste, the feel of his huge glans between my lips . . . I was wet with desire, trembling with lust.

'Where are you?' Sue called from the patio as her husband was about to shoot his spunk into my mouth.

'Here,' I replied, rising to my feet and stepping out from behind the bushes. 'I was just talking to Neil about having these bushes removed.'

'That's an idea,' she said, walking across the lawn towards me. 'You'd have a lot more space.'

'The roots will be pretty deep,' Neil said shakily, trying to conceal the bulge in his trousers as he stood next to me.

As Rod wandered across the lawn and joined the discussion, I felt a shot of adrenalin bolt through my veins. The danger, the excitement . . . My panties were soaked with my juices of lust, my clitoris solid in expectation. Sucking my brother-in-law's cock while our partners were nearby had aroused me no end. It was a shame that I'd not had the pleasure of a mouthful of spunk, I reflected, as Rod and Sue suggested that we join them for a drink and went back to the house. This was a new and exciting game. But it was also blackmail.

'You'll have to finish the job,' Neil breathed softly,

adjusting the crotch of his trousers. 'There's no way I can stay like this.'

'You'll have to have a wank,' I returned. 'We almost got caught just now.'

'Come on, Cindy. It won't take a minute. You don't want Rod to see the photographs, do you?'

'Of course I don't.'

'Then, you'd better do as you're told. You've had more men than –'

'It's funny to think that I've been playing around for years; you have your bit on the side and . . . well, Sue has her male friend.'

'What?' he breathed, staring into my blue eyes. 'Her male friend?'

'It's been going on for about a year now.'

'You're lying.'

'Am I? I was in town last summer when I noticed Sue go into a bar.'

'You must have been mistaken. She never goes into bars.'

'That what I thought, at first. I peered through the doorway and saw her having a drink with a young man. I thought he was just a friend she'd bumped into. Until they kissed each other.'

'I don't believe a word of it.'

'I must have seen them together half a dozen times over the last year or so.'

'Why tell me?'

'I thought that you should know, Neil. It seems that, apart from good old Rod, we're all fucking around on the side.'

'I don't believe you, Cindy. Sue isn't like that.'

'Isn't she?'

'Has she told you about this man?'

'No, she hasn't. Maybe I shouldn't have mentioned it. I just thought that . . .'

133

'You'd try to cause trouble?'

'Not at all. Seeing as you know about me and I know about you, I thought you should know about Sue.'

'As I said, I don't believe you.'

'That's up to you. We'd better go inside. They'll be wondering what we're doing.'

'What about —'

'Have a wank, Neil. Or go and see your bisexual slut. By the way, does she live locally?'

'Why do you want to know?'

'Because I've seen her around. Has Sue met her?'

'Sue? Of course not.'

'I could have sworn that she was in the bar with Sue and her young man last year.'

'Hardly.'

'Maybe I'm wrong.'

Watching Neil mooch across the lawn to the house, I wondered whether he believed my lies. He was worried, that was for sure. But what was the point in worrying him? What would I achieve? What would I gain by lying about Sue? I couldn't carry on like this, beholden to my brother-in-law, forced to suck his cock as and when he needed his balls draining . . . I had to put an end to the nightmare.

'Aren't you coming in?' Rod called from the back door.

'In a minute,' I replied, wishing that he'd leave me alone with my thoughts. He was always there, hovering, fussing . . .

'What is it, love?' he asked as he approached. 'Something's bothering you, I know it.'

'It's Neil,' I began, wondering what the hell I was about to say.' He keeps . . .'

'Keeps what?'

'Chatting me up.'

'What? You must be mistaken, Cindy. Neil would never –'

'Rod, I am not mistaken. You suspected him the other day. When you came home and found me naked, you said something about Neil being a man and –'

'I didn't suspect him. All I meant was –'

'Rod, he keeps chatting me up and I don't like it.'

'What's he said, exactly?'

'That I have a nice body, that he'd like to see me naked . . .'

'I'll have a word with him. He's probably just messing about, having a bit of a laugh. I'll tell him to back off, OK?'

'All right. I'm going to stay here for a while. I need to relax.'

Watching him walk back to the house, I wondered what the hell I'd done. Neil wouldn't be at all happy once he discovered that I'd gone running to Rod with my tales. But I had to do something. A mistake or not, I had to try to put a stop to Neil. I half expected him to come marching down the garden and have a go at me. But, with Sue and Rod around, he obviously thought better of it. He'd be round the following day, I knew. He'd threaten me, have a go at me. At least I'd made some sort of stand.

Sue came to the back door and said goodbye, but Neil didn't bother. When they'd gone, I sat in the lounge with Rod. He seemed awkward, nervy. This was ridiculous, I mused. He'd not mentioned Neil, not said anything about having a word with him. What was going on? I'd thought that he'd question me, ask me what Neil had been saying. He finally announced that he had to go to the office for an hour or so. I was pleased, but didn't show it.

135

'I thought we were going to watch a film,' I sighed as he moved to the door.

'I had a word with Neil,' he said, forcing a smile. 'He was shocked by your accusation.'

'I thought he'd deny it.'

'Cindy, he reckons that you're making this up.'

'As if I'd . . . God, I wish I'd not said anything to you.'

'How long has this been going on? Neil chatting you up, I mean.'

'A week or so,' I breathed, wishing that Rod would go and leave me in peace. 'Look, just forget about it. I shouldn't have said anything. Do you have to go out?'

'I've got to get some papers from the office. And I need to . . . I'll see you later.'

It was unlike Rod to go out on the spur of the moment. But I was pleased to have a little time alone to think and plan. Plan? Plan what? I didn't know how I was going to deal with my brother-in-law. I could have gone along with him, screwed and sucked him now and then. But to have sex with his lesbian slut? He had photographs, I reflected. Photographs of the slut licking my pussy. How the hell had I got myself into this horrendous mess?

Deciding to take a shower, I went up to my bedroom and slipped out of my clothes. I needed a holiday, I decided. I needed to get away for a week or two and relax, calm my mind. Greece would be nice, I mused, crossing the landing to the bathroom. The sun, the sea, good food and drink . . .

Hearing a noise downstairs, I thought that Rod must have come back for something. I called out, but he didn't answer. Reckoning that he must have gone into the garden to look for me, I trotted down the stairs.

'We need to talk,' Neil said, standing in the kitchen doorway grinning at me.

'What the . . . How dare you walk into my house! Rod will be back any minute, so –'

'I want to talk to you, not Rod.'

'Get out, Neil. I've just about had enough of this.'

'So, you went running to Rod? You said that I'd been chatting you up, didn't you?'

'Yes, and I'll tell him that you came here and started again.'

'That wouldn't be a wise move, Cindy.'

'Why have you come back? What do you want?'

'I dropped Sue off and decided to come back and chat to Rod about your lies. When I noticed that his car wasn't in the drive . . . You have a beautiful body, nice hard tits.'

'Get out, Neil.'

'Not until we've had a talk. You don't seem to realise the severity of the predicament you're in. I have photographs . . .'

'Yes, I know. But I don't care. You can threaten me, you can –'

'Tell Rod about Richard and Ian?'

'I . . . I don't know what you're talking about.'

'I've done my homework, Cindy. As I said the other day, I've known about you for three years.'

'OK, so you know about my male friends. Look, if Rod gets back and sees your car –'

'I've parked down the road. More to the point, if he gets back and finds you standing naked in front of me . . .'

'You're hell bent on causing trouble, aren't you?'

'No, I'm not. The last thing I want is trouble, Cindy. If we hear Rod's car, I'll slip out the back way. But only if you finish what you started earlier.'

'For God's sake, Neil. I can't have you walking

into my house demanding sex as and when you feel like it.'

'If Rod walks in and find us, what's he going to think? You go running to him saying that I've been chatting you up, and he then finds you naked with me? I'll say that I rang the bell and you opened the door completely naked and invited me in.'

'He'll be back any minute, Neil. Please . . .'

'Suck it,' he demanded, hauling out his flaccid cock. 'Kneel before me, your master, and suck it.'

My head spun as I gazed at the veined shaft of his cock. I couldn't believe his audacity. My master? He was crazy, but what could I do? How the hell did he know about Richard and Ian? What else did he know about me? Trying to come to an arrangement, I said that I'd have sex with him whenever he liked. But not with his lesbian slut. He just laughed and again ordered me to kneel before him and suck out his spunk.

His cock waving from side to side as he gazed at the crack of my pussy, he retracted his foreskin and exposed his swollen knob. It was too late to say no. Had I told him to sod off on day one, this might not have turned into a nightmare. There again, he knew so much about my once-secret life that telling him to sod off wouldn't have done me any good. Why did Rod have to go out tonight of all nights? I wondered. Why the hell had I decided to have a shower and strip naked?

'Bend over,' Neil ordered me. 'You need to be taught a lesson, my girl. You need a damned good spanking.'

'A spanking?' I echoed. 'For fuck's sake, Neil. If you think that I'm going to allow you to –'

'I am your master, Cindy. The sooner you accept that, the better.'

'You might treat your slut like a slave, but you're not doing the same to me.'

'Bend over, or I'll wait for Rod to get back and have a long chat with him. Is that what you want? A ruined marriage?'

'Of course it's not what I want. But I'm not going to be treated like a lump of shit.'

'That's all you are, Cindy. A cheating, lying, dirty, filthy little –'

'Get out, Neil. Get out of my house and my life.'

'I'll sit in the lounge and wait for Rod. I have the photographs in the car. I'm sure that he'll be –'

'All right,' I finally conceded, realising that I had no choice.

I bent over and touched my toes. As Neil stroked the firm orbs of my buttocks, I imagined Rod walking into the hall and staring in disbelief at the crude scene. He'd said that he'd be an hour or so. What if he was only half an hour? Neil was taking unnecessary risks. Having me suck his cock in the garden when Rod and Sue were in the house, and now about to spank me in the hall . . . He could come to the house for sex when Rod was at work. Why take risks like this? Unless he thrived on danger. Perhaps the prospect of getting caught fired his libido. My mind was in turmoil as he ran his fingertip up and down the deep ravine between my tensed buttocks. I prayed for him to get this over with and leave the house.

The first slap of his hand across my buttocks jolted my naked body. I held on to the radiator to steady myself. My long blonde hair veiling my flushed face, cascading over the hall carpet, I let out a gasp as the second slap stung my naked bottom. I'd always enjoyed a good spanking, but not by my brother-in-law's hand. The slaps resounding around the hall, I knew that we wouldn't hear Rod's car pull up. If he opened the front door and witnessed his loyal wife's debauchery . . .

'I'll teach you not to go running to your husband,' Neil breathed, landing the hardest slap yet. 'You're my slave, Cindy. And don't you forget it.'

'Please, that's enough,' I whimpered as his hand caught the backs of my thighs.

'You should have been spanked years ago.' He chuckled, unbuckling his leather belt. 'I'll teach you a lesson you'll never forget.'

The first crack of his leather belt reverberated throughout the house. I squeezed my eyes shut and bit my lip. Again, the leather strap flailed my stinging buttocks, the pain permeating my tensed flesh as he let out a wicked chuckle. I found it difficult to comprehend the situation. I was naked in the hall, receiving a gruelling whipping from my brother-in-law. And my husband might walk in at any time. I'd enjoyed many a thrashing in my time, but not under threat.

My burning buttocks became numb as the leather belt repeatedly swished through the air and thrashed me. I felt my juices run between the engorged lips of my vulva. Blackmailed, threatened, forced to submit to a cruel thrashing . . . If it hadn't been for the fear of Rod catching me, I'd have loved every minute of the gruelling punishment. The sound of leather swishing through the air, the crack of the belt across my fiery buttocks, the numbing sensation . . . And the danger? Was that why my pussy was dripping with desire?

'That's just a taste of what you'll get if you misbehave again,' Neil said, halting the punishment. 'Sluts like you need disciplining. Sluts like you need –'

'May I dress now?' I asked him. 'Rod could be back at any minute.'

'You'll stay where you are,' he snapped. 'I've nowhere near finished with you.'

His bulbous knob slipped between my milk-smeared inner lips. I looked up between my parted legs at his heavy balls. They were huge, rolling, heaving, swinging beneath his massive cock. My head on the floor, my feet wide apart, the sexual centre of my young body lay bared to my blackmailer. I watched his solid cock entering me, stretching my outer lips wide apart, driving deep into my tightening pussy and impaling me completely. Grabbing my hips, he withdrew slowly. His veined shaft glistening with my pussy cream, he drove into me, ramming his knob hard against my ripe cervix as he let out a grunt of pleasure.

'You're a tight-cunted little bitch,' he gasped, again withdrawing and ramming his massive organ into my tightening sex sheath. Finding his fucking rhythm, his lower belly slapping the glowing flesh of my buttocks, his swinging balls battering my mons, he rocked me back and forth like a rag doll. His cock was huge, the shaft stretching my pussy to capacity as his knob repeatedly buffeted my cervix. I gasped as he pushed his thumb into my anus, stretching the delicate brown tissue and sending quivers rippling through my young womb. His thumb entering my rectum, his rock-hard cock repeatedly thrusting deep into the wet heat of my contracting pussya, he let out a long low moan of pleasure as he fucked me.

The sight of his pussy-wet cock sliding in and out of my cunt sent quivers of pleasure rippling through-out my body. I parted my feet further and watched his huge balls swinging between my thighs. The squelching sound of my sex juices resounding around the hall, the slapping of his lower belly against my burning buttocks filling my ears, I was tempted to slip my hand between my thighs and massage my clitoris to orgasm. But I couldn't allow Neil to know of the immense pleasure he was bringing me. I'd just have to frig my clitty later, I mused, as he again let out a gasp of male pleasure.

I heard a car pulling up in the drive as Neil's spunk jetted from his throbbing knob and flooded my pussy cavern. The creamy liquid gushed from my bloated sex hole and streamed down my thighs in rivers of milk. I knew that Rod was about to open the front door and discover not only his wife's adultery but also his brother's betrayal. Hadn't Neil heard the car? I wondered as he continued to fuck me.

'Rod's back,' I gasped as Neil slowed his thrusting rhythm. 'For God's sake . . .'

'I'll be in touch,' he breathed, sliding his sex-wet cock out of my pussy.

'God, no,' I whimpered shakily as he grabbed his belt and made his escape though the back door as the front door opened. 'Christ . . .'

'Cindy?' Rod gasped, his dark eyes frowning as he looked me up and down. 'What the –'

'I fell down the stairs,' I lied shakily, brushing my sex-matted blonde hair away from my flushed face.

'How the hell did you manage that? Are you all right?' he asked me concernedly.

'Yes, I think so. I was about to take a shower and . . . I came over dizzy and fell down the stairs.'

'Go and sit down, love. I'll make you a cup of tea.'

'I'll get my dressing gown first,' I said, trying to conceal the cocktail of spunk and girl juice running down my inner thighs. 'You go and put the kettle on. I'll be down in a minute.'

'Are you sure you're all right?'

'Just a little shaken. I'll be fine.'

Dashing up to the bathroom as he went into the kitchen, I washed my spunk-dripping pussy and my sex-stained legs. My buttocks stinging like hell, I couldn't believe how close I'd come to complete and utter ruination. Neil was such a bastard, I reflected, grabbing a towel and drying myself. He was also insane, I decided. It was almost as if he wanted to get caught. Would that be some kind of turn-on for him? Caught fucking his brother's wife? After slipping into my dressing gown, I went downstairs and joined Rod in the lounge.

'What was Neil doing here?' he asked me as I sat on the sofa.

'Neil?' I echoed, my heart banging hard against my chest. 'He came here with Sue, to see us.'

'I mean, what was he doing here just now?'

'I'm not with you, Rod,' I breathed, sure that he couldn't have seen his brother escaping.

'His car is parked down the road.'

'Is it?'

'I passed it when I came home.'

'Rod, I'm still very shaken. I don't want to talk about Neil's car. He hasn't been here and I have no idea why his car is parked down the road. End of subject, OK?'

'I just thought that he might have come back for something or . . .'

'Then he'd have parked outside. If he had been here, then where is he now?'

'I don't know, Cindy. It all seems rather odd to me.'

'Look, if you're that concerned, phone him. Phone him and ask him why he parked down the road.'

'I'm not concerned, just curious.'

'Did you do whatever it was at the office?'

'Yes, yes, I did. I had to go through some papers

143

and clear my desk for the morning. I think I'll take a look around the garden.'

Watching him leave the room, I knew that he was suspicious. Neil was a fool, I thought, wandering into the kitchen. To take a risk like that was crazy. Gazing out of the window, I wondered what Rod was up to as he hovered by the bushes at the end of the garden. What the hell was he looking for? Signs of sex? Spilled spunk? He wasn't looking for his brother, surely? Neil would have slipped around the side of the house and . . . Unless he'd hidden in the garden.

'Shit,' I breathed, again thinking what a bloody mess my life had become. My buttocks stinging, my pussy leaking spunk, Rod seemingly searching the garden . . . There was no way I could live like this. Dashing into the lounge as the phone rang, I dreaded to think who it was. Had Neil decided to ring and wind me up? Was Sue now suspicious?

'How are things?' Alan asked me.

'Dreadful,' I replied, hoping that Rod hadn't heard the phone.

'I thought I might come over tomorrow morning.'

'No, Alan. Things are pretty dodgy at the moment.'

'Just for a few minutes?'

'Look, Rod is highly suspicious. He went to the office this evening and Neil came round and –'

'Did you say that Rod's been to the office?'

'Yes.'

'I've been here all evening, Cindy.'

'You didn't see him?'

'No. I had some work to catch up with and . . . Rod hasn't been here.'

'But . . . he said that he'd been to the office and cleared his desk ready for the morning.'

'He's not been here, Cindy. Look, I'll call round in the morning.'

'Yes, yes, all right.'

Replacing the receiver, I felt my stomach churning. If Rod hadn't been to the office, where had he been? Why lie about it?

I went into the garden and sat on a patio chair. Rod was still hovering behind the bushes, poking about by the shed. I decided not to confront him. He'd lied, and was obviously up to something behind my back. By confronting him, he'd realise that I was on to him. Why lie to me? I mused, as he walked across the lawn towards me. As far as I knew, he'd never lied to me before. Was he seeing another woman? No, not Rod.

'Did you find what you were looking for?' I asked him.

'Looking for? I wasn't looking for anything. I was wondering about your idea of digging up the bushes to make more space by the shed. Neil reckons that the roots will be massive, running deep into the ground. Still, I could pay someone to do it.'

'What's happening at the office tomorrow?'

'Nothing, why?'

'You said that you'd cleared your desk. I thought there might be something on in the morning.'

'Oh, that. I just wanted to clear up some papers. My desk was looking like a tip.'

'Does Alan ever go in during the evenings?'

'Not as far as I know. He's on the road most of the time so his desk is hardly ever used. Are you feeling all right after your fall?'

'Yes, I'm fine. I called you at the office and then decided to take a shower. I don't know why I came over dizzy.'

'You rang the office?' he asked me, staring hard into my blue eyes.

'Yes, but I must have missed you.'

'Er . . . the phone rang but I didn't answer it. I thought it might be a client so I didn't bother.'

Lies, I mused, wondering what the hell he had to conceal. Was he seeing another woman? I didn't know what to think. Perhaps I should have followed him. My buttocks stung, and spunk oozing between the inflamed lips of my pussy. I held my dressing gown over the firm mounds of my breasts and moved to the back door.

'Well, I think I'll go up to bed,' I said. 'I'll probably be covered in bruises in the morning.'

'At least nothing's broken,' Rod murmured. 'I'll lock up and catch the news before I join you.'

'I'll probably be sleeping by the time you come up.'

'OK, I won't wake you. Goodnight, love.'

Leaving him in the garden, I climbed the stairs to my room with a thousand thoughts battering my tormented mind. Why would Rod say that he'd been to the office when he hadn't? Perhaps he *was* seeing another woman, I mused, as I slipped beneath the quilt. That was highly unlikely. Or was it? Neil was a cheat; I was a slut . . . Perhaps Rod had a lady friend. There again, perhaps he'd been spying on me. If he'd seen Neil arrive . . . I closed my eyes. I was too tired to think about it.

Eight

Rod seemed fine in the morning. He had a good breakfast and kissed my cheek before leaving, and I reckoned that I'd overreacted. So, he'd not been to the office. That was no big deal, I decided. He might have wanted to spend some time alone, walking in the park or whatever. Rather than explain, he'd probably thought it easier to say that he'd been to the office. We all need time alone now and then, I mused, as I cleared the kitchen.

I remembered that Alan was coming round, but wondered why I'd not seen anything of Richard or Ian. It was unlike them to stay away from me for so long. Ian loved mouth fucking me and Richard enjoyed playing the teacher and enacting his naughty schoolgirl fantasies, so why hadn't they come to see me? Again, I couldn't help thinking that Rod had warned them off. Ridiculous though it was, I could think of no other reason for their keeping away.

I was relieved when Alan rang and said that he couldn't make it. He was visiting a client fifty miles away, and wouldn't be back until late afternoon. He had a life; he was getting out and about and meeting people. I felt that I should get out of the house more often and meet people. Although I had my male lovers, my world was almost insular. Besides, it was a beautiful summer day. A walk in the park would do me good. Especially dressed as a schoolgirl, I thought in my wickedness. Apart from a change of scenery, I also needed some excitement.

Changing into my school uniform in my bedroom, I recalled my schooldays. I used to love winding up middle-aged men by sitting with my legs parted and the swell of my tight panties exposed. I'd always come across as innocent, of course. Sitting on the grass in the park with my panties showing, I'd love watching the men watching me. Although older now, I could still get away with playing the role. In my uniform with my hair in pigtails, my white socks and gymslip . . . I looked every part a schoolgirl. Checking my reflection in the mirror, I grinned. I was ready to launch myself into the world of male fantasy.

Leaving the house, I wondered whether Rod was lurking as I walked briskly down the street in my very short gymslip. There again, I doubted that he'd recognise me. If he did see me, or one of his spies reported back to him, then I'd say that a schoolgirl came to the house asking for directions. Lies had always come so easy to me. But now? The lies were still easy but, with Rod's suspicious mind, were they believable? Rod was at work, I reflected, as I walked across the park. He had a lot to do and couldn't waste time watching and following me.

My buttocks were still sore from Neil's gruelling thrashing. I hovered by the long grass edging the woods and began picking wild flowers. I knew only too well that there was something alluring about a girl in a short skirt picking flowers. Nature and virgins somehow go together. At an early age, I discovered that exposing my panties in the garden excited male visitors to our house. Sitting on the grass with the triangular patch of my panties exposed not only excited men, but also turned me on.

There were a couple of middle-aged men in the park; one walking a dog and the other sitting on a bench staring at the pond. A young mum pushing a pram glanced at me several times. She stopped by the man sitting on the bench and said something to him. Did I know her? I wondered. What was she talking about? The man turned and looked at me, so I carried on picking flowers. Perhaps he was a spy. The mum finally left the park, and he made his way towards me.

'Shouldn't you be in school?' he asked me as he approached.

I stood up and smiled at him. 'Yes, I should,' I replied sheepishly. 'But there was a fire in the library and we were all sent home.'

'Who are the flowers for?'

'No one in particular. I often come here and pick flowers.'

'They're nice,' he said as I squatted and picked some more.

My school blouse fell open to reveal my cleavage, and I wondered whether he was talking about the flowers or my breasts. He'd be thinking about my tits, I knew. He'd imagine squeezing the hardness of my firm mounds, tweaking the ripe teats of my erect nipples, sucking the brown protrusions into his wet mouth. Allowing my blouse to open a little further, exposing the half-moons of my breasts, I felt my outer lips engorging, puffing up as my arousal heightened.

Making sure that my thighs were parted enough to display the bulge of my white cotton panties, I knew that his balls would be heaving in anticipation, his cock twitching expectantly. He was a very lucky man, I mused, as I picked another flower. An innocent schoolgirl displaying her tight panties, her rounded breasts . . . But he didn't know just how lucky he was. The long grass tickled my inner thighs and I felt my clitoris stir as I looked up at him.

'Most of these are weeds,' I said. 'Either that or wild flowers. But they're still nice to look at. They're pretty.'

'You're nice to look at,' he breathed, his wide eyes focused on the tight material of my straining panties. 'And you're very pretty.'

'Thank you.' Climbing to my feet, I decided to tempt him further. 'I think I'll go into the woods,' I said. 'To look for more flowers.'

'Mind if I join you?'

'No, of course I don't mind.'

Following me along the narrow path between the trees, he remarked on the nice weather and chatted about wild flowers. My hips swaying, my long legs striding, I knew what he was thinking as we ventured deeper into the woods. He was picturing my naked pussy, my tight little girlie crack. Would he make a move? I wondered, as we entered a clearing surrounded by thick bushes. How would he broach the subject of sex? Would he dare to reach out and touch me? With the excitement wetting my panties, swelling the sensitive nub of my pining clitoris, I sat on the soft grass with my chin resting on my knees and my panties now blatantly exposed.

'It's nice here,' he said, settling before me with his dark eyes locked between my legs. 'I've always loved the countryside. The trees, the fresh air, the flowers . . . We could meet here again, if you like.'

That was his first step towards my seduction. 'Yes, I'd like that,' I replied. 'My friends aren't interested in nature. They prefer to hang around town whereas I like the woods.'

'I'm Colin, by the way.'

'Oh, I'm Kirsten.'

'You're a very pretty girl, Kirsten. Do you have a boyfriend?'

'No,' I replied with a silly girlish giggle. 'I'm not interested in boys. They're young and stupid.'

'Perhaps you'd prefer to be with an older man?' he proffered. 'Someone like me, for example.'

His second step towards sex. 'I've always liked older men. I get on better with older men because . . . Well, I suppose they're not silly like boys.'

Obviously wondering what to do next, he couldn't take his eyes off my pussy-bulged panties. My stomach fluttering, I knew how desperate he was to move the veil of my panties aside and gaze at the swollen lips of my pussy. How far would he go? I pondered, keeping my knees together and parting my feet a little further.

Sitting in the woods with a stranger staring at my tight panties, I felt really good inside. Away from Rod and Neil, I felt free, at ease. I could enjoy myself, relax and play my sex games in complete safety. This is how I'd spent my five years of marriage, I reflected, as I reclined on the grass with my legs slightly parted. Free to play my sex games and enjoy my private life, my young body. But then, Neil had reared his ugly head and ruined everything. He thought me a wanton whore, and he was right. But it was no business of his.

Was I so bad? I wondered, making sure that my gymslip rode up my thighs as I made myself comfortable on the soft grass beneath the trees. I was the perfect wife, always keeping the house pristine, having nice meals ready for my husband when he came home from work. As far as Rod was concerned, he had a loyal, loving wife. Until now, I reflected dolefully, trying to push all thoughts of Neil from my mind. Was Rod suspicious? Did he have spies following me? Or was I making mountains out of molehills?

'You say that you've always liked older men,' Colin breathed as I stretched my limbs, deliberately showing more of my tight panties. 'I was wondering . . . perhaps we could . . . I suppose you think me too old to be your friend?'

Step three towards pushing his cock into my tight little pussy. 'You're not old,' I said with a giggle. 'You haven't got grey hair or anything.'

'I'm in my forties,' he confessed.

'That's not old. I like you. You're sensible, unlike boys of my age.'

'And I like you, Kirsten. I like you very much.'

Settling by my side, he stroked my knee and told me how attractive I was. Attractive or fuckable? I mused dreamily. My hair in pigtails, my white blouse partially open, my panties displayed as I lay beneath the sun, I knew exactly what he meant. A young virgin girl lying on her back in the woods and a middle-aged man admiring her nubile body . . . A recipe for sex. Was he married? I wondered. Did he have a loving, trusting wife at home? Rod had a wife, ut she wasn't at home. Neither was she to be trusted. But what Rod didn't know couldn't hurt him. Neil could hurt him. Would he really destroy his brother's life?

Colin's fingers moved slowly up my thigh. I wondered how far he'd go. Meeting a schoolgirl in the park, following her into the woods, stroking her knee as she lay on her back with only the flimsy material of her panties veiling her tight virgin crack . . . He must have thought this a dream come true. He probably reckoned that I was about eighteen, I mused, closing my eyes and parting my legs a little wider. Eighteen, and incredibly naïve and innocent. As his fingers moved dangerously close to the swell of my panties, I decided to give him a little more encouragement.

'It's nice here,' I sighed. 'We'll have to come here again.'

'Yes, we will,' he replied eagerly.

'It's nice to think that you might become my boyfriend.'

'Really? Kirsten, do you mean . . .'

'I mean that I'd like you to be my boyfriend. I've never had a boyfriend. I've never met anyone I've liked enough to even think about having a relationship.'

'I know that we've only just met, but I think you're an amazing girl. You're an angel, heaven sent.'

An angel? I was the devil's daughter, hell sent. As he leaned over and kissed my full lips, his hand slid up my thigh and his fingertips pressed into the soft bulge of my panties. I writhed a little and parted my legs wider as he massaged me there, sending him the message that I liked what he was doing. I knew from experience that I'd have to make a perfunctory protest at some stage, just to remind him of my innocence. He thought me a virgin, I giggled inwardly. I was a married woman, a married slut.

'Colin, no,' I breathed as his finger slipped beneath my panties and massaged the fleshy cushion of my lips.

'What's the matter?' he asked me, retracting his hand. 'I thought . . .'

'I'm a virgin,' I whispered, loving my naughty game. 'I've never done anything before.'

'Yes, I know. If you'd rather I didn't touch you . . .'

'Touch me, if you want to,' I conceded, my pussy muscles tightening. 'But I don't want –'

'I understand,' he said, and kissed me again. 'Don't worry, Kirsten. I'll look after you.'

Look after me? Did he think that slipping his fingers into a girl's panties with a view to fucking her senseless was looking after her? He was a normal man, I decided, as his fingers massaged the tight material veiling my girl slit. He'd recall my young body every time he wanked, I mused. Every time he wanked and brought out his fresh spunk, he'd imagine my young body, my petite breasts, my little virgin crack. A normal man, a dirty old man.

Pulling my panties aside, he slipped his finger between my engorged inner lips and massaged the creamy wet entrance to my hot pussy. I let out another sigh and writhed as his finger ventured into my sex sheath. His cock would be solid, I thought, imagining his full balls rolling. Should I allow him to fuck my tight pussy or my pretty mouth? Both, I concluded, as my womb rhythmically contracted. Slipping his wet finger out of my sex, he moved up to the bulb of my clitoris and massaged me there. He knew exactly what to do, I thought dreamily, gasping as his fingertip encircled my sex spot.

'Have you ever masturbated?' he asked me, probably imagining me slipping my hand down the front of my panties and frigging myself off.

'No,' I breathed. 'I've never done anything.'

'You've never touched yourself there?'

'Well, I've sort of explored myself,' I confessed. 'But nothing else.'

'I think it's time you had an orgasm. Just relax, and I'll look after you.'

Time I had an orgasm? I thought. I must have had thousands of massive orgasms in my life. Rarely a day went by without my clitoris pulsating in orgasm. But now, with this very lucky middle-aged man, I was the innocent little schoolgirl who'd never touched herself let alone writhed in the grip of a massive climax. Lifting my buttocks clear of the ground as he tugged my wet panties down, I allowed him to pull them off my feet. He parted my feet wide, opening the crack of my vulva as he spread my legs. The innocent little schoolgirl? The experienced whore, more like.

Positioning himself between my legs, he spread my pussy lips with his thumbs and ran his tongue up and down the gaping valley of my vulva. I arched my back and let out a whimper as his tongue repeatedly swept over the sensitive tip of my erect clitoris. My juices gushed from my neglected sex hole, and I decided that I would meet him again. He had no idea who I was or where I lived, so I'd be safe enough. We'd meet in the woods for crude sex and, unless Neil followed me and caused trouble, I'd be free to enjoy my body to the full.

I'd played this game several times over the years. Making out that I was a naïve virgin, allowing a middle-aged man to initiate me into the fine art of fucking . . . Rod and I had only just moved into our house when a man had called and asked me whether my mother was in. I was dressed in a miniskirt with no make-up, and he'd obviously thought me to be the daughter of the house. I'd seized the opportunity to play my naughty games. I'd invited the man in and, within ten minutes, he was fucking me over the dining-room table. He came back for more on several occasions. I finally said that my mother was suspicious and I never saw him again.

'Come for me,' Colin breathed, his wet tongue slurping as he licked my clit. Stretching my swollen lips further apart and sucking the nub of my clitoris into his hot mouth, he pushed a finger into my burning sex and massaged my inner flesh. Finger fucking me, sucking on my sex button, he took me to the brink of my climax and held me there. He was good, very good. How many girls had he licked and fucked? Desperate for the release of orgasm, I writhed and gasped and begged him to suck me harder. I knew that he'd like my begging, my pleading for more. Dirty old man. Normal?

The explosion of lust finally came, and I let out a scream of pleasure. Digging my fingernails into the soft grass, arching my back and parting my legs to the extreme, I shuddered uncontrollably as my lover sucked a massive orgasm out of my pulsating clitoris. On and on, waves of pure sexual bliss rolled though my trembling body as my orgasmic juices spewed from my contracting pussy. My head lolling from side to side, my nostrils flaring, my young breasts heaving, I again let out a scream.

Before my pleasure had begun to wane, Colin was stabbing at the tight entrance to my pussy with his bulbous knob. Obviously thinking that he was about to strip me of my virginity, he managed to push his purple crown into the wet heat of my pussy. I didn't protest as his penile shaft glided along the well-creamed sheath of my pussy until his glans pressed hard against my cervix. His balls rested against the naked flesh of my firm buttocks, and my pussy lips stretched tautly around the root of his cock. He withdrew slowly and rammed into me.

'God,' he breathed, rocking his hips and fucking me. 'You're so tight and hot.'

'Slowly,' I whimpered. 'Do it slowly.'

'You're beautiful, Kirsten. You're an angel.'

'You're so big,' I gasped. 'Please, do it slowly.'

'It's all right, sweetheart. I'll look after you, I promise.'

'Not hard,' I gasped. 'Slowly.'

Ignoring my words, he repeatedly drove the entire length of his cock deep into my tight pussy with amazing force. Lost in his arousal, his fantasy come true, he fucked me with a vengeance as my cries of bliss resounded throughout the trees. If only Rod could see me now, I thought, imagining him walking into the clearing. Why was I thinking like that? Did I want Rod to catch me revelling in my adultery? Perhaps, somewhere deep in the dark recesses of my mind, that was my ultimate goal.

If Rod caught me, Neil's blackmail threats would come to an end. I'd be free of Rod, free of Neil, free to fuck a dozen men every day. But the excitement I derived from my secret life was because it *was* secret. The danger, the lies and deceit, the adulterous betrayal ... Sex alone wouldn't be enough. Sex without infidelity and cheating and lying wouldn't be the same. This was real sex, I reflected, as my pussy flooded with spunk. Reaching another mind-blowing climax as the man above me shuddered in his illicit coming, I wrapped my long legs around him and hooked my feet together behind his back as he fucked me.

'Yes,' he cried, increasing his fucking rhythm as his spunk squelched deep inside my pussy. I rode the crest of my orgasm as my spasming cunt overflowed and spewed out a cocktail of spunk and girl juice. This was my sexual heaven, the ultimate in adultery. Rod was at work, and I was lying on my back in the woods with a stranger fucking me senseless. I was a schoolgirl, innocent, naïve ... Colin had brought me womanhood.

I was pleased to have met Colin. Not every man fell prey to my school uniform; the allure of my young body. One middle-aged man I'd tried to entice to seduce me had been disgusted. He'd called me a filthy slut and had said that he'd go to my school and report me. As he'd walked off, I'd said that I'd only wanted to suck the spunk out of his hard cock. I remember thinking that he must have been gay. As Colin pumped the last of his spunk deep into my cock-hungry pussy, I thought again how happy I was to have met him.

'Kirsten, you're beautiful,' he breathed, finally stilling his deflating cock with his knob resting against my spunked cervix. 'I've never met anyone like you.'

'You were amazing,' I whispered shakily. 'Thank you.'

'Thank *you*,' he said with a chuckle, sliding his cock out of my hot pussy. 'We'll meet again, yes?'

'Yes, we will. And we'll love again.'

'There's so much I can teach you,' he said, zipping his trousers as I grabbed my panties and stood up. 'We'll have great times together.'

There was nothing he could teach me, I mused, as I tugged my panties up my long legs and covered the inflamed crack of my pussy. He probably planned to introduce me to oral sex, cock sucking and spunk swallowing. Or, possibly, anal sex. Was he married? I again pondered, as we left the clearing. Did he spank his wife's naked buttocks? He'd probably enjoy putting me across his knee and spanking me. No, there was nothing he could teach me. If anything, I might teach him a thing or two.

'Your flowers,' he said as we emerged from the woods and walked across the park. 'You forgot your flowers.'

'I don't need flowers any more,' I replied, smiling at him. 'I have you now.'

'Kirsten, you don't know what it means to me to have you. Never have I known anyone like you. We will meet again, won't we?'

'Definitely,' I trilled. 'After the amazing things you did to me, I definitely want to go to the woods with you again.'

'Tomorrow?' he asked me eagerly.

'Yes, tomorrow after school. I'll be here at four o'clock.'

'How long will you have? I mean, do you have to be home at a particular time?'

'We'll have an hour together. As long as I'm home by five, Mum won't be suspicious. What about you?'

'Me? What do you mean?'

'What time do you have to be home?'

'Oh, er . . .'

'Are you married?'

'Er . . . goodness me, no. I . . . I live alone.'

'Perhaps I could visit you?'

'Well, I think for the time being . . . we'll meet in the woods.'

'All right.'

As we reached the road and went our own ways, I became aware of my spunk-soaked panties clinging to the swollen lips of my pussy. I felt happy, satisfied. Another conquest, I mused, as I neared my house. I'd been fucked in the woods by a stranger. Another man had fallen prey to my young body. What more could I have asked for on such a beautiful summer day? Another man, another cock, another fuck . . .

I walked through the hall to the kitchen, opened the back door and stepped out on to the patio. I knew that boredom would soon set in as I wandered across the lawn. With the rest of the morning ahead of me, I didn't know what to do. I pondered on going into town, and then wondered whether I should go back to the park to find another gullible man. Hearing James kicking a football around in his garden, I wondered whether he'd appreciate my hot, wet mouth.

I slipped into the bushes and spied on young James. He was wearing shorts, the crotch bulging beautifully as he bounced the football on his knee. Was he in need of draining his balls? I wondered as I squatted in the bushes. I could feel Colin's spunk oozing between my swelling pussy lips and filling the tight crotch of my panties. Colin had been good, fucking me senseless and satisfying me. But my libido had risen again, and I was in dire need of a solid cock.

'Cindy, where are you?' Rod called from the back door. What the hell was he doing home? I wondered fearfully. Cowering in my hiding place, there was no way I could allow him to see me in my school uniform. He called again. Remaining perfectly still, I was sure that he'd not search the bushes. He'd probably think that I'd walked down to the local shop or gone to post a letter. But he would think it odd that I'd left the back door wide open.

'She's not here,' he said as I peered through the foliage to see Neil emerge from the house. 'The back door was open. Where the hell has she got to?'

'Gone for a walk, I expect,' Neil said, plonking himself on a patio chair.

'It's unlike her to leave the house unlocked.'

I couldn't hear what they were saying as Rod joined Neil on the patio. Only catching the odd word, I wondered what the hell they were talking about. Rod mentioned me, and then said something about the shed. Had they arranged to meet at the house? I wondered, keeping one eye on young James. Rod was supposed to be at the office. Why bring Neil round in the middle of the morning? Again catching a few words, I froze. Neil said something about a horny little slut, and Rod laughed. They weren't talking about me. They couldn't have been.

'She's bloody good,' Neil said, raising his voice above Rod's laughter. 'And damned tight. Still, you don't need me to tell you that.'

I couldn't hear anything after that as James repeatedly kicked the football against a fence. *You don't need me to tell you that.* If they weren't talking about me, then ... Surely, they weren't seeing the same woman? Jackie, the slut. Had Neil introduced his brother to the filthy tart? There was no way Rod would cheat on me, I was sure of that. In which case, if they were talking about me ... My mind dizzy with confusion, I didn't know what to think. They were obviously expecting me to be home, I mused. What had they planned?

They finally walked into the house and closed the back door. I waited until I'd heard a car drive off before slipping out of the bushes. *You don't need me to tell you that.* My heart sank as I discovered that Rod had locked the back door. I held my hand to my head. Dressed in my school uniform, my panties soaked with Colin's spunk, I was locked out of the bloody house. The downstairs windows were closed, and I'd left my key on the hall table ... This was a nightmare.

Wondering what Rod had meant about the shed, I wandered down the garden to take a look. Opening the door, I had an idea. I could tell Rod that I'd been tidying up in the shed, not heard him calling me, and had then been unable to get back into the house. Not much of a plan, I mused, gazing at the work bench. But it was the best I could come up with. I'd have to get out of my school uniform, I decided, noticing Rod's overalls hanging on a hook.

Stripping out of my uniform, I donned the overalls and again looked around the shed. What *had* Rod been talking about? Perhaps he'd been thinking about

161

digging up the bushes and getting rid of the old shed. We only used it to store junk, and it did take up quite a bit of the garden. If that was the case, then what had Neil meant about a girl being damned good and tight? Men's talk, I concluded, leaving the shed and hiding my school uniform beneath the bushes. They'd been chatting about sex, that was all. But I instinctively knew that there was more to it than that.

Looking up at the back of the house, I grinned. The bedroom window was open. If I could get in, there'd be no need for my lies, I mused, wondering whether I could scale the drainpipe. Young James was the man for the job. He'd have no trouble shinning up the pipe and clambering through the window. Calling him over, I hoped that Rod wouldn't come back and discover James in our bedroom. That would be all I needed. There again, I could go back to my original story. I called out for James again. He obviously thought that I wanted sex as he emerged from the bushes and grinned at me.

'What can I do for you?' he asked as he approached me.

'James, I'm locked out. Could you climb up to the window?'

'No problem,' he replied, looking up at the drainpipe. 'No sooner said than done.'

Watching him scale the pipe, I noticed his bulging shorts. I'd have to reward him for helping me, I thought in my rising wickedness. It would only be fair to give him something in return for coming to my rescue. A blowjob? I pondered, imagining his ballooning knob spunking in my thirsty mouth. My pussy was overflowing with another man's spunk, but my tight bottom was free. No sooner had he climbed through the window than he opened the back door and smiled at me.

'Thanks,' I said. 'You're brilliant.'

'How did you manage to lock yourself out?' he asked me, gazing at my overalls.

'It's a long story. I've been tidying the shed, hence the overalls.'

'Oh, right.'

'I suppose I'd better give you something for coming to my rescue.'

'Give me something?' he breathed as I dropped to my knees. 'Oh, I see.'

Tugging his shorts down, I licked the flaccid shaft of his young cock. He stiffened quickly, his cock standing bolt upright before my wide eyes. Fully retracting his fleshy foreskin and taking his bulbous glans into my wet mouth, I sucked hard. He gasped and shuddered, clutching my head as I rolled my tongue over the silky-smooth surface of his ripe plum. He tasted wonderfully salty. After playing football, his male scent was strong. Breathing in the fragrance of his pubes, I kneaded his heavy balls and took his swollen knob to the back of my throat.

Sinking my teeth gently into his shaft, sucking hard on his beautiful organ, I wondered whether his young friend would appreciate my wet mouth. Was he visiting James today? Would he creep through the bushes with his cock stiff and his heavily laden balls in dire need of draining? The thought sent quivers through me as James began to tremble uncontrollably. I moved my head back until the bulb of his knob was between my succulent lips. Tonguing his spunk slit, gobbling and slurping on his granite-hard member, I hoped that he'd not shoot out his spunk so soon.

Unfortunately, he came quickly. His spunk flooding my mouth, bathing my tongue and filling my cheeks, he moaned softly as he came. He rocked his hips and mouth fucked me. What did he think of me? The woman next door, the married woman he'd politely greeted in the street from time to time. Did he think me a common whore? Repeatedly swallowing the fruits of his teenage loins, I didn't care what he thought as I drank from his teenage fountain head. Slurping and sucking, wanking his hard shaft and toying with his balls, I lost myself in my arousal. This was a dream, I mused. A teenage lad fucking my spunk-thirsty mouth . . .

Working on him until I'd drained his balls, I swallowed the remnants of his orgasm before licking my lips and standing before him. His face was flushed, his breathing fast and shallow. He tugged his shorts up and leaned against the wall to steady himself. The taste of his spunk lingered on my tongue. I asked him whether that was payment enough for his help. Shuddering, he nodded appreciatively as I pulled my overalls to one side and exposed the firm mound of my breast, my erect nipple. I was about to suggest that he fuck me over the patio table when I heard the front door open. Now what? I thought angrily, as Rod called out.

'Oh, James,' he said, appearing in the doorway.

'James kindly climbed through the window and let me in,' I said.

'I'd better get back,' James murmured sheepishly, heading for the bushes.

'Cindy, what the hell . . .' Rod began, staring at my overalls. 'Why are you wearing my overalls? And what was James doing here? You say he climbed in through the window?'

'I was tidying the shed and . . . I was locked out of the house. God knows how it happened.'

'You were in the shed?'

'Yes, tidying up. When I came out, the back door

was locked. James climbed up the drainpipe and went in through the window.'

'I came home earlier. I thought you were out so I locked the door.'

'Rod . . . you idiot.'

'I called you, Cindy. I called and thought that you must have gone out.'

'Leaving the back door wide open? Hardly.'

'I'm sorry, love. I didn't realise. Why didn't you hear me calling you?'

'All I could hear was James kicking his football against a fence. What did you come back for?'

'I was passing and thought I'd call in for a coffee.'

'And why are you here now?'

'I've come back because I was worried about you. I thought you'd gone out and —'

'Luckily, James was around,' I cut in, wondering why he'd not mentioned Neil. 'Locking the bloody door . . . You always seem to be calling in. You never used to leave the office during the day, let alone come home every five minutes.'

'It's not every five minutes, love,' he whined.

'It seems like it.'

Having made him feel guilty, I thought how well things had turned out. I'd sucked young James, swallowed his spunk, and Rod had come back to find him in the garden. And I'd had the perfect excuse. I could taste one young man's spunk on my lips, and feel another man's spunk soaking my panties. It had been a good morning, I mused, as Rod checked his watch and announced that he had work to do. A damned good morning of crude sex. And I had the afternoon to look forward to.

'I'll see you this evening,' Rod said, smiling at me.

'Had you any plans for the shed?' I asked him, wondering why he'd mentioned it to Neil.

'Plans? No, why?'

'I just wondered. Seeing as we're thinking about digging up the bushes to make more room, I thought you might have decided to get rid of the shed.'

'Oh, I see. No, the shed's fine. Anyway, I'll see you this evening.'

As he left, I felt confused. He'd not mentioned bringing Neil to the house, which was most odd. And he'd definitely said something about the shed when he was talking to his brother. Something was going on, I was sure. Was I becoming paranoid over nothing? I pondered. I'd ask Neil about it the next time I saw him. Which wouldn't be too long, knowing my sex-crazed brother-in-law. One thing was for sure, I was going to have to be very careful. I was safe enough playing the role of a schoolgirl in the park, under cover of the woods. But closer to home?

Nine

Stuck in the house, feeling hemmed in, I was becoming increasingly edgy. Rod had gone to work and I'd cleared the breakfast things as usual. Feeling fidgety, I knew that boredom would come to me again as I gazed out of the kitchen window at the rain. There'd be no playing games in the park today, I thought. And James wouldn't be in his garden. Bored, edgy, in dire need of illicit sex.

Wandering into the lounge as the phone rang, I hoped that Richard or Ian was going to visit me for crude sex. A long, hard cock to suck, fresh spunk to swallow, my clitoris licked and sucked to a massive orgasm ... That would have brightened up my day nicely. But it was Neil on the phone. My stomach sank as he informed me that he'd be over to see me later. I told him that I was going out and wouldn't be back until the evening.

'I'll be there in an hour,' he said.

'Neil, I'm going out,' I repeated. 'I won't be here, don't you understand that?'

'You'll be there,' he returned. 'And I want you to shave your pussy.'

'What?' I gasped, thinking that I must have misheard him.

'Shave your pussy, Cindy. If you don't –'

'No,' I stated firmly.

'Then I'll post the photographs to Rod's office.'

'Why the hell . . . Neil, I am not going to shave.'

'Just do it, Cindy. Unless you want your marriage to come to an abrupt end. I'll be there in an hour.'

Slamming the phone down, I held my hand to my head and sighed. I was fuming, my stomach churning. How dare Neil order me to shave my pussy? What did he think I was? He knew what I was, I thought. But didn't he think that Rod would notice? How would I explain my shaved pussy to my husband? There again, I didn't suppose that Neil was bothered. I couldn't shave my pubic hair, my blonde fleece. I'd look awful, and it would itch like hell.

Not knowing what to do, I paced the lounge floor trying to come up with an idea. I could go out, I thought. But I'd only be delaying the inevitable. Neil wanted sex and, sooner or later, he'd get it. This was getting worse, I reflected anxiously. I'd already been licked by a lesbian slut, fucked by my brother-in-law, blackmailed . . . And now I was to shave my pubes for the bastard. For my master? Was I becoming a slave to Neil?

I climbed the stairs to the bathroom and I recalled the last time I'd shaved my blonde pubes. I'd just left school and had met an elderly man I'd taken a liking to. He'd said that he'd always dreamed of licking and fucking a hairless pussy. I'd refused to do it but, when he offered me cash, I'd grabbed the money and shaved for him. He'd loved the sight and feel of my hairless pussy lips. Soft, smooth . . . And I'd loved the feel of my puffy lips rolling back and forth along his cock as he'd lived out his fantasy and fucked me.

The old man had paid me well. But the only reward I'd now get for shaving was a saved marriage. Stripping and sitting on the edge of the bath, I wondered whether it was worth it. Putting up with Neil and his lesbian slut just to hang on to Rod and my beautiful home? I had some money an aunt had left me, just about enough to buy a house. Perhaps that was the way to go. Leave Rod and, in the process, say goodbye to Neil and set up on my own.

I took Rod's shaving foam from the shelf recalling the old man I'd shaved for as I lathered the swelling lips of my vulva. Perhaps I should find other old men who'd pay well to lick and finger a naked pussy. In my own house somewhere far away from Rod and his brother, I could do anything. Shave, dress as a schoolgirl, take money from men in return for committing obscene sexual acts . . .

Massaging foam into the gentle rise of my mons, I knew that, yet again, I had no choice. Neil had a hold on me, a hold that I couldn't wriggle out of. What would he demand of me next? I pondered, taking a razor and dragging the blade over my sensitive flesh. I realised that the situation could only get worse as I watched my blonde curls falling away from my pussy. The risks I was taking, the risks Neil was forcing me to take, would eventually lead to Rod's discovery of my adultery. It was only a matter of time before he caught me.

Working the razor over my vulva, I finally grabbed a flannel and wiped away the foam and blonde curls. The transformation was amazing. Gazing at my reflection in the full-length mirror, I couldn't believe what I'd done. My pubes gone, my pussy lips smooth and swollen, years had been stripped away from my young body. Rod was bound to notice, I thought anxiously as I dried myself with a towel and dressed. We rarely had sex but . . . I'd just have to make sure that he didn't see me naked. If he did glimpse my hairless pussy, then I'd say that I'd shaved for him.

169

Would he believe that I'd done it to try to brighten up our sex life? Probably not.

Neil let himself in with his key, which riled me. He marched into the house as if he owned the place. Finding me in the lounge, a grin furling his lips, his dark eyes fell to my miniskirt. I felt beholden to him as he stared at my naked thighs. I was his sex slave, I thought angrily. He snapped his fingers and I jumped. If I didn't, then all hell would be let loose. Should I leave Rod and buy a house? I again pondered. I could only afford a smallish house, but it would be all mine. All I needed was enough room to entertain sex-starved men, take their cash and offer them my naked body . . .

'Have you done it?' Neil finally asked me. 'Have you shaved?'

'Yes,' I sighed, wondering whether Rod would call in for a cup of coffee.

'Show me.'

'There,' I said, lifting my skirt and lowering the front of my white cotton panties. 'Satisfied?'

'I will be,' he said, chortling, his dark eyes widening as he gazed at my hairless sex crack. 'You look just like –'

'I know what I look like,' I cut in angrily. 'Shall we get this over with?'

'We'll start with you stripping naked,' he instructed me, adjusting the bulging crotch of his trousers.

After tugging my skirt and panties down, I pulled my top over my head and unhooked my bra. As Neil gazed at the firm spheres of my breasts, my erect nipples standing proud from the dark discs of my areolae, I realised that I'd almost reached the stage where I wanted Rod to discover what was going on. If he found out about his brother's blackmailing, at

170

least the nightmare would come to an end. I might not have a marriage, but I'd be free of Neil for good. Was that the answer? I wondered, stepping out of my skirt and panties and standing naked before my brother-in-law. Before my master.

'Over the dining-room table,' Neil ordered me, leaving the lounge.

'I don't have a great deal of time,' I said, following him into the dining room.

'Don't give me that crap. You have all the time in the world.' Grabbing several lengths of rope from beneath a chair, he grinned at me. 'I prepared for this the other day,' he said, chuckling.

'You . . . When did you come here?'

'Lean over the table, Cindy. We're going to enjoy a little bondage.'

'Neil, I don't want this,' I protested. 'I'll have sex with you, but . . .'

'I know you will. Bend over the table, please.'

Taking my position, I allowed him to pull my arms out across the table and bind my wrists. Having secured the end of the rope to one of the table legs, he moved behind me and parted my feet. I knew that I should stop him as he tied my ankles. The sexual centre of my body crudely exposed, vulnerable to his every perverted whim, I knew that I should never have allowed him to treat me like this. Blackmail or not, I was going to have to put an end to my horrendous dilemma.

Standing behind me and cupping the naked lips of my pussy in his palm, he squeezed my hairless sex flesh. I decided I'd tell Rod everything as Neil pushed a finger deep into the wet heat of my tight pussy. I wondered what his reaction would be. He'd either understand and forgive me, or throw me out of the marital home. If Neil told him that I'd cheated and lied for five years, that I'd fucked man after man, swallowed enough spunk to make a river, enjoyed two teenage lads on the lawn ... Rod would never understand, let alone forgive me. Should I move out and buy that house?

Neil had me exactly where he wanted me, literally. He knew as well as I did that I had no way out of my predicament. I either go along with him, play his crude sex games, or ... Or what? Even if Rod did understand, forgive and forget, where would that leave me? With no sex life at all. No excitement, no massive orgasms, no spunk to swallow ... I was a nymphomaniac, a whore, a cumslut – and I couldn't live without cocks. If Rod discovered my wicked ways and forgave me, I'd have to leave him.

'So, what have you been up to?' Neil said, kneeling behind me and kissing my bulging pussy lips. 'Fucked any men recently?'

'When did you put the rope beneath the chair?' I asked him.

'The other day, why?'

'Yesterday? Were you here yesterday?'

'No, I wasn't. Now, I think it's time for another thrashing.'

'Rod will be home soon.'

'Really?'

'As I said, I'm going out. We're going shopping.'

'In that case, we'd better not waste any more time.'

Squeezing my eyes shut as he unbuckled his leather belt, I tensed my naked buttocks in readiness for the merciless thrashing. He didn't seem at all bothered about Rod, which intrigued me. I could have easily arranged to go shopping with Rod. It wasn't something we did very often, but we had been out for the odd day. We used to go out for walks, I reflected. Take a walk in the countryside, enjoy a pub lunch ...

Rod was too busy for such things now. But why wasn't Neil worried?

The first lash of the belt landed across my naked buttocks with a loud crack. I let out a yelp. I'd been tied over my dining-room table and thrashed by dozens of men. I loved a cruel whipping, a good spanking. But not by my brother-in-law. The second crack of the leather strap jolting my young body, I again yelped. My buttocks beginning to numb, I felt my milky juices soaking my pussy lips and trickling down my inner thighs.

Continuing with the arduous whipping of my burning buttocks, Neil didn't realise that, yet again, I'd found my sexual heaven. He had no idea how much I enjoyed a damned good spanking and thrashing. But my pleasure was marred by worry. Why the hell wasn't Neil concerned about Rod turning up? Had he spoken to him? Had he called the office and checked up on Rod's movements before coming to see me? Something was wrong, I knew, as the belt again flailed the fiery orbs of my naked bottom.

'That should have warmed you up,' Neil said and chuckled, running his fingertips over the glowing cheeks of my bum.

'What were you doing here yesterday?' I gasped, finally relaxing my muscles.

'I wasn't here yesterday.'

'Rod said that you came here with him.'

'I wasn't here, Cindy. If Rod said that, then . . .'

'He was lying?'

'He must have been talking about some other time. I wasn't here yesterday,'

As he left the room, my suspicion began to grow. Rod hadn't mentioned that he'd brought his brother to the house and Neil had denied it. Why? What were they up to? Crazy though it was, I began to think that

Rod was in on the sexual abuse. My thinking was going way off track, I was sure. Rod, allowing his brother to blackmail me, to sexually abuse me? I knew Rod well, I reflected. He'd never agree to such a scam. As Neil returned, I couldn't get the crazy thought out of my head.

'Why do that?' I asked him as he wrapped a tea towel around my head and blindfolded me. 'Neil, I don't want . . .'

'It's a little fantasy of mine,' he replied, moving behind me. 'I like to think that I've taken a girl prisoner.'

'You don't have to blindfold me, for God's sake.'

'It's all part of my fantasy, Cindy. Blindfolded, tied over the table with your hairless pussy lips bulging between your naked thighs . . . It's all part of my little fantasy.'

Listening to the zip of his trousers, I wondered whether he was going to force his huge cock into my pussy or my bum. More thoughts swirled in the mist of my confused mind, and I wondered why Neil reckoned that he could get away with this. Blackmailing me, using and abusing me when he knew that Rod might walk in at any minute and . . . He wasn't working alone, I was sure. He had Jackie, his tart. Was Rod in on the game? If Rod had discovered my secret life, he might have put his brother up to this. But why? What would he gain?

Wondering whether Rod thought this to be some kind of punishment for my adultery, I let out a rush of breath as Neil's solid cock entered the tight sheath of my hot pusy and drove fully home. Rod was too busy at the office to keep coming home to check up on me, I thought, as Neil withdrew his hard cock and rammed into me. Even if he had discovered something about me, he'd have confronted me rather than involve his brother like this. Turning my thoughts to Alan Johnson, I wondered whether he was working with Neil. Perhaps all three men were ... My thinking was going crazy again.

'You're a tight little whore,' Neil breathed. 'I can feel your hairless pussy lips gripping my cock. If you're a good little girl, I'll fuck your tight arse once I've done your cunt.'

Remaining silent, I listened to the squelching of my pussy juices as Neil's cock repeatedly impaled me. His lower belly slapping my burning buttocks, his swinging balls smacking my naked mons, his bulbous knob battering my cervix, he grabbed my hips and increased his fucking rhythm. I could feel my inner labia rolling back and forth along his veined shaft, repeatedly dragged into my sex hole and then pulled away from my body.

This was my sexual heaven, I again mused dreamily. My naked body bound with rope, my buttocks burning from a severe whipping, a beautiful cock fucking my spasming pussy ... What more could a girl ask for? Freedom, I reflected. Freedom to live and lust. But there was no way I'd find freedom unless I got my hands on the photographs. And the chances of that were zero. Buying my own house wasn't an option; it was the only way out.

Enjoying the moment, the driving of Neil's hard cock, the repeated thrusting and withdrawing, I listened to the gasps of male pleasure resounding around the dining room as my tethered body rocked back and forth with the forbidden fucking. Sucking sounds echoing around the room, low moans, deep breathing, flesh meeting flesh ... My pelvic cavity inflating and deflating, I waited for the spunk to jet deep into my pussy and lubricate the illicit union. What was Rod doing? I found myself wondering. My clitoris now solid, my juices flowing in torrents, I imagined Rod sitting at his desk. He'd be totally oblivious to his wife's adulterous debauchery, unaware that his loving wife was betraying him.

Pulling his pussy-wet cock out of my tight sex, Neil pressed his knob hard against my anal ring. I let out a yelp as his cock forced its way into my rectum. The delicate brown tissue surrounding my anus stretched to capacity, and I revelled in the exquisite pleasure. Waves of pure sexual bliss rolled through my naked body as my brother-in-law repeatedly withdrew his massive organ and rammed into me. Squelching, sucking, smacking flesh, gasping . . . The sounds of crude sex.

Desperate for his spunk to flow and lubricate my burning arse, I wondered whether blackmail was so bad after all. I was getting plenty of sex, more than enough spunk . . . But this wasn't the way I'd wanted it. I'd always hand picked my lovers, chosen my men carefully. To be forced to have anal sex, blackmailed and threatened wasn't what I wanted. I had no control, no say in the matter, and I didn't like it.

'Here it comes,' Neil breathed, increasing his anal fucking rhythm. His cock swelled, stretching me painfully. His spunk jetted from his orgasming knob and flooded my hot bowels. Thrusting, pistoning, spunking, squelching . . . The exquisite sensations of crude sex rippling through my naked body as spunk oozed from my bloated anus and ran down to my pussy, I hoped that Neil would soon be able to restiffen and fuck me again. I could feel his spunk running in rivers down my thighs, and I prayed for him to find the strength, and the hardness, to do my bum again before leaving. Having endured the leather belt and an anal fucking, I was in desperate need for the release of orgasm. Would he lick and suck my clitoris? Or would I have to resort to masturbating when he'd satisfied his male lust and fled the marital home?

His cock finally slid out of my rectal tube. I could feel my anus gaping wide open. With spunk oozing from my inflamed hole, I again prayed for Neil to find the potency to ram his beautiful cock deep into my tight arse and fuck me there again. If only he hadn't resorted to blackmail, I reflected. If only he'd come to me for sex without his threats and . . . But I would never have entertained him. I would never have played my dirty sex games so close to home.

'Did you enjoy that?' he asked me.

'No,' I lied. 'Will you please take the blindfold off and let me go now?'

'Not yet, Cindy. I'm stiffening up nicely for the second round.'

'You're vile,' I hissed, my stomach somersaulting at the prospect of another anal shafting. 'Vile, vulgar, despicable . . .'

'And you're a tight-cunted little whore. God, I'm as hard as rock already. You see how you turn me on?'

As he moved about behind me, I knew that my prayers had been answered. He was all man, I thought happily, as I felt the swollen bulb of his cock pressing hard against my spunk-dripping anal ring. Relaxing my muscles to allow him entry, I gasped as he drove his cock deep into my very core. Trembling uncontrollably as he impaled me completely on his magnificent cock, I grinned. He thought that he was using and abusing me, forcing me to endure his anal violation, when, in truth, I was revelling in his crude act. He withdrew his slimed member, the vacuum almost sucking my insides out, then rammed into me with a cruel vengeance. My stomach was almost pushed into my mouth with the thrust of his cock.

I wished that Rod was more like his brother. I couldn't understand how Neil had such staying power, such virility. His cock was rock solid, stretching my anal duct open to the extreme as he swung his hips and fucked me hard. He was all man, that was for sure.

Like a rag doll, I flopped back and forth. His belly slapped my stinging buttocks, his balls battered the fleshy pads of my shaven pussy lips, and he finally reached his goal and pumped his second load of creamy spunk deep into me. Would he find the strength to repeat his crude fucking for a third time? I wondered in my sexual haze. Would he restiffen and shaft my arse yet again?

'God,' he breathed, making his last thrusts into my spunk-flooded rectum. 'I've never known such a tight-arsed little whore.'

Saying nothing as he finally withdrew his slimed cock, I looked into the darkness of my blindfold and wondered what other sexual delights he had in store for me. Another whipping? More anal abuse? My aching bottom hole gaping wide open, spunk draining from my inflamed rectal sheath and coursing down my inner thighs, I listened to movements behind me. What was he doing? What was he planning? Finally, he removed my blindfold, released the ropes and helped me to haul my exhausted body off the table. Steadying me on my sagging legs, giving me no time to recover from the abuse, he ordered me to masturbate in front of him.

'No,' I breathed, rubbing my aching wrists.

'After two anal shaggings, you must be desperate to come,' he said, chuckling as I folded my arms and covered the firm mounds of my breasts. 'You look nice without any pubes.'

'Just leave now,' I snapped.

'How many men have you had since you married Rod? Fifty, sixty . . .'

'Go to hell, Neil. You've had what you wanted, so get out of my house and leave me alone.'

'Have you counted the number of cocks you've had spunking up your tight little arse?'

'You can ask as many questions as you like, but I won't –' I dashed into the lounge as the phone rang, surprised to hear Rod's voice.

'I'm in Birmingham,' he told me. 'I'm going to be home pretty late tonight.'

'Oh, right,' I breathed, watching Neil out of the corner of my eye as he ambled into the lounge.

'Are you all right, love?'

'Yes, of course.'

'I'm sorry about this. It's a damned client I'm having major problems with.'

'Do you want me to wait up for you?'

'No, no. By the time I've finished here and then driven back . . . If it gets too late, I might stay here overnight.'

'Oh, er . . . all right.'

'I'm sorry, love. It just can't be helped. I really don't think that I'll be home before the morning.'

'Well, I'll see you tomorrow.'

'I'll ring you this evening.'

'OK, speak to you later.'

I replaced the receiver, grabbed my clothes and began to dress. Neil watched me, grinning as I pulled my panties up my long legs. Wondering how long he was going to hang around, I pondered on my hairless pussy. I could have some real fun dressed in my school uniform, I mused. Lurking in the park, looking out for sad perverts, I'd not have to worry about getting home for Rod. But I had to get rid of Neil first.

'Rod won't be back until tomorrow?' he asked me.

'That's right,' I replied coldly. 'Not that it has anything to do with you.'

'So much for your shopping trip,' he quipped. 'What will you do for the rest of the day? Fuck the young lads from next door?'

'Housework,' I lied. 'Now, if you'll excuse me.'

'I think we need to talk, Cindy.'

'Do we? What about?'

'The situation.'

'Go on.'

'I want more from you. I want –'

'Neil, I don't care what you want. You're not getting it, OK?'

'And you're not understanding the situation. Don't you realise that I could destroy your marriage, just like that?'

'Yes, I do. But –'

'There are no buts, Cindy. I have photographs of you with those lads from next door. You, naked on the lawn, getting fucked rotten by two teenage lads. Take your clothes off.'

'Take them off? No, I won't. You've had what you wanted, so get out.'

'Clothes off, Cindy. If you don't, then I'll be forced to –'

'Surely, you're not man enough to do it again?' I quipped.

'Just take your clothes off. Do as you're told, like a good little girl.'

Undressing, I couldn't believe that he was going to fuck me again. What sort of man was he? I wondered, tugging my skirt and panties down and kicking them aside. A bloody miracle man? At least Rod wouldn't come barging in, I thought as I again stood naked before my brother-in-law, my blackmailer. If Neil was able to raise an erection, I'd at least enjoy another crude sex session. I could do this all day every day, I mused, as he took a length of rope and pulled my arms out in front of me.

'What are you doing?' I asked him as he bound my wrists with the rope.

'You'll see,' he said, chuckling, leading me into the kitchen. He opened the back door.

'Neil, it's raining hard.'

'I realise that,' he returned, leading me down the garden.

'For God's sake,' I complained as he forced me to bend over. Having tied the free end of the rope to the base of a bush, he stood up and slapped my wet bum. 'What the hell do you think you're doing?' I hissed. 'You must be bloody mad.'

Unable to believe, or understand, what he was doing as he dashed back to the house, I watched him grinning at me through the kitchen window. My naked body bent over, my long blonde hair becoming matted as the rain lashed my naked body, I didn't know what to do. Neil had lost his senses, I was sure, as I did my best to huddle beneath the bush. The rain splattering my naked body, my hair now in rats' tails, I could see him laughing at me through the window. What the hell did he think he was playing at? Was this supposed to be some kind of punishment? Had Neil planned this well in advance? How did he know that it was going to lash with rain?

'Let me go, for God's sake,' I called as he stood in the kitchen doorway.

'Not until you've learned your lesson, Cindy. You'll do what I say, when I say. Do you understand?'

'I've done everything you've asked,' I returned.

'It doesn't look like the rain's going to let up.'

'Neil, unless you . . .'

This was ridiculous, I thought angrily, my naked body now drenched. Returning with another length of rope, he ordered me to stand up. The rope securing my wrists to the bush was too short to allow me to stand upright. All I could do was drag myself to my feet with my body bent over and my naked buttocks projected out. After tying the rope around my waist and securing the end to the branch of a tree above me, he stood back and admired his handiwork. Neither able to stand or kneel, there was no way I could move. Was he going to ram his cock into my rectum yet again? Surely not.

The first lash of a length of rope across the crimsoned flesh of my bottom sent a jolt through my naked body. I let out a harsh yelp. Why in the garden? I wondered, as the rope swished through the air and again bit into the glowing flesh of my buttocks. Why in the pouring rain? My naked body swaying, almost hanging from the tree branch, I could do nothing to defend myself as the rope repeatedly flailed the burning globes of my rain-wet bottom. Again and again, the rope lashed my naked flesh, the pain permeating the firm mounds of my buttocks as he chuckled in his devilry.

Discarding the rope he snapped a branch off a bush, raised it above his head and brought it down across my buttocks with a loud crack. The rough leaves of the branch were biting into my stinging flesh, and I let out another yelp. Neil had definitely lost his senses, I knew, as he repeatedly brought the branch down, chuckling wickedly as he flailed my glowing bottom. The leaves caught the backs of my legs, striking the fleshy cushions of my hairless pussy lips bulging between my thighs. I was enjoying the abuse. But I didn't think that I could take much more. Again and again, the branch swished through the air, lashing my wet bottom, the swollen lips of my exposed vulva, until I cried out and begged him to stop.

'It looks as though your bum's on fire,' he said, lowering the rope to his side.

'Rod is bound to notice the weals,' I breathed shakily. 'For fuck's sake, let me go now.'

'You're right, Rod will notice,' he said, chortling. 'A glowing arse, shaved cunny lips . . . Of course he'll notice.'

'Why are you doing this? I can understand your wanting sex with me, but why do this?'

'You're an animal, Cindy,' he breathed. 'You've cheated on my brother, betrayed and deceived him from day one of your so-called marriage. You're an animal, and that's how I'm going to treat you.'

'If I'm an animal, what are you?'

'Your master. You're nothing but a dog, and I'm your master.'

'Are you going to release me or –'

'No, not yet. Jackie wants to have some fun with you.'

'If you think . . .' I began as he called the slut. 'How the hell did she get into my house?'

'I let her in,' he said as the girl approached. 'There we are, Jackie. The slut has been spunked and whipped. She's all ready for you.'

The girl said nothing as she kneeled behind me and ran her fingertips over the glowing orbs of my stinging bottom. Ignoring my protests, she parted my firm buttocks and licked the spunk-bubbling entrance to my rectum. She was wearing a red leather miniskirt and tight T-shirt. The nipples of her firm breasts pressing through the rain-wet material, her white panties on show, she looked like a right tart as she attended to my exposed bottom hole.

Locking her lips to the delicate brown tissue of my anus, she sucked hard. Drawing out the spunk, she slipped two fingers between the hairless lips of my vulva and drove them deep into the tight sheath of my hot pussy. I squirmed as I watched her between my legs, horrified at the thought of a girl sucking my bottom hole and fingering my pussy. My head upside down, my long blonde hair spread over the wet grass, I watched the slut's fingers stretching my pussy lips wide open. She was a filthy lesbian. Neil was a bastard, and I'd make sure that he paid for treating me like this.

'She tastes lovely,' the slut murmured, her tongue lapping at my anal hole as her fingers massaged the inner flesh of my contracting pussy.

'I'll pump her full of spunk again in a minute,' Neil said. 'And then you can have another drink of arse-flavoured spunk.'

'Mmm,' the slut breathed appreciatively, pushing her tongue deep into my arsehole.

My clitoris swelled as she fingered my pussy and tongued my anus. I couldn't believe that my arousal was soaring. I wasn't a lesbian, I reminded myself. The very thought of another woman tonguing and fingering me had always left me cold. But now? After pushing more fingers into my bloated pussy, the slut again locked her lips to my anus and sucked my bottom hole. Drawing out the remnants of Neil's spunk as he watched the crude lesbian show, she was obviously in her element.

'Please,' I gasped. 'My back aches and –'

'Fill her up again,' the slut trilled, withdrawing her fingers from my bloated pussy and leaping to her feet. 'Fill her with fresh spunk and I'll suck it out of her.'

'With pleasure,' Neil said, stabbing at the wet eye of my anus.

Amazed as he again slipped his knob past my defeated anal sphincter muscles, I couldn't believe that he was going to fuck me there for the third time. His cock shaft entered me, stretching my rectal tube wide open. I let out a gasp as the girl positioned herself beneath my naked body and began licking the sensitive tip of my clitoris. My pussy juices flowed freely between my engorged inner lips and streamed down my thighs, and I knew that I'd be unable to hold back my orgasm. I couldn't allow another girl to bring me off, I thought, as she expertly attended to my aching cunt.

The slut's tongue slurped between my shaved lips, as Neil's huge cock repeatedly drove deep into my anal canal. I quivered as fingers entered my pussy. I gazed at the triangular patch of the slut's white panties as she sat on the wet grass fingering and licking between my thighs. Where the hell had Neil picked her up? I wondered as she groped at my breasts with her free hand. I'd always thought him to be happily married to Sue. How wrong I was.

There again, I was as bad as Neil. I'd had dozens of men, sucked spunk from dozens of rock-hard cocks. We were as bad as each other, I decided, as the slut managed to force more fingers into my pussy. But I would never have stooped so low as to blackmail someone for sex. Neil had his wife and his bisexual slut, so why bother with me? It was the excitement, I mused. The danger, the thought of fucking his sister-in-law, the betrayal . . . If Rod ever discovered the shocking truth about his seemingly loyal and faithful wife . . .

'Yes,' Neil gasped, his huge cock pumping spunk deep into my bowels for the third time as the slut sucked hard on my clit. Her fingers pistoning my contracting pussy, Neil's spunk deluging my rectal tube, I finally reached my own mind-blowing orgasm. The rain lashed my naked body, and I shook uncontrollably as the girl sustained my incredible pleasure. Never had I known an orgasm of such strength and duration. On and on, waves of pure sexual ecstasy rolled through my tethered body as my brother-in-law fucked my tight arse. Shuddering, whimpering, I hung from the rope tied to the tree branch as the wicked pair abused my body. The slut was good, I decided, as she mouthed and tongued my pulsating clit. And Neil was bloody amazing. But this was blackmail.

My orgasm finally waning, Neil dragged his deflating cock out of my arse and his accomplice slipped her fingers out of my drenched pussy. I was hanging from the rope like a lifeless puppet, and fell to the ground as Neil released me. Writhing on the wet grass, curling up into a ball as the rain lashed me, I watched the evil pair walking across the lawn to the house. They'd finished with me. They'd used and abused me and finished with me. For the time being, at least.

Ten

Sue looked up from her coffee cup and smiled at me. 'I haven't come here to cause trouble or argue with you,' she said. 'I've come to tell you of my suspicions.'

'So, you're saying that Neil and Rod were together yesterday?' I asked her. 'And you saw them together today?'

'Yes.'

'Sue, Rod was at the office all day yesterday. And now he's in Birmingham. He won't be home until tomorrow morning.'

'I drove past yesterday. I was going to call in and have a coffee with you when I saw Neil's car parked down the road. I then saw Neil walk up your drive, with Rod.'

'I was here all day. Are you sure it was yesterday?'

'Of course I'm sure. I saw Neil and Rod walking up your drive.'

'I just don't understand it.'

'Are you sure that you were here all day? You didn't pop out for anything?'

I stared at her across the kitchen table. I didn't know what to think or say. I'd spent an hour or more with Neil and his slut. I'd been tied up in the garden, whipped, fingered, sucked and fucked ... Rod had phoned me to say that he was in Birmingham. Today or yesterday, Sue couldn't have seen him. Why would he lie to me? If he had lied and he'd not gone to Birmingham, if he'd come to the house with Neil . . . Surely, he wouldn't have watched his brother treat me like an animal?

I'd had these suspicions before, I reflected, toying with my coffee cup. This was by no means the first time I'd thought that there was something going on between Rod and Neil. But I couldn't imagine Rod watching his brother use and abuse me. If that was the case, then Rod must have been in on the scam from day one. Perhaps Rod had taken the photograph of me in my bondage gear. I was confusing myself, my mind going way off track. The idea that Rod was working with Neil was ludicrous.

'Cindy?' Sue breathed, breaking my reverie. 'Are you sure that you were here all day yesterday?'

'Er . . . no, no. I went out for a while,' I lied, not knowing what else to say.

'Perhaps that's when Rod and Neil came here,' she persisted.

'You couldn't have seen him today. He's in Birmingham, Sue,' I persisted. 'He rang me.'

'He could have rung you from the end of the road and told you that he was in Birmingham.'

'That's true, but . . . Where is he now then? It's eight o'clock. Surely, he would have come home by now.'

'He might be staying at a local hotel or . . . As I said, I'm not trying to cause trouble. To be honest, I've had my suspicions about Neil for some time. He goes off out; he says that he's working late when I know damned well that he isn't . . . Has Rod ever lied to you? Has he said that he's had to work late?'

'The other evening, he said that he had to go back to the office. I later found out that he'd not been there.'

'Where had he been?'

'I don't know. I didn't ask him because . . . because I thought that he might have needed some time alone. Have you asked Neil about this?'

'No, he hasn't been home. He's been out all day. God only knows where he is. I don't know what's going on, Cindy. But there's no doubt in my mind that Neil and Rod walked up your drive yesterday. It must have been when you were out. And they were together today. I saw them coming here.'

'I can't think why they'd come here,' I breathed pensively, frowning at her. 'I mean, why would Rod phone and say that he was in Birmingham and then come to the house with Neil? Had I been here . . . what would he have said to me?'

'Your guess is as good as mine.'

My mind swirled with a thousand thoughts. I couldn't imagine Rod going along with Neil's blackmailing. Why would he do that? Why would he allow his brother and the slut to abuse me like that? Unless he got his kicks from watching his wife . . . No, Rod just wasn't like that. Although Sue was adamant, I came to the conclusion that she was mistaken. She'd seen Neil, I was sure of that. Perhaps, as she'd peered through the windscreen in the driving rain, she'd thought that Rod was with him.

'I don't know what to think,' I said, finishing my coffee.

'I think we should keep an eye on them,' Sue suggested. 'I'm not saying that Rod is playing around behind your back, but he's definitely up to something.'

'If he was, what would that have to do with his coming here with Neil?'

'I have no idea, Cindy. Look at the facts. The other evening, Rod said that he went back to the office, and

189

you found out that he was lying. This morning, he rang and told you that he was in Birmingham, and yet I saw him walking up your drive. Neil told me that he was working away today, and yet I saw him with Rod.'

'There's got to be a simple explanation, Sue. Perhaps they're planning something? Yes, that's it. A surprise party or ...'

'A party? Christmas is months away; there are no anniversaries or birthdays ...'

'A surprise holiday for the four of us?'

'Hardly. Neil's been acting strangely recently. He goes out; he comes back late; he lies ... I'm not trying to plant seeds of doubt in your mind, Cindy. You and Rod are the perfect couple, everyone knows that. You couldn't be happier. But ...'

'But what?'

'But I instinctively know that something's going on. I can sense it, Cindy. Something's going on.'

She was right, but *what* was going on? All I could do was wait until the morning and then confront Rod. There again, what was the point? He'd only lie to me. I was in two minds whether or not to tell Sue about Neil. Perhaps she should know that he was blackmailing me for sex, that he was screwing a bisexual slut ... But I'd only cause trouble and probably end up the worse for it. I didn't know what to do. Be honest with Sue? Confront Rod? Or leave the marital home and buy a house somewhere far away from problems and trouble.

'I suppose I'd better be getting back,' Sue said, finishing her coffee.

'Will you ask Neil about this?'

'Not yet. I'll do a little detective work before confronting him. And I think you should check up on Rod's movements. Ask a few searching questions when you see him tomorrow. It should be easy enough to find out whether or not he stayed at a hotel in Birmingham.'

Seeing her out, I wondered what her detective work would unearth. If she followed her husband to my house, witnessed the crude sexual acts . . . But that was the least of my worries. What the hell was Rod up to? Where was he? Finally, I climbed the stairs to my bedroom, and snuggled beneath the quilt and recalled the day's events. I'd shaved my pussy, had my naked body bound with rope and whipped, my clitoris sucked to orgasm by a girl, endured my brother-in-law's cock driving deep into my arse . . . And, to top it all, Sue was on the case.

Rod was home in time for breakfast. He talked about Birmingham, the client he'd seen, the hotel he'd stayed in . . . He was so convincing that I had to stick to my conclusion that Sue had been mistaken. Besides, had he witnessed the crude acts I'd committed with his brother, he'd not have been able to hide his . . . disgust? Or perverted pleasure? Sue was wrong. There was no way my husband was a voyeur.

'Were you all right on your own?' he asked me, finishing his breakfast.

'Sue came round,' I said, suddenly realising that he must have left Birmingham very early to get home in time for breakfast. 'What time did you leave the hotel this morning?'

'The hotel? Oh, er . . . about five, I suppose. The roads were pretty quiet.'

'Quiet? They must have been empty,' I quipped. 'By the way, Neil called in yesterday.'

'Oh?'

'He was passing so he came in for a cup of coffee.'

The atmosphere was tense. We were talking as if we were reading lines from a script. Did he know about my dark side? I pondered. Did he know about Neil and his slut? Wearing my dressing gown, I wondered whether to show him my shaved pussy and gauge his reaction. If he knew, if he got his kicks from watching his brother fuck his wife ... Coming up with an idea as he was about to leave for the office, I grinned.

'I have a new friend,' I said mysteriously.

'A new friend? Who's that?'

'Jackie.' He didn't flinch an eyelid. 'She's a friend of Neil's. He brought her round yesterday.'

'He's not mentioned her. He was saying something about getting a new secretary. Does she work for him?'

'Yes, something like that. She's coming round this morning.'

'Does Neil know?'

'That she's coming round? I have no idea.'

'Right, well, I'd better be going.'

As he left the house, I felt that we were like strangers. No kiss on the cheek, no smiles. Was he seeing someone else? I reflected. He might have stayed at a local hotel with some slut or other. Perhaps he was sharing Jackie with his brother? I couldn't imagine my husband shafting the slut's arse. Slipping my dressing gown off as I climbed the stairs, I knew that I was going to have to watch my back. Whatever Rod was up to, I was going to have to be extremely careful.

Gazing at the reflection of my hairless pussy lips in the mirror, I couldn't believe the transformation. Running my fingertips over the smooth flesh of my mons, I decided to go to the park and play the role of a schoolgirl again. Boredom would soon have me in its grip unless I did something exciting, and what could be more exciting than luring a middle-aged man into the woods and allowing him to fuck me senseless? Rod was at the office, Neil ... Gazing out of the bedroom window, I didn't care where Neil was. The sun was shining, the birds singing. It was a lovely summer day, a day made for wandering through the park in my school uniform. A day for getting fucked.

Frowning as I thought I saw someone peep out from behind the shed, I wondered whether young James was looking for his football. Perhaps he was looking for me; looking for a mouth fuck. My stomach fluttered as I pictured his beautiful cock pumping fresh spunk over my tongue. Spying through the net curtains, I couldn't see anyone. But I was sure that someone had been there. Was Neil lurking at the end of the garden? I wouldn't have put anything past him. As I was about to go and investigate, the phone rang.

'It's me,' Alan said as I pressed the receiver to my ear. 'I thought I might call round and see you.'

'Was Rod at the office yesterday?' I asked him, dreading the answer.

'Rod was in Birmingham. He stayed overnight. Surely you knew that?'

'Yes, yes, I did.'

'What's going on, Cindy? Why ask about Rod?'

'It doesn't matter. Look, I have to go out this morning. I have several things to do in town.'

'Oh, that's a shame. I was rather hoping that we could ... well, you know?'

'Yes, I know. How is Rod this morning?'

'He hasn't arrived yet. I doubt that I'll see him as I have to go out and see clients.'

'Oh, right. Look, come round later. After lunch.'

'Great. I'll see you at, say, two o'clock?'

'I'll look forward to it.'

'So will I, Cindy, so will I.'

Replacing the receiver, I felt a lot easier. Rod and Alan worked closely together. Alan would have known about the problems with a client in Birmingham. Rod could have hardly made up such a story. Unless Alan was also in on the blackmail scam. My thinking was going crazy again. I was becoming increasingly paranoid.

I donned my school uniform. My long blonde hair in pigtails, tied with pretty red ribbons, a very short gymslip and white blouse, navy-blue knickers, white ankle socks and black shoes . . . This time, my name was Belinda. I was out of school because I'd been to the dentist. I loved acting, playing the role of an innocent girl. I loved watching middle-aged men ogling my young body. Thinking their dirty male thoughts, they'd give anything to get their hands inside my school knickers. My arousal soaring, my pussy wetting, I was about to leave the house when the doorbell rang.

Slipping into the lounge, my heart racing, my hands trembling, I spied through the net curtains. 'Shit,' I breathed, staring at Jackie, the slut. What the hell was she doing? Where was Neil? Having waited until she'd given up and walked down the drive, I left the house and stopped at the end of the drive. She was nowhere in sight; I was safe. Walking down the street, looking over my shoulder every few seconds to make sure that I wasn't being followed, I didn't think that she'd recognise me in my school uniform. Again wondering why she'd called at the house, I thought that she might have wanted sex. But where was Neil?

I reached the park and walked across the grass towards the trees. Apart from a woman with a dog, the park was deserted. I felt despondent, and a little anxious. Seeing Jackie at my front door had unnerved me. Hovering by the long grass and wild flowers

194

edging the wooded area, I turned my thoughts to Rod. If he was in on the scam, then he'd keep a very close eye on me, even go as far as to follow me. I was surprised that Neil wasn't watching the house and . . . Who had been behind the shed? Was it James?

Sitting with my chin resting on my knees, my navy-blue knickers bulging alluringly between my thighs, I pushed my anxiety to the back of my mind as I noticed a man walking towards me. He was in his fifties with greying hair. Dressed in black trousers and an open-neck shirt, he was an ideal candidate for my sex games. He reminded me of Richard. Where was Richard? And Ian, for that matter. Had Rod and Neil got to them, threatened them? Whatever Rod and Neil were doing, wherever they were, I didn't care.

'No school today then?' the man asked.

'I've been to the dentist,' I replied, looking up at him.

'Teeth all OK?'

'Yes, yes, fine,' I said, my chin still on my knees as I parted my feet a little wider. Did he like the sight of my navy-blue knickers?

'So, what are you doing here all alone? Aren't you going back to school?'

'I don't have to go back until after lunch. It's a nice day, so I thought I'd sit here and . . .' My words tailed off as I saw a man in the distance. I was sure that it was Rod. 'I think I'll walk in the woods,' I said, leaping to my feet.

'I'll come with you, if you don't mind?'

'I don't mind.'

I followed the narrow path into the trees with the man close behind me. Was it really Rod I'd seen? And what had the slut wanted? What the hell was going on? I imagined all the more that there was a conspiracy working against me. Rod was at the office,

I told myself, and I had nothing to worry about. After leading the man into the small clearing, I stopped and looked about as if I was lost.

'Oh,' I breathed. 'There's no way out.'

'We took the wrong path,' he said, his eyes falling to my partially open blouse. 'Still, it's quite nice here. What's your name?'

'Belinda,' I replied. So far, so good.

'I'm John.'

Sitting on the ground in my usual position, I wondered what my would-be sexual conquest was thinking as he sat opposite me and stared at the bulge of my navy-blue knickers. He was no doubt imagining my pink pussy slit, wondering how to get his hands inside my knickers and play with my puffy girl lips. I'd done pretty well so far, I mused. A man had found me, followed me into the woods and was now gazing at the bulging crotch of my school knickers. Time to take things a little further.

'I'm sorry that I'm not very good company,' I said, my blue eyes locked on to his. 'It's just that I have a lot on my mind at the moment.'

'Oh? Do you want to talk about it?'

'My boyfriend ... We've been together for a month now and ... He wants to do things.'

'Do things?' he echoed. 'Ah, I see what you mean. So, you don't feel that you're ready for sex?'

'Well, no. I've never done anything before. To be honest, I don't want him to think that I'm no good. He's had other girlfriends, you see. He's done things and ...'

'You're afraid that he'll leave you and find some other girl?'

'Well, yes.'

'It's nice to think that you can tell me about your problems. We've only just met, and yet you obviously feel that you can confide in me.'

'You don't mind?'

'No, not at all. In fact, I'm very pleased. I reckon that we're going to become good friends.'

'I hope so,' I murmured, smiling at him. 'I don't have anyone I can talk to. My dad's always at work; my mum's always busy with my little brother; my friends ... They all have boyfriends, and they all have sex. I feel so alone, so left out.'

'What do you know about sex?' he asked me, his eyes transfixed on my knickers. 'If you don't mind my asking, what have you done?'

'Well, nothing. That's the trouble, I haven't done anything.'

'You don't masturbate?'

'No, no, I don't.'

My stomach fluttered with butterflies. I knew that my plan was working well. I loved the game, the lies and deceit, the pretence. Poor little schoolgirl, alone and worried, virginal and desperate to learn ... My games were so easy. Easy to play, and win. John was a nice man, warm and friendly and anxious to help me. Little did he know that he was going to do more than help me. He was going to show me how to masturbate, how to have full-blown sex. But, as always, I had to retain my air of innocence, come across as extremely naïve – and very gullible. Was his cock solid? I wondered, my knickers wetting with my rising arousal. Talking to a schoolgirl about masturbation must have turned him on.

'Even though you don't masturbate, you must have sexual thoughts?' he persevered.

'I'm always having sexual thoughts,' I confessed sheepishly. 'I suppose I shouldn't be talking to you like this.'

'No, no. You carry on. It helps to talk.'

'You're very kind.'

'The thing is, I don't think I can help you.'

'Oh? But I thought that talking . . .'

'Talking's fine, it can help a lot. But, when it comes to sex . . . To be honest, Belinda, the only way I could really help you is by . . . Never mind. I suppose you're too young to understand.'

'Understand what?'

'You're too young and I'm too old.'

'For what? I don't know what you mean.'

'The only way I can teach you about sex, about masturbation, is to show you.'

'Show me?'

'This boyfriend of yours . . .'

'Derek.'

'Yes, Derek. You'll lose him unless you get some experience.'

'I know that.'

'I would suggest that you slip your knickers off and allow me to teach you, but . . .'

'Oh, I see,' I sighed, averting my gaze as he stared into my eyes.

That was a very direct line, I mused. *Slip your knickers off and allow me to teach you.* He obviously realised that he was going to get nowhere by stalling, holding back. I was about to shock him, please him, by slipping my knickers off, when I heard a twig cracking underfoot. Someone was in the woods, lurking. Kids? I wondered. John was too busy eyeing my school knickers to notice as another twig cracked. Was it Rod? I wondered anxiously. The man I'd seen . . . Reckoning that it was an animal, probably a rabbit, I tried not to worry.

'Belinda . . .' John began hesitantly. 'I was wondering . . .'

'Wondering about what?' I breathed.

'Would you take your knickers off for me?'

'I . . . I don't know,' I replied, trying to appear embarrassed.

'Please, Belinda. It's been a long time since . . . Will you at least allow me to look at you?'

Standing before him, I lifted my gymslip and pulled my knickers down to my knees. He stared open mouthed at the hairless lips of my pussy, my tightly closed sex crack. Licking his lips, he moved forwards for a better view of my feminine intimacy. He'd have given anything to touch me there, I knew. To touch, stroke, caress . . . Hearing a bush rustling somewhere in the woods, I knew that I wouldn't be able to enjoy my sex games all the time I was worrying about Rod. It seemed that there was no escaping him. Even though I was sure that he was at the office, he was ruining my dirty games. Should I leave him? I wondered, as John reached out and stroked each outer lip in turn.

'You're beautiful,' he breathed, squeezing the fleshy pads of my swelling labia. 'I've never seen such beauty.'

'You said that you only wanted to look,' I said.

'Yes, but . . . May I kiss you there?'

'Well, I suppose so,' I sighed, hoping that I wasn't giving the game away by producing too much pussy milk.

Pressing his lips against my naked vulva, he pushed his tongue out and licked my crack. I could hear his heavy breathing as he tasted me there. I could also hear a bush rustling. The old man moved back and looked up at me, his eyes frowning as he, too, heard something. My plan had worked so well, but . . . Leaping to his feet, he looked about the clearing. The game was over, I knew, as he told me to pull my knickers up. Telling me to meet him in the woods after school, at four o'clock, he slipped into the bushes and made his escape.

After pulling my knickers up, I adjusted my gymslip and brushed my blonde hair away from my face. My stomach sinking, I was silently fuming. Who the hell was lurking in the woods? Was it Rod? Perhaps Neil and his slut had followed me? Deciding to stay where I was and hope that they'd go away, I sat on the grass and pondered on the situation. Blackmailed by my brother-in-law, forced to have sex with him and his bisexual slut . . . The time had come to do something. I couldn't live like this, I thought dolefully. The old man had taken the bait, followed me into the woods, kissed my naked pussy . . . and then left me wanting, craving.

'Ah, there you are,' the slut breathed as she entered the clearing and dumped a leather bag on the ground.

'What the hell . . .' I gasped, unable to believe that she'd had the audacity to follow me.

'You've been a naughty little girl, haven't you?'

'Piss off,' I hissed, rising to my feet.

'That's not very nice,' Neil said, emerging from the bushes and standing by the slut's side. 'I like the school uniform.'

'What the fuck do you want?' I asked him as he grinned at me. 'For God's sake, can't you leave me alone for five minutes?'

'It seems not, Cindy. If Rod discovers that you've been to the park dressed as a schoolgirl and lured some old man into the woods . . .'

'To be honest, I don't give a damn,' I returned. 'Go and tell him; go and show him the photographs. I'm beyond caring.'

'All right, if that's the way you want it.'

'Yes, it is the way I want it. I've had enough if this. Go running to your brother and –'

'And your mother?'

'What?'

'I think it only right that your mother should see the photographs. She should know what sort of girl her daughter is, don't you agree?'

'You leave my mother out of this.'

'Clothes off,' the slut ordered me.

'No.'

'Think about it, Cindy,' Neil breathed. 'Imagine your mother's reaction when she sees photographs of you enjoying lesbian sex, enjoying two teenage cocks . . . Think about it.'

I was more concerned about my mother discovering the truth than my husband. I was her little girl, the apple of her eye. Rod would leave me if he discovered my secret life. He'd throw me out of the marital home. But my mother would be heartbroken and undoubtedly disown me. I'd not expected this. All along, I'd thought that Rod was my worry. Neil was a bastard. To bring my mother into the equation was despicable.

I slipped out of my gymslip, unbuttoned my blouse and dropped it to the ground as my blackmailers looked on. They'd won, I thought angrily, unhooking my bra. There'd be nothing I could say to my mother by way of an excuse. The photographs clearly depicted the real me; showed beyond all doubt that I was a common slut. My mother had always liked Rod. Like everyone else, she'd always thought us to be the perfect couple. There'd be nothing I could say to excuse my wanton whoredom.

Ordering me to stand against a tree with my arms around the trunk, the slut opened her leather bag and pulled out several lengths of rope. I complied, clinging to the old oak tree as she bound my wrists. The rough bark pressing into the sensitive teats of my nipples, I knew that I was in for a spanking as she pulled my feet wide apart and ran another length of rope around the tree. My naked buttocks positioned for a thrashing, the swollen lips of my hairless pussy bulging between my parted legs, I was in for a gruelling spanking.

'There's something about hairless pussy lips,' the slut said, taking something from the bag and kneeling behind me. 'Something extremely arousing. But I think yours need puffing up a little.'

'I'm going to enjoy this,' Neil said, chuckling as he moved behind me.

Saying nothing as the slut pressed something against the lips of my vulva, I'd never felt more despondent in all my life. I couldn't cope with the thought of losing, especially to my bloody brother-in-law. I'd enjoyed my dirty games, my clandestine life, for five years. Rod had been happy in his ignorance; I'd been happy in my sexual heaven . . . And now my world had fallen apart. Neil had said that I was his sex slave, and that's exactly what I'd become. I could no longer fight. I had no strength left in me to fight my master.

My outer lips swelled as I listened to the sound of air hissing. I knew what the slut was doing. A vacuum pump, I mused, recalling the device advertised in a magazine. My hairless labia sucked into the plastic container, inflating painfully as she pumped the rubber bulb, I wondered how long my pussy lips would remain puffed up, grossly oversized. I also wondered how long I'd be tied to the tree and sexually abused.

'You're going to look wonderful,' the slut said, leaving the pump clinging to my inflated pussy lips and standing up. 'Puffy, swollen, hairless . . . I'll need to pump you every day for a lasting effect. You'll have a beautiful front bottom before long.'

'What about her nipples?' Neil asked her. 'We could puff them up nicely.'

'Don't worry, I won't forget her nipples,' the slut said.

Hearing a branch snapping off a bush, I knew what Neil intended to do as he moved behind my tethered body. Brushing the rounded cheeks of my bottom with the rough leaves, he let out a wicked chuckle. The vacuum pump sucking hard on my outer lips, I squeezed my eyes shut and clung to the oak tree in readiness for the gruelling thrashing. Neil was a bastard, I thought for the umpteenth time. He was also my master.

The branch swished through the air, landing across my tensed buttocks with a loud crack. I let out a yelp which sent the birds fluttering from the trees. Again, the branch flailed my stinging buttocks, the rough leaves biting into my bared flesh as Neil chuckled again. The slut announced that she was going to take some photographs as the cracking of the branch across my bottom orbs resounded throughout the woods. More evidence of my debauched ways; more ammunition.

Imagining my mother staring at the photograph as the slut clicked the camera shutter and caught the branch landing squarely across the globes of my bottom, I shuddered. She'd be absolutely horrified, I knew. Neil and his slut had so much evidence against me now that I'd be for ever at their beck and call, for ever their sex slave. Although I loved bondage and whipping, my anxiety wouldn't allow me to enjoy the pleasure. My poor mother, I reflected. If she laid eyes on the photographs . . .

'Grease her arse,' Neil ordered his accomplice. 'Give her a good helping of butter and I'll do her tight little arse.'

'My pleasure,' the girl replied, taking a tub of butter from the bag. 'I'll pump her up a little more,' she breathed, squeezing the rubber bulb.

My swollen lips were sucked into the plastic container. I closed my eyes as she smeared butter between the stinging cheeks of my bottom. Massaging the butter into my anal ring, she said that she was looking forward to drinking a blend of fresh spunk and butter from my bum. She was a dirty little slag, I thought, as she stepped aside. As Neil pressed his knob hard against my well-greased anus, I tightened my grip on the tree. I was nothing but a lump of female meat, I thought, as his cock head slipped into my anus. Nothing but a lump of meat with three holes.

His solid cock drove deeper into my rectum, his swollen knob coming to rest deep in my bowels. I gasped as he found his rhythm and arse fucked me in his crudity, my breasts stinging against the rough tree bark. I could feel his huge knob journeying along my rectal tube, stretching me wide open and repeatedly entering my bowels. My face was pressed against the trunk of the oak tree, and I knew that my naked body would bear scratches as evidence of my adultery, my debauchery.

I'd tell Rod everything, I decided, as the slut took photographs of the anal coupling. I'd tell him about my secret life, the way his brother had blackmailed me, treated me worse than an animal . . . There'd be no arguments, no blazing rows, because I'd leave the marital home and buy a house somewhere far away. All I needed to take with me was my school uniform – and my young body.

My plan sounded good. But what about my mother? Would Neil really send her copies of the photographs? Would he stoop so low as to destroy my mother's life? More than likely, I thought, as he repeatedly rammed his ballooning glans into the fiery depths of my arse. There again, if I told Rod of his brother's intentions, he might be able to stop him.

Rod wouldn't want to see my mother upset any more than I did. That was the answer, I concluded, as Neil let out a gasp. His spunk creamed my rectal tube, lubricating his pistoning cock, and he grabbed my hips and fucked me harder than ever.

The slut giggled as she took several photographs of the anal spunking. Where did she live? I mused. Where had she come from? If I could get hold of her address . . . But what would be the point? I had to concentrate on my own life, I decided, as the slut pumped the rubber bulb, the vacuum sucking hard on my inflamed clitoris. I had to talk to Rod, tell him everything, and then move far away. I'd talk to Rod that evening.

As Neil withdrew his cock from my rectum, the slut kneeled behind me and yanked my buttocks wide apart. Locking her full lips to the greased ring of my anus, she sucked hard and drew out Neil's spunk. She was a vile whore, I thought, my mind brimming with thoughts of talking to Rod. I'd thought myself to be a dirty little slag, but she was a sewer rat in comparison. Her tongue entered my burning arsehole and she licked deep inside me and again sucked out the bubbling spunk.

I'd have loved to get my own back on the slut; tie her to the tree and whip her buttocks with the branch until she screamed for mercy. But, again, I realised that there was no point in seeking vengeance. Besides, she'd probably enjoy a damned good thrashing. My plan to move away was best, I thought, as she drank from my anal canal. A new town, a new house, a new start. And a new hunting ground. No one would know me. I could walk the local park dressed as a schoolgirl, check out the pubs and bars for new sexual conquests . . . That was the answer.

'Are you going to fill her up again?' the slut asked Neil as she sucked my arse dry.

'Not now,' he breathed. 'I think we'd better get out of here.'

'So soon?' she complained. 'But, I thought ...'

'I have things to do, Jackie. Important things.'

'Oh, right.'

Removing the vacuum pump and releasing the ropes, Neil waited for the slut to pack her bag before leaving me naked in the clearing. Without a word, he'd simply walked off and left me with weals fanning out across my buttocks, my rectal tube inflamed ...

I wondered where John, the old man, had gone. He obviously didn't want to be seen in the woods with a schoolgirl with her navy-blue knickers pulled down to her knees. We'd not meet again, I mused, as I left the clearing. I'd not visit the park again, or the woods.

I was horrified to see Rod's car in the drive when I reached the house. What the hell was he doing home, yet again? I wondered anxiously. Was Neil with him? I couldn't understand why Rod had been taking so much time out of the office recently. It was so unlike him to leave his desk for five minutes, let alone go home at odd times throughout the day. Trying not to read things into the situation, I turned and headed back down the street.

How long would he be there? Had he decided to take the rest of the day off? Returning to the park, I sat on a bench and stared at the ground. Perhaps now was the time to confess? I deliberated. But not dressed as a schoolgirl. I'd have to wait until he went back to work, *if* he went back to work. I wondered whether it *had* been him in the park earlier. My buttocks stung like hell and my breasts were sore from the tree bark. I desperately needed to have a shower and change. All I could do was wait, I decided. Perhaps an old man would come my way. Perhaps an old man who loved schoolgirls would help me to pass the time.

Eleven

Rod didn't come home until seven o'clock. His excuse was that he'd had to go and see a client. Recalling Sue's words, my suspicion heightened, and I decided not to believe Rod. What was he up to? Why hadn't he phoned to say that he'd be late? He kept asking me searching questions about my day. Where had I been, who was I with. The time had come to tell him the truth. The time had come to put an end to my nightmare.

'I want you to listen to me,' I said authoritatively as he sat on the sofa. 'I have something important to tell you.'

'Oh? Is everything all right, love?' he asked, looking up at me as I stood before him.

'No, it's not.'

'Look, I'm sorry that I had to work late. I would have phoned but –'

'Rod, it has nothing to do with your being late.'

'I'll get that,' he said, leaping to his feet as the doorbell rang.

This was hopeless, I mused, pacing the lounge floor. I'd built up the courage to tell him the truth, rehearsed my lines . . . Nothing was going to stop me, I decided. Once he came back and sat down, I'd tell him about my lovers, my dirty sex life, my five years of adultery – and his brother's blackmailing. I had enough money in the bank to buy myself a modest house, and I was all set to leave. Nothing was going to stop me now.

'Oh, Alan,' I breathed surprisedly as he walked into the lounge with Rod. 'Er . . . how are you?'

'Fine, thanks,' he replied, winking at me. 'I've just called in to give Rod some papers.'

'Coffee, Alan?' Rod asked.

'Thanks.'

'Papers?' I whispered as Rod went into the kitchen.

'Actually, I've come to see you. I'm sorry that I couldn't make it this afternoon.'

'See me? What about?'

'We need to talk. Any chance of getting rid of Rod for a while? Or could you go out and I'll meet you somewhere?'

'What, now?'

'It's important, Cindy.'

'I can't really go out. I suppose I could ask Rod to go and get some vodka.'

'Yes, do that.'

Alan seemed nervy as I went into the kitchen to speak to Rod. Hovering in the lounge doorway, he was obviously desperate to talk to me about something. Changing my mind, I knew that I couldn't ask Rod to go out. He'd think it highly suspicious if I asked him to go and buy some vodka the minute Alan had called to see him. Watching him pour the coffee, I didn't know what to say.

'You all right, love?' he asked me.

'Yes, I . . . I think we're low on vodka. I wouldn't mind having a few drinks this evening, but . . .'

'Shall I nip out and buy a bottle?'

'Would you mind?'

'Of course not. I'll just take Alan his coffee, and then I'll go.'

Rod was a pushover. Thanking Alan for the papers, he made his excuses, grabbed his jacket and left the house like an obedient dog. Waiting until I heard the front door close, I moved to the window and watched him walking down the drive to his car. He'd only be twenty minutes at the most, but that would give me time enough to talk to Alan. Time enough to suck Alan's beautiful knob and drink his fresh spunk?

'Well?' I said, joining Alan in the lounge. 'What is it?'

'Rod went out today,' he whispered, sipping his coffee.

'Alan, you don't have to whisper,' I sighed. 'He's gone.'

'Sorry. I rang you to say that he'd left the office, but there was no reply.'

'I had to go out for a while. Did Rod say where he was going?'

'No, he didn't. When he came back, he spoke to Neil on the phone. I was in the side office, but I could hear what he was saying.'

'And?'

'He mentioned you, and he said something about the park. Does that mean anything to you?'

'God,' I gasped, flopping on to the sofa. 'Er . . . yes, it means everything to me. What else did he say?'

'He obviously didn't realise that I was there because he didn't keep his voice down.'

'What else did he say, Alan?' I snapped.

'That's about it, really.'

'That's it? He must have said something else?'

'He said that he'd go out at eight o'clock this evening.'

'Go out?'

'Yes.'

'It's seven-thirty, and he's said nothing to me about going out.'

'I reckon that he's planning something with Neil. Do you think Neil has dropped you in it?'

'I wish you'd told me about this earlier.'

'I rang several times but you weren't here. Oh, there's one more thing.'

'Yes?'

'He mentioned the shed.'

'What about it?'

'I don't know. He just said something about the shed.'

'I'm beginning to put two and two together,' I sighed. 'He went out to the shed when he came home earlier.'

'So, what does it all mean?'

'It's nothing for you to worry about, Alan. Look, I think you'd better go.'

'Go? But . . .'

'Just go, Alan. I'll speak to you tomorrow.'

'All right. Will be you OK?'

'Oh, yes. I'll be just fine.'

After seeing Alan out, I walked down the garden and opened the shed door. What the hell I was looking for, I had no idea. But this was the second time that Rod had mentioned the shed to Neil, and I was determined to discover his secret. Why had he gone out to the shed the minute he'd got home? Unable to find anything untoward, I headed back to the house. I didn't like mysteries. Had James said something about the shed? No, of course he hadn't. What was it about the bloody shed?

The phone was ringing as I walked into the kitchen. Dashing into the lounge and grabbing the receiver, I knew who the caller was before I answered.

'Sorry, love,' Rod whined. 'I've just had a call on my mobile from a client. I'm going to have to see him.'

'What, now?'

'I'm afraid so. Is Alan still there?'

'No, he left.'

'I'll only be a couple of hours. I really am sorry about this.'

'That's all right,' I said cheerily. 'There's something I want to watch on television, so don't worry.'

'OK. I'll bring some vodka home.'

'All right, I'll see you later.'

Replacing the phone, I couldn't work out what was going on. I poured myself a large vodka and tonic, knocked it back and refilled my glass. The alcohol kicked in. I took a deep breath and wondered what to do, how to play the game. Was this a game? Were things fitting into place? Or was I just too paranoid? I knew that the pieces of the puzzle were coming together, but I couldn't see the picture.

Climbing the stairs to my bedroom, I changed into my red miniskirt and skimpy white blouse. My pussy lips were still swollen from the vacuum pump, and I wondered whether they'd ever return to normal. Lifting my skirt and eyeing my vulva in the mirror, I was amazed by the sheer size of my hairless labia. My front bottom, I mused, stroking the soft hillocks of flesh rising either side of my sex slit. Resisting the temptation to masturbate, massage my clitoris to a massive orgasm, I finally lowered my skirt.

Something was about to happen, I knew, as I slipped into a very tight pair of white cotton panties. But what? Instinct was telling me something. Would Neil come round? Rod had planned to go out at eight o'clock. Why? Finally returning to the lounge to finish my drink, I once more paced the floor. When the doorbell rang, I grinned. Things were obviously going to plan, I mused, opening the front door. Whatever the plan was.

'John?' I gasped, staring at the old man I'd met in the park. He was the last person I'd expected to find standing on the doorstep. 'What are you doing here?'

'Are your parents in?' he asked me. 'There's no car in the drive, so I thought . . .'

'How did you find out where I lived?'

'I followed you, Belinda. I went back to the park some time later; and I saw you sitting on the bench. I followed you here. I know it was wrong, but . . .'

'You'll have to go,' I said firmly. 'My . . . my father will be home soon.'

'I just wanted to talk to you. After meeting you today, I . . . I was desperate to see you again. I only want to talk to you for a minute or two.'

'Come in,' I said, looking over his shoulder at the street.

Taking him into the lounge, I thanked God that Rod was out. If John had come knocking on the door and Rod had answered . . . This was worse than a nightmare. I had to get rid of him, and quickly. As he looked around the lounge, I thought that he'd realise that I wasn't a schoolgirl. Fortunately, there were no photographs of me, no pictures of a happy wedding day. But I hardly looked like a young girl dressed in my miniskirt and skimpy blouse.

'You'll have to be quick,' I said. 'What do you want?'

'Belinda . . . I have to see you again. You're so beautiful, so angelic.'

'All right, I'll see you again in the park.'

'When?'

'Tomorrow after . . . after school.'

'That's great. You will be there, won't you?'

'Yes, I'll be there. Now, you must go.'

'May I hold you? Just for a minute.'

'All right,' I conceded.

As he took me in his arms, I felt my clitoris swell, my juices wetting my tight panties. His hand moved down my back and clutched my bottom. I knew how desperate he was to strip me naked and ogle my young body. He'd already kissed and tasted my hairless pussy crack and ... Rod would be out for some time, I mused in my soaring arousal, wondering whether to allow the old man the pleasure of licking my girl crack again. But the plan ... I had to think about the plan. What plan?

'You must go now,' I breathed softly as he slipped his hand beneath my skirt and fondled the firm cheeks of my rounded buttocks. 'John,' I gasped as his fingers moved beneath the tight material, delving into my bottom crack. 'John ...'

'Please ...' he murmured. 'Just let me feel you.'

'My dad will be back soon.'

'How soon?'

'I don't know. Maybe half an hour.'

'Is there somewhere we could go? How about the park?'

'No, I can't go out. Look, come out into the garden. If my dad comes back, you can escape around the side of the house.'

In the garden, I led him across the lawn to the bushes by the shed. This wasn't a good idea, I thought, gazing at the shed. Was I right about Rod? I wondered as John kneeled on the ground before me. Was he up to something with Neil? Concealed by the bushes, John and I couldn't be seen from the house. But what about the shed? There was a small window in the side of the shed ... I was confusing myself. I'd thought that I'd worked out what was going on, but now?

As John lifted my miniskirt and pulled my panties down to my knees, I felt a quiver run through my womb. His wet tongue running up and down the length of my juiced-up girl crack, I knew that I was putty in his hands. But I had to try to think clearly. Rod had said something to Neil about me and the park. Had he been there? I'd thought that I'd seen him, but couldn't be sure. Had Neil carried out his threat and told Rod about my dirty secret?

Closing my eyes as John peeled open my hairless pussy lips and pushed his tongue into my sex-drenched love hole, I gazed at the shed window through my eyelashes. The shed, I mused, wondering what the hell Rod's interest was in the rickety shack. This had nothing to do with digging up the bushes; I knew that much, as John licked and slurped fervently between my slender thighs.

'You're beautiful,' John said, his pussy-wet mouth smiling as he looked up at me. 'What have you done to your pussy? Your lips are puffy, beautifully puffy and . . .'

'You shouldn't have come here,' I sighed.

'I had to see you, Belinda. I had to . . .'

'Yes, I know. The thing is . . . if my dad catches us, there'll be big trouble.'

'He won't, I promise you. Should he come back, I can hide here, in the bushes, and then slip away later. I just can't get over your beauty, Belinda.'

His mouth pressed hard against my vulval lips and he again pushed his tongue deep into my sex hole. I wasn't in the mood for sex. My mind was swirling with thoughts of Rod and Neil, wondering what they were up to. I couldn't concentrate on my dirty game with the old man. At least I'd allow him the pleasure of realising his schoolgirl dream, I thought, as he clutched my naked buttocks and pushed his tongue deeper into my pussy.

Hearing a dull thud come from inside the shed, I froze. John had obviously heard nothing. Slurping at my juicy cunt, he was oblivious to his surroundings. Someone was in the shed, I was sure, as I closed my eyes and gazed through my lashes at the small window. It was probably James, I mused. He must have slipped into the garden just before ... Unless it was Rod. Was that what he'd meant about the shed? Had he planned to hide and ... Is that why Neil had taken me down the garden in the pouring rain? So that Rod could watch and enjoy the animalistic abuse of his wife?

I was sure that I was wrong as John eased two fingers deep into my contracting pussy. Although things were beginning to fall into place, I couldn't imagine Rod as a voyeur. We were happy together, the perfect couple. The idea of Rod watching his brother fuck and whip me, the slut licking my pussy, was ludicrous. I might have been wrong about Neil, obviously not knowing him at all, but ... I knew Rod of old. He was virtually asexual. His life consisted of his work; revolved around his office.

But things were falling into place rather too well. Rod had said that he was in Birmingham, and then turned up with Neil. Perhaps the plan had been that Neil would fuck me over the patio table while Rod watched from the house. Unbeknown to me, my hiding in the bushes had ruined their plan. No, I just couldn't believe it. I was wrong, I had to be. As John sucked out my pussy milk, drinking from my young body, I wondered whether to take a look in the shed. If Rod was in there ... I didn't want to know.

'Lick my bottom,' I instructed John, turning and touching my toes. 'I've heard my friends at school talking about bottom licking, and I want to see what it's like.'

'Yes, yes, of course,' he breathed, obviously stunned as I pulled my skirt up over my back.

Parting the firm cheeks of my naked bottom, exposing my anus, he lapped fervently at my private hole. The idea that Rod might be watching me sent my libido rocketing. I was positive that I was wrong, but the notion excited me. I'd heard about husbands watching their wives get fucked, deriving immense pleasure from watching the adulterous acts. If Rod was like that, if he . . . I was fantasising, I knew. The thud in the shed had probably been something falling over, or the wood contracting as the sun went down.

Hearing John's zip, I knew that he was going to fuck me. He had his fantasies, and I had mine. To fuck a little virgin schoolgirl's cunt was obviously his dream. What was my dream? I mused as his bulbous knob ran up and down the drenched groove of my hairless vulva. To play my schoolgirl games in the park? To lure men to my house and commit crude sexual acts with them? Or to buy my own house and play my games in the comfort and privacy of my own home?

'Belinda,' John murmured, his glans between the engorged petals of my inner labia. 'Belinda, I'm going to –'

'I know,' I cut in. 'I want you to do it.'

'Are you sure?'

'Yes, do it. I want to be like my friends. I don't want to be a virgin any more.'

Breathing heavily, John let out a gasp as he pushed his cock deep into the hugging sheath of my school-girl cunt. Whether or not he knew that I was deceiving him didn't matter. As long as he was enjoying his fantasy, nothing mattered. He was big, his beautiful cock stretching me to capacity as he grabbed my hips and forced his knob hard against the creamy-wet ring of my cervix. He withdrew slowly, then again pushed the entire length of his solid cock deep into my quivering body. He was in his sexual heaven, I mused, and he found his fucking rhythm.

My long blonde hair cascaded over the grass as my body rocked back and forth with the illicit fucking. I listened to the familiar squelching sounds of my pussy juices as his cock repeatedly withdrew and entered me. How many men had fucked me in the garden? I pondered. How many times had I dropped my panties or stripped naked and been fucked senseless? Was this the end of the road? Was John to be the last in a long line of men to screw me rotten?

This was my life, I mused, again thinking about Rod and his evil brother. I'd reached the stage where I wanted to take control of my life, my destiny. Although I'd been free to screw around throughout my five-year marriage, I'd not enjoyed complete freedom. My own house, I mused dreamily, as John drew closer to his orgasm, his pussy spunking. No Rod or Neil, no Alan ... Richard and Ian had obviously been frightened off. Neil was the likely culprit, I reflected. Wanting to keep me for himself, for his bisexual slut, he'd not want other men around. What had he said to my lovers? Had he threatened them?

'Do my bottom,' I said as John began to gasp. 'The other girls ...'

'All right,' he breathed, slipping his rock-hard cock out of my burning cunt. 'Are you really sure that you want this?'

'Yes, yes. You're teaching me, remember?'

His bulbous plum pressing hard against my tightly closed anal iris; he let out a rush of breath as his glans slipped into my rectal sheath. I was tight and hot, desperate for the feel of his solid cock stretching me wide open. I shuddered and whimpered in the grip of my debauchery. My anal ring finally stretched tautly around the root of his cock, and I slipped my hand

217

between my thighs and massaged the solid nub of my sensitive clitoris.

John came quickly, his spunk jetting deep into my rectum as I massaged my clitoris to a massive orgasm. Wailing in my coming, my trembling body rocking back and forth with the crude anal fucking, I knew that I could never give up my life of adulterous sex. Again and again, John rammed his solid cock deep into my arse as I rode the crest of my incredible climax. With John's spunk spewing from my bloated anal hole and running down my thighs in rivers of milk, I hoped that Rod *was* watching. The time had come for him to discover the truth. The time had come to end the farcical marriage.

'God, Belinda,' John cried, making his last penile thrust deep into the very core of my quivering body. 'You're an amazing young girl.'

'Don't stop,' I ordered him, my pleasure peaking as I sustained my orgasm with my vibrating fingertips.

After repeatedly driving his cock into my burning arsehole until he began to deflate, he finally stilled his penis with his knob absorbing the inner heat of my spunk-bubbling bowels. Massaging the last ripples of sex from my inflamed clitoris, I fell forwards, his cock leaving my arse as I crumpled on the ground in a quivering heap. Panting for breath, my eyes rolling in the aftermath of my amazing climax, I rolled over and lay on my back as he zipped his trousers.

'Belinda, I . . .' he began. 'Are you all right?'

'I've never been better,' I gasped. 'That was incredible.'

'I will see you again, won't I?'

'Definitely,' I lied. 'After school tomorrow, I'll meet you in the woods.'

'I'll be there,' he said, his face beaming as he looked down at my hairless, gaping pussy crack.'

'You'd better go now.'

'Yes, yes, I will. I'll see you tomorrow.'

As he scurried across the garden, I clambered to my feet and adjusted my dishevelled clothing. Fucked and spunked by yet another man, I mused happily, staggering back to the house on my trembling legs. Turning as I reached the back door, I gazed at the shed. Slipping into the kitchen, I closed the back door and spied out of the window. I was sure that no one was hiding there, but kept watch for ten minutes or so. Finally, I left the house and walked across the lawn; I opened the shed door. Nothing. It must have been the wood creaking, I decided, returning to the house. My thoughts about my husband had been wrong. Rod was no voyeur. He'd never agree to watch his brother fucking and whipping me.

After a shower, I slipped into my dressing gown and went into the lounge. Pouring another large vodka and tonic, I felt pleased with myself. I'd come to the decision to leave Rod, and wasn't going to change my mind. No matter what happened, I'd buy a house and make it my home. Beginning to plan my new home, picturing the way I wanted the lounge, I pondered on the idea of a sex den. A special room set aside for sex. Handcuffs, whips, chains, vibrators . . . I'd lure men to my house and spend hours fucking them.

'Hello,' I said, grabbing the ringing phone.

'Hi, love,' Rod breathed. 'I'm on my way home.'

'Oh, that's good. Did you get the vodka?'

'Yes, I did. Have you been all right?'

'I've been fine.'

'I seem to be working odd hours of late. What with Birmingham and –'

'It doesn't matter,' I cut in. 'Things are about to change so –'

'Change? What do you mean?'

'I mean things . . . We'll talk about it when you get back.'

'Are you sure you're all right?'

'Yes.'

'What's the problem, Cindy? I can tell that something's on your mind.'

'As I said, we'll talk about it when you get back.'

'I'll only be five minutes. I'll see you soon.'

'OK.'

Dropping the receiver into its cradle, I sighed. This wasn't going to be easy, I knew, as I paced the lounge floor. Making my plans, I decided to confront Rod with Birmingham. He'd come to the house with Neil when he was supposed to be in Birmingham. Why had he lied? I'd follow that by asking him why he'd said that he'd been back to the office the other evening when I knew damned well that he hadn't. Alan had been there, and not seen Rod. My husband had lied to me. Why?

'All right?' he called, closing the front door and joining me in the lounge.

'Pour me a vodka and tonic, please,' I ordered him.

'Of course. Cindy, what's the problem?'

'We need to talk,' I said, watching him pour my drink.

'What about?'

'Birmingham, for one thing.'

'Birmingham? Look, I know that you don't like my staying away overnight. But it couldn't be helped. We're getting pretty busy at work. So busy that I've asked Neil to join the company.'

'Neil?'

'He's not happy where he is. He's a good man, and we need him to take on some of the clients to share out the workload.'

'Oh, I see. The other day, when you supposedly went to Birmingham . . .'

'Supposedly?'

'Why did you bring Neil here?'

'How do you know that?'

'It doesn't matter how I know. Why did you lie to me about it?'

'I didn't lie to you. Yes, I did bring Neil here. I also brought him here the other day. And I didn't tell you because he doesn't want Sue to know that he might be leaving his job.'

'But you were supposed to be in Birmingham.'

'I called in to see you. I was going to take Neil with me but it was difficult. He had things to do at work so . . . May I ask you a question?'

'Yes, of course.'

'I've called in a couple of times over the past few days, and you've not been here. Where have you been?'

'Shopping, walking . . . I don't stay here all day every day, Rod. What's all this about the shed?'

'The shed? Cindy, what are you driving at?'

'You've been talking to Neil about the shed.'

'Oh, that. He wants to store something in the shed. A few bits and pieces from his garage so that he can get his car in there.'

'Oh, well . . . What about the park? You said something to Neil about me and the park.'

'How the hell do you know about that?'

'It doesn't matter how I know. What were you talking about?'

'He said that he thought he'd seen you walking across the park. He mentioned it in passing, that was all. Cindy, what's this all about?'

'You've not been to the park then?'

'*Me*? God, with the pressure on at the office, how the hell would I get the time to go walking in the park?'

'Are you going to pass me my drink, or stand there holding it?'

'Oh, er ... sorry. Cindy, tell me what this is all about. The shed, the park, Birmingham ...'

'Things seem odd,' I said, knocking back my drink. 'I'll have another one, please.'

'Right. What things seem odd?'

'You know about the photographs, don't you?'

'Photographs? Now you really have lost me. Look, I've been under pressure at the office lately. I know that I've been vague, and I've had to work late now and then ...'

'The other night, you said that you'd been back to the office. Do you remember that?'

'Yes.'

'I rang the office and Alan answered. He said that you'd not been there, Rod. He'd spent half the evening at his desk, and you didn't go there. You told me that you'd heard the phone ring and you didn't answer it because you thought that it might be a client. You lied to me.'

'Yes, I did lie to you. And I'll tell you why. Neil's been acting strangely recently. I don't know whether it's his job or Sue, but he's been feeling down about something. I told you that I was going back to the office because I didn't want you to know that I was seeing him. As it happens, I didn't see him. He'd said that he'd be in the pub near to his place, but he wasn't there. When I got back, I was going to tell you about it but you'd fallen down the stairs and I was worried about you. I know that you wouldn't go running to Sue, but Neil doesn't want her to know about him working with me until it's all sorted out. You know what she's like. Worry, worry, worry.'

'Yes, I do know. Rod, I'm sorry. I suppose I've been concerned because ... You lied to me, and you've never done that before.'

'We've never lied to each other, Cindy. And that's the way it's going to stay. OK?'

'OK.'

Feeling as guilty as hell, I couldn't tell Rod that I was leaving him. How wrong I'd been, I reflected. In my mind, I'd accused him of being a voyeur, lying, cheating, shagging Neil's slut ... When, all along, he'd been working hard at the office. Although I didn't relish the idea of Neil working with Rod, there was nothing I could do about it. But why the big secret? Why not tell Sue about the job? She wasn't that much of a worrier.

Sue had fired my suspicion, I reflected. Going on about Birmingham and Rod taking Neil to the house ... There again, her suspicions about her husband weren't unfounded. The bastard was screwing the slut. At least I now knew that Rod didn't suspect me. He wasn't sneaking home to spy on me; he knew nothing about the photographs or my dirty secret ... And that was the way it was going to stay.

'Don't mention this to Sue,' Rod said. 'Neil will tell her that he's changing jobs if and when it happens.'

'OK,' I breathed, still feeling incredibly guilty. 'Rod, have you had suspicions about me?'

'Suspicions? No, why?'

'Alan said something about your being worried about me.'

'All I said to Alan was that I was concerned about leaving you alone so much. What with working late, going to Birmingham ... I've been worried about you, Cindy. Worried, not suspicious.'

'There's no need to worry about me. I like being here alone during the day. Don't worry, Rod.'

'I'll try not to. Right, I think I'll have a shower.'

As he left the room, I finished my drink and wandered out into the garden. The sun was sinking below the trees; it was a lovely evening. Holding my dressing gown together, I walked to the bushes by the shed and grinned. The old man had enjoyed his time with the daughter of the house, I reflected. He'd enjoyed fucking a schoolgirl's bottom hole. Deciding that I would meet him in the woods the following afternoon, I felt a lot easier about Rod. Apart from Neil and his bloody blackmailing, I had nothing to worry about. Believing Rod to be a voyeur, I'd obviously allowed my mind to run wild.

'Hi,' James said, emerging from the bushes and joining me.

'Oh, James,' I breathed. 'You made me jump.'

'Sorry.'

'My husband's in,' I said, glancing at the house.

'I only came to tell you about that man who was here the other day.'

'Which man?'

'The one with the dark-haired girl. I saw them the other day, do you remember?'

'Yes, I do. That was Neil.'

'I was in the bushes this morning, looking out for you, and I saw him go into your shed.'

'I was out this morning,' I murmured pensively. 'Did you see what he was up to?'

'He had a large brown envelope when he arrived, and he didn't have it when he left.'

'Was my husband with him.'

'No, he was alone.'

'I see,' I breathed, grinning at him. 'James, you're an angel.'

'I just thought that you should know. Seeing as he was here with that girl the other day and . . .'

'All right, I'll take a look in the shed.'

'I'd better get back before your husband comes out.'

'Yes, you do that. Don't go too far away though. I might be out here a little later.'

'Oh, er . . . I'll hang around in the bushes then.'

After waiting until he'd gone, I slipped into the shed and looked about. A large brown envelope? Neil would have to be pretty stupid to hide the photographs in the shed, I mused. There again, Rod had said that Neil had wanted to keep a few bits and pieces in our shed. But not the photographs, surely? Rummaging about beneath the bench, I found what I was looking for. Peering inside the envelope, I pulled out the photographs.

'God,' I breathed, gazing at a picture of James and his young friend fingering my sex holes on the lawn. I was delighted to have found the evidence of my debauched ways. But why would Neil keep the photographs in our shed? Gazing at a picture of Neil whipping my naked buttocks in the hall, I froze. Who the hell had taken the photograph? From the angle, I knew that the shot had been taken from the kitchen, but . . . Neil and I had been alone in the house, or so I'd thought. Had the slut sneaked in through the back door?

Stuffing the photographs back into the envelope, I didn't know what to think. If the slut had been with Neil, then why would she hide? Surely she'd have joined in with the debauchery? Having slipped the envelope back beneath the bench, I grabbed the padlock and key from the hook on the wall and left the shed. We never bothered to lock the door as there was nothing of value in the shed. But now? Padlocking the door, I slipped the key into my dressing-gown pocket and hovered by the bushes.

I should have been over the moon about finding the photographs. But I was more confused than ever. Were there copies? Why would Neil hide photographs in the shed if he had copies at his house? Reckoning that they were the originals, I was sure that my nightmare had come to an end. I should have destroyed the evidence, but I was intrigued. Would Rod ask me why the shed was locked? My thinking was going crazy again. He knew nothing about the photographs. Rod, in his innocence, knew nothing about anything other than his work.

Looking up at the house and noticing that the bathroom light was on, I knew that Rod was still in the shower. I had time to give young James a quick blowjob, I decided, moving to the bushes dividing our gardens. Peering out of the foliage, he grinned at me as I opened my dressing gown and exposed the hairless crack of my pussy. Raising his eyes and focusing on the ripe teats of my breasts, he asked me what I wanted him to do.

'Lick my cunt,' I ordered him. 'Stay in the bushes and kneel down. If my husband comes out, he won't see you.'

'You've shaved,' he whispered, kneeling with his head emerging from the foliage. 'God, you're amazing.'

'Do you like my hairless pussy?'

'Yes, yes I do. You look like a –'

'Lick me,' I breathed, holding my gown open. 'Lick my schoolgirl cunt and make me come.'

Closing my eyes as he ran his wet tongue up and down the groove of my pussy, I felt a quiver run through my pelvis. This was sexual bliss, I mused dreamily. The thought that my husband was in the house while a teenage lad licked out my cunt in the garden sent thrills throughout my trembling body. The sheer decadence of the adulterous act sent my libido rocketing to frightening heights. Gasping, swaying on my sagging legs, I knew that I was about to come.

'Suck out my cunt milk,' I ordered my young pupil, my crude words further heightening my arousal. 'Push your tongue deep into my hot cunt and lap up my juices.'

'Mmm,' James moaned through his nose as he complied.

'That's it. Lick deep inside my tight cunt.'

James was good, I thought in my sexual haze. Moving up to the solid nub of my expectant clitoris, he licked and sucked, taking me closer to my orgasm. His fingers entered the tight sheath of my adulterous pussy. He massaged deep inside, inducing my sex milk to flow in torrents. Moving closer to the bushes, I reached up and held a branch as if I was looking at it. Should Rod happen to look out of the window, he'd only see me examining the bush. He'd have no idea that young James was fingering my hot cunt and sucking pleasure out of my clit.

'Don't stop,' I breathed huskily, teetering on the verge of my climax. 'I'm going to come, James. I'm going to ... God, yes.' I gasped as the explosion of pleasure erupted within my pulsating clitoris. 'Finger fuck my cunt. Harder, harder ...' Swaying on my trembling legs, I half-hoped that Rod was looking out of the window. The thought of my husband watching as I rode the crest of a massive climax turned me on no end. He'd have no idea that I was in the grip of a tongue-induced orgasm.

Slipping his free hand behind me, his fingers delving into the deep gully of my buttocks, he teased the sensitive eye of my anus. Trying to not let out a cry of pleasure as his finger entered me, driving deep into the spasming sheath of my rectum, I thought that I was going to pass out as he double finger fucked my sex holes and sucked hard on my orgasming clitoris. He *was* good, bloody good. And he was getting better.

Parting my feet wider, I whimpered and trembled as my sex sheaths tightened around his thrusting fingers and my clitoris pulsated wildly within his hot mouth. For one so young and inexperienced, James was doing far better than many men I'd known. He was my star pupil, that was for sure. And I had so much more to teach him. Wondering when his friend, Simon, would next call round to see him, I decided to take both young men in hand. They'd enjoy becoming my sex slaves, I mused as my orgasm finally began to recede. I'd initiate them in the fine art of bondage, naked buttock spanking . . .

'Are you all right, Cindy?' Rod called from the back door.

'Oh, er . . .' I gasped as James withdrew his fingers and crouched in the bush. 'I was just . . . just looking at the bushes. I think they need trimming.'

'You face is flushed, love,' he whined as he approached.

Moving away from the bushes, I smiled at him. 'It's so hot,' I complained. 'I think I'll go up to bed.'

'You're trembling, Cindy.'

'Yes, I . . . I feel a little dizzy. It's all right; it's only the heat. I'll go and lie down and I'll be fine.'

Rod followed me into the house and offered me a cup of tea as I climbed the stairs. It was a shame that I'd had to leave James to wank, I reflected. His cock must have been solid, his full balls heaving and rolling. But there was always tomorrow. Accepting Rod's offer of tea, I slipped beneath the quilt and hoped that he wouldn't want sex. My buttocks still lined from the thrashing Neil had given me, my pussy lips devoid of hair, my juices of lust streaming from my gaping pussy . . . No, he wouldn't want sex. He never did.

Twelve

Rod had enjoyed a good breakfast and had gone to work. Everything was normal – quiet. The photographs were under lock and key in the shed; the sun was shining; my suspicions about Rod had left me . . . I felt good, happy. I'd arranged to meet John in the woods that afternoon, so I had something to look forward to. But I knew that Neil would rear his ugly head before long. Neil was like a dark cloud looming in the sky, threatening to bring me a storm.

Clearing the breakfast things, trying to forget about Neil, I wondered whether James would be kicking around in his garden. He might enjoy a quick blowjob, I mused, imagining his youthful cock pumping fresh spunk into my thirsty mouth. The gap in the bushes dividing our gardens was very useful. Recalling James hiding in the bushes, licking my pussy slit as Rod had stepped out on to the patio, I felt a tremble run through my womb. Rod had been totally oblivious to my crude act, I thought happily. The danger, the excitement . . . The bushes were very useful indeed.

Deciding to wear my very short skirt and skimpy blouse with no bra or panties, I thought that I might spend some time in the garden. I enjoyed wandering around without panties. The immense feeling of freedom with my naked pussy veiled only by my skirt was a terrific turn-on. Wafts of fresh air cooling my hairless sex lips, my love hole ever ready for a solid cock . . . I loved walking around with no panties.

I was about to go up to my bedroom to change when the front doorbell rang. Hoping that it wasn't Neil, I walked through the hall and hesitated.

'Oh,' I sighed, finally opening the door to find Neil standing on the step. 'I thought you had a key. You normally come barging into my house uninvited.'

'I left it at home,' he said, walking past me into the hall. 'I hear that you've been talking to Rod about Jackie?'

'Hardly,' I breathed.

'You said that you'd met her, that she was working for me and –'

'Oh, yes, so I did. What about it?'

'I don't want anyone to know about her, Cindy. I would have thought that obvious.'

'Then why bring her here? If you want to keep your slut secret, then why –'

'I'll ask the questions,' he cut in. 'I don't like the way things are going. I don't like you talking to Rod and –'

'He *is* my husband,' I cut in.

'From now on, you'll not go to the park to meet other men. You'll not have other men visiting you here or –'

'I'll do what the hell I like,' I returned angrily.

'No, Cindy, you won't. You see, I have so much on you now that –'

'You could ruin my marriage and destroy my mother? Why don't you go ahead and ruin everything? You're always threatening to destroy all I have, so why not go ahead and do it?'

'Is that what you want?'

'Yes, yes, it is. You see, I don't need Rod. I don't need anyone.'

'Rod needs you, Cindy.'

'Then, why threaten to split us up? You'd be destroying your brother's life, Neil – not mine.'

'OK, so you don't need Rod. What about your mother? She needs you, Cindy. If she discovers the truth about her sweet little daughter . . . There's no need for me to go through that again.'

He was right, I knew. That was the only real hold he had on me. Following him out into the garden, I wondered what his ultimate goal was. Was it simply to have sex with me, as and when he felt like it? He had Jackie, the slut, so why bother with me? I was his sister-in-law, I thought. That's what fired his libido. The thought of fucking his brother's wife; using and abusing his sister-in-law . . . I sat on a patio chair as he wandered across the lawn to the shed. I felt that this was a turning point. Neil had taken things this far, but where to now?

'I hear that you might be working with Rod,' I said as he ambled across the lawn towards me. 'That'll be interesting.'

'Working with Rod?' he echoed, frowning at me. 'What are you talking about?'

'That's what Rod said.'

'Oh, er . . . yes, yes, that's right.'

'Surely you hadn't forgotten?'

'No, of course not. How about a cup of coffee before we start?'

'Before we start what?'

'Sex, Cindy. Rampant sex.'

Leaving my chair and walking into the kitchen, I felt that something was wrong as I filled the kettle. Neil couldn't have forgotten that he was planning to work with Rod. His reaction had been most peculiar.

231

Unless he was surprised that I knew about it. Why did he want coffee? I wondered, taking the cup from the cupboard. He'd obviously come round for sex, so why waste time wandering around the garden and drinking coffee? Perhaps he was waiting for the slut to arrive, I thought, imagining the girl sucking a massive orgasm out of my clitoris. Jackie, the filthy little bisexual slut . . .

'Why is the shed locked?' Neil asked me, walking up to the back door.

'I didn't know that it was,' I replied nonchalantly.

'Have you got the key?'

'No, I haven't. Rod must have locked it.'

'He wouldn't have . . . Are you sure the key isn't hanging up somewhere?'

'Positive, Neil. Rod must have locked the shed, and he must have the key.'

He frowned as he walked back down the garden, and I wondered whether he wanted to get hold of the photographs. Why had he hidden them there in the first place? It was a pretty daft place to hide the evidence of my adulterous life. And why did he want them now? Perhaps he had some more to add to his collection. I should have destroyed them, I thought, pouring the coffee. Why hadn't I burned them? Subconsciously, perhaps I liked the thought of being blackmailed into illicit sex.

Watching Neil hovering by the back door, obviously concerned about the padlock, was rather amusing. There was nothing he could do, other than force the padlock. I didn't know what he'd planned, but I'd obviously made things difficult for him. I asked him why he wanted to go into the shed as I placed the coffee cups on the patio table and sat down. He hesitated, looking awkward as he again gazed at the shed.

'Rod said that I could borrow something,' he finally replied.

'Borrow what?'

'Er . . . a spade. I have one or two jobs to do in my garden.'

'Oh, right. When are you going to put your things in our shed?'

'What things?' he breathed, obviously confused.

'I thought that you wanted to get your car into your garage?'

'My car? Cindy, what are you talking about?'

'Sorry, I was confusing you with someone else.'

Sitting opposite me and sipping his coffee, he obviously knew nothing about clearing his garage and storing a few things in the shed. Rod had lied to me. Neil knew nothing about the shed, or changing his job and working with Rod. Unable to work out what the hell was going on, I again felt that we'd reached a turning point. As Neil dashed into the house to answer the front doorbell, I reckoned that his slut had arrived. Should I slip into the bushes and hide? I could always sneak into James's garden. That would upset Neil and his bisexual accomplice.

'Cindy, this is Evans,' Neil said, leading a middle-aged man out of the back door. 'He's a good friend of mine.'

'What the hell . . .' I gasped, leaping to my feet. 'You can't invite –'

'He wants to have a little fun with you.'

'Fun? Fuck off, both of you.'

'She's a little fiery at times,' Neil told his friend. 'She'll calm down once she's naked.'

'Neil, for God's sake.'

'Clothes off, Cindy. All of them.'

'No, I won't.'

'Fuck me about and you'll be very sorry,' he hissed. 'You don't want Rod's company to know what you're like as well as your mother, do you? Rod's wife is a prostitute – is that what you want everyone to know?'

Rod's company? I thought fearfully. Rod was in line for promotion; he was doing so well . . . If head office got to hear about his young wife . . . A prostitute? I wouldn't have put anything past Neil. He was a first-rate bastard, and would think nothing of destroying not only me, but my mother and my husband. I had no choice, I knew, as the middle-aged man looked me up and down. Although I'd played my dirty sex games for five years, I'd never wanted to see Rod hurt. His life was his work, his office. To destroy that would be . . . I had no choice.

Unbuttoning my blouse, I gazed at Neil's so-called friend. He was in his fifties with greying hair swept back from his suntanned face. Not bad looking, I mused. Had I been in my school uniform and met him in the park, I'd have lured him into the woods and allowed him to fuck me senseless. But I wasn't in the park, and I was going to have to allow him to fuck me senseless because I was being blackmailed. After dropping my blouse on to the patio table, I unhooked my bra and exposed my firm breasts to his widening eyes.

'Nice tits,' Evans breathed.

'Nice everything,' Neil quipped. 'Wait until you see her little cunt. I'm sure you'll agree that she's worth the money.'

'Every penny,' Evans said and chortled.

Worth the money? I thought angrily. Every penny? Had Neil taken money from the man? Was he selling me for sex? He'd said that Rod's company would hear that I was a prostitute. Was that his goal? Apart from using and abusing me to satisfy his perverted whims, he was making money from my body. Slip-

234

ping my skirt down, I could hardly believe that this was my brother-in-law. He was a despicable bastard, I'd discovered that much. But to sell me to strangers for sex?

Standing before my audience in my tight panties, I felt a bolt of arousal course though my young body. Sold for sex? The notion excited me, wet the groove of my hairless vulva. I'd not only learned what sort of man Neil was, but I'd also discovered the incredible depths of my debauchery. I was a whore; I'd known that from an early age. But, it seemed, there were no limits to my nymphomaniacal behaviour. Sold for sex? A whore, a prostitute, a filthy little slut . . .

'What did I tell you?' Neil asked his friend as I slipped my panties down and kicked them aside. 'Just feast your eyes on her sweet little cunt.'

'Yes,' Evans breathed as he focused on my sex crack, my swollen pussy lips. 'A beautiful specimen.'

'Bend over the table, slut,' Neil ordered me.

'Neil, please . . .'

'Do it.'

They were talking about me as if I was nothing more than a lump of meat. But that's all I was to my brother-in-law. A lump of female meat to be fucked, whipped, used and abused, sold for crude sex . . . As Neil tied me to the table with several length of rope, binding my wrists behind my back and securing my ankles to the table legs, I reckoned that I was to endure a damned good whipping. How many more men would he bring to the house to abuse me? I wondered, as he blindfolded me with a tea towel.

As Neil announced that he'd grabbed a tub of butter and half a cucumber from the fridge, I knew that I was in for a gruelling session of depraved sex. He yanked my buttocks wide apart and massaged a good helping of butter into my anal ring, then let out a wicked chuckle as his friend whispered something. My head resting on the table, my eyes closed, the sun warming my back, I realised that I was in my element as Neil suggested that his friend give me a good cucumber fucking.

What had my life become? I wondered as the rounded end of the cucumber slipped between the pumped-up lips of my vulva. A tart during my schooldays, I'd fallen deeper and deeper into the mire of sexual deviancy. But I was happy, wasn't I? This was the life I'd chosen. The day I'd married Rod, I knew that my life wouldn't change. Cocks, spunk, fingers, tongues . . . My young body was made to bring men and me immense sexual pleasure. Marriage had changed nothing.

As the solid cucumber slipped into the tight sheath of my very wet pussy, I wondered why Neil had greased my anal portal. Probably to fuck me there, I mused, my lower stomach inflating as the cucumber impaled me completely. As one of my abusers ran his fingertips up and down my inner thighs, all I could do was stare into the darkness of my blindfold. My womb contracted and my juices of arousal warmed the cold shaft of the cucumber. I let out a rush of breath as something pushed hard against the well-greased eye of my anus.

A second cold cucumber straight from the fridge entered the tight duct of my rectum. I imagined Rod stepping out on to the patio and gazing in disbelief at my abused sex holes. Was that what I wanted? I asked myself in my sexual haze, the cooling shaft driving deeper into my restricted anus. My husband staring at two cucumbers emerging from my bloated sex ducts . . . The ultimate in sexual deviancy; blatant adultery.

'Suck that,' Evans ordered me, grabbing a tuft of my long blonde hair and lifting my head up. 'Suck the spunk out of my cock.' Opening my mouth and taking his swollen glans inside, I savoured the taste of his salt. I ran my wet tongue over the silky-smooth surface of his cock head, probing his spunk slit. I breathed heavily through my nose as Neil pumped both my sex holes with the cucumbers. My naked body glowed with sex as I sucked on the man's knob. Lost in their debased sexual acts, neither man spoke as they abused my sex holes; my spunk-thirsty mouth.

Rocking his hips, Evans clutched my head as he forced his mouth fuck upon me. I couldn't see him, but I could smell the aphrodisiacal scent of his pubes, his balls. His bulbous knob gliding back and forth over my tongue, repeatedly driving to the back of my throat, I moaned through my nose as Neil yanked the cucumber out of my bumhole with a loud sucking sound. His cock slipped past my inflamed anal ring and thrust deep into me. He grabbed my hips and began his anal fucking.

My pussy muscles gripped the cucumber, my mouth bloated with a solid cock. My naked body flopped back and forth over the table as Neil repeatedly rammed his knob into my hungry arse-hole. The brown tissue surrounding my anus dragged back and forth along his shaft, the thin membrane dividing my sex sheath sandwiched between the cucumber and his cock. I moaned through my nose as my clitoris inflated and threatened to explode in orgasm.

My mouth filling with spunk as Evans gasped, I ran my tongue around the rim of his orgasming knob and repeatedly swallowed his creamy offering. Neil's knob exploded in orgasm, pumping cooling spunk into the fiery depths of my bowels. I finally reached my own massive climax. Shaking violently in the grip of my incredible pleasure, my naked body fucked at both ends by two beautifully hard cocks, I imagined a third cock ramming deep into my spasming pussy. This was real sex, I thought in my orgasmic delirium. A crude double fucking, an enforced double spunking . . . This was debased sex in all its depraved glory.

'Tight-arsed little bitch,' Neil gasped as he shafted my arse and flooded my bowels with his spunk. 'Dirty, filthy little whore.'

'Swallow it all,' Evans breathed, clutching my head tight as he fucked my spunk-bubbling mouth. 'Swallow every last drop of my spunk.'

Listening to their crude words as they used and abused my naked body, I wondered whether young James was watching the debauchery from the safety of his hide in the bushes. Was he waiting for his turn to fuck me and drain his heavy balls? As Neil finished his anal fucking and slipped his deflating cock out of my rectum, my mind-blowing orgasm finally began to recede. Shuddering as Evans made his last penile thrusts into my bloated mouth, I swallowed the remnants of his creamy spunk before his cock withdrew.

Gasping and writhing on the table, my naked body trembling uncontrollably, I wondered what the men were planning next as they moved about behind me. Would they remove my blindfold and allow me to see? Again, a bulbous knob pressed hard against the spunk-dripping eye of my inflamed anus, trying to gain entry to my inner core. It must have been Evans, I assumed. He'd restiffened quickly after his mouth fucking, his throat spunking. Perhaps, like Neil, he had amazing virility and staying power?

'Straight in,' Neil said as the man's cock entered me, his knob travelling along my rectal sheath and coming to rest deep within my bowels. The stretching sensation, filling me, bloating me . . . As he withdrew and rammed into me again, his lower belly slapped the firm flesh of my naked buttocks. I felt my pussy muscles tighten around the cucumber bloating my pussy. The teats of my breasts pressed hard against the patio table. The rope securing my wrists bit into me. I gasped as the man grabbed my hips and fucked me hard.

I could hear Neil's spunk squelching within my inflamed arse and the man pistoned me there. Squelching, oozing from the burning ring of my anus and running down to the cucumber shaft bloating my pussy. How many times could each man manage to fuck my tight arse? I wondered, as I rocked back and forth over the table. How much spunk could they produce between them? They must have had bionic cocks, I thought happily.

Neil should share the money from the sale of my young body, I mused. The least the bastard could do was go halves with me. After all, it was my mouth, my arse and my cunt he was being paid for. A prostitute? That's what I'd become. A whore, sold for crude sex to anyone and everyone willing to pay to use and abuse my body. Where was the slut? I wondered, surprised that she wasn't taking part in the sexual deviancy. Perhaps she was fucking some man or other in the park. Or some girl or other.

The man fucking my arse grabbed my hips. I felt other hands running over my back, between my parted thighs. Frowning within the dark of my blindfold, I was sure that I counted five hands. I couldn't have done, I reflected. Two clutching my hips, one between my thighs and one running up and down my spine . . . Perhaps the slut had arrived. Why hadn't she spoken? Why hadn't the men greeted her?

My rectum flooded with a deluge of spunk. I thought that I must have been mistaken until I again counted five hands. Or were there six? Confusion reigning, I listened for identifying noises but heard nothing other than heavy breathing and flesh smacking flesh. The man's spunk was streaming from my bloated anus and running down my thighs. I gasped as he finally withdrew his spent cock. My bumhole gaping wide open, bubbling with spunk as people moved about behind me, I wondered what the hell was going on.

'We'll allow you to rest,' Neil said, removing my blindfold and untying the ropes.

'Who was here?' I asked him, hauling my aching body upright and shielding my eyes from the bright sun. 'Who was it?' I asked him again, sure that I heard the front door close.

'No one was here,' he replied. 'Put your panties on to keep the cucumber in place.'

'Neil, I'm not leaving it –'

'Do as you're told, slut,' he hissed. 'You'll leave the cucumber up your dirty little cunt, do you understand?'

Pulling my panties up my long legs, concealing the juice-dripping end of the cucumber, I grabbed my clothes and dressed. Someone had been with Neil and his friend, I knew. It couldn't have been the slut, I reflected, watching Evans adjust his trousers and brush his greying hair back. Mumbling something to Neil, he went into the house. Again, I heard the front door close as he made his escape. Two people had left the house, I was positive.

'I want half the money,' I said, scowling at Neil. 'How much did you sell me for?'

'Half the money?' he echoed, laughing at me as I adjusted my wet panties to keep the cucumber in place. 'You get nothing, Cindy. Slaves don't get paid.'

'Presumably you plan to bring other men here to fuck me?'

'Of course. I'm going to build up a nice little business. There are plenty of men around who'd pay well to fuck a whore like you. By the way, Jackie will be round later for your vacuum-pumping session.'

'She bloody well won't,' I returned. 'I'm not having that slut anywhere near me.'

'Don't argue with me, Cindy. You know what will happen if you defy me. I'll be back later,' he said, stepping into the kitchen. 'And I want to find the cucumber where I left it. If I don't then . . .'

'Yes, yes, I know,' I sighed.

Once he'd gone, I pulled my panties aside and slipped the sex-dripping cucumber out of my inflamed pussy. After tossing it into the bushes, I went up to my bedroom and grabbed the key to the shed. The time had come to destroy the photographs, I decided, bounding down the stairs and taking a box of matches from the kitchen drawer. Marching across the lawn, I opened the shed and took the envelope from beneath the bench. There may have been copies, I mused, but I very much doubted it. Stepping out of the shed, I opened the envelope and decided to burn one photograph at a time.

'What?' I gasped, finding the envelope empty. 'How the hell . . .' The key had been hidden at the back of my underwear drawer. There was no way Neil, or anyone else, couldn't have used it. There had only ever been one key to the padlock, so how on earth could Neil . . . I suddenly doubted myself; wondered whether I'd taken the photographs, but I was positive that I'd not removed them. Was I going mad?

Returning to the house, I noticed Rod's mobile phone on the hall table. He'd taken it to work with him, I was sure. He never went anywhere without his phone, and it certainly hadn't been there earlier. I couldn't believe that Rod was the third person; the third abuser. Had he forced his cock deep into my anus and spunked my bowels? Rod, my asexual husband, fucking my tight arse in front of his brother and Evans? No, it just wasn't possible.

I wandered out into the garden, as confused as ever. Everything pointed to Rod. He was the last piece of the puzzle, fitting nicely into place to complete the picture. Recalling the time Neil had tied me to the dining-room table and blindfolded me, I wondered whether Rod had been there. Neil had shafted my tight bottom hole twice. Was he really that virile? Or had the second rock-hard cock belonged to my husband?

'Hi,' James said, emerging from the bushes and looking at the house. 'Are you alone?'

'I'm not sure,' I sighed.

'Shall I go?'

'No, no. I'm alone, James. I don't suppose you were lurking in the bushes earlier?'

'No, I've been in my room. I didn't realise that you knew Josh.'

'Josh? Who the hell is Josh?'

'His friends call him Evans.'

'What?' I gasped. 'You know him? You know Evans?'

'I was looking out of my window and saw him leave your house.'

'But . . . who is he?'

'He works at the college.'

'Rod does work for the college,' I breathed pensively. 'They're a client of his. Did you see anyone else leaving my house?'

'No, I just happened to glance out of the window. Are you all right? You seem a little shaky.'

'I'm fine, James. Wait there a minute,' I said, leaving him on the lawn and heading for the house.

Deciding to check the numbers on Rod's mobile phone, I wondered whether I'd find the slut listed. It was a long shot, but . . . Eyeing the hall table, I couldn't believe that the phone had gone. Rod was lurking, spying, I knew, as I checked the lounge. My husband was not only a voyeur, but also obviously loved joining in the gang bangs. How could he treat me this way? I mused. It was no wonder that he'd not wanted sex recently. He was getting sex – anal sex with his wife.

I was wrong, I had to be. We were the perfect couple. When had Rod decided to use and abuse me like this? Had he discovered my secret life and decided to use me rather than divorce me? Had he discovered the truth, he might have planned to throw me out of the house, I reflected, and then thought that he might as well use me to satisfy his lust for anal sex. Was he sharing the slut with his brother? Did they give her a double fucking? Hearing a dull thud upstairs, I was sure that it was Rod. What the hell was he up to? Or was it Neil? Back in the garden, I reckoned that Rod was watching me, spying on me. And I decided to put on a sex show for him. If I was wrong, and he knew nothing about my dirty life, then he'd throw me out of the house and divorce me.

'Why don't you take my clothes off?' I asked James as I stood before him in the middle of the lawn. 'It's hot today, James. Take my clothes off for me.'

'Here?' he breathed, looking about him. 'In the middle of the garden?'

'Why not? No one can see us.' No one apart from my husband. 'I think the time has come to give you another sex lesson. Would you like that?'

'Very much,' he replied eagerly, his face beaming as he unbuttoned my blouse.

'Tear my clothes off,' I ordered him. 'Tear them off as if you're raping me.'

He ripped my blouse open and tore the garment from my body. After grabbing my bra and tearing the garment in two, he tossed it to the ground and yanked my skirt down. Ripping my wet panties off, he gazed longingly at the swollen lips of my pussy, my very wet sex crack. Was Rod watching? I wondered, instructing James to do as he wished with my naked body. Was he at the bedroom window watching his wife's adulterous act? Or was Neil the voyeur?

Following the teenage lad's instructions and positioning myself on all fours, I glanced up at the bedroom window as he kneeled behind me. I couldn't see anyone as James parted the firm cheeks of my bottom and ran his tongue up and down my anal gully. Licking the delicate brown tissue surrounding my inflamed anus, I wondered whether he could taste spunk there. He pushed his tongue deep into my rectum, licking inside me and sucking out the creamy spunk as I quivered and whimpered in the grip of the decadent act. His hand groped between my parted thighs, his fingers entering the tight sheath of my hot cunt. He slurped at my bottom hole as he finger fucked me.

His cock would be rock hard, I knew, as he slipped his tongue out of my anus and drove at least two fingers deep into the heat of my inflamed rectum. How much crude sex could I endure in one day? I wondered, my aching pleasure sheaths lovingly gripping the lad's pistoning fingers. How many cocks could I take up my arse in one day? Four, five, ten . . . Recalling the time I'd spent an evening with four young men, I'd had my arse fucked six or seven times in succession. Could I have endured ten cocks shafting my hot rectum?

'Fuck me now, James,' I gasped, again looking up at the bedroom window. 'Fuck me like you've never fucked me before.'

'Are you sure that no one's in the house?' he asked me, tugging his zip down.

'There's no one there,' I said. 'Why are you worrying?'

'I thought . . . It doesn't matter.'

'Thought what?'

'I thought I saw the dining-room curtain move.'

'It was probably the breeze.' Either that, or my husband watching my lewd adultery. 'Don't worry, James.'

Did Rod have his stiff cock in his hand? I mused. Was he wanking as he watched his young wife commit crude acts of sex on the lawn with a teenage lad? What were his thoughts? The idea of my husband watching me commit adultery sent my arousal rocketing once more. I let out a gasp as James pushed his swollen glans hard against my well-salivated anal mouth. His glans slipped past my sphincter muscles and glided into my creamy arse. I felt myself inflate. He pushed his cock fully home, his beautiful knob embedded within the hot depths of my bowels, then he grabbed my hips and withdrew slowly.

Another anal shafting, I mused. More spunk pumped deep into the core of my body. With young James living next door, I'd never want for a beautifully hard cock. I'd ask him to call on me every day, I decided, as he repeatedly withdrew and thrust into me. The sensitive tissue of my anus dragging back and forth along his rock-hard shaft, his knob sinking deep into my bowels with each indriving of his cock, he mumbled words of sex as he fucked me.

He came quickly, his spunk lubricating my rectal cylinder as he pistoned me. His balls swinging, pummelling the soft swellings of my hairless pussy lips, he must have thought me a dirty little whore. On all fours on the lawn, my buttocks projected out, my knees wide apart, a teenage cock shafting the tight tube of my rectum . . . I *was* a whore. But I was also a wife, a housewife. Two sides, two vividly contrasting worlds.

As James shafted me, draining his heavy balls, I again wondered whether my voyeur was Neil or Rod. Would I ever discover the truth? I reflected. If it was my husband, and he loved watching other men fuck me, use and abuse me, then I could continue with my debauchery, my adulterous life. Knowing that my husband was watching my crude fucking would add to the excitement. He'd come home from the office and ask me whether I'd had a good day, knowing that I'd had cocks spunking in my mouth, my rectum and tight pussy. We'd play a game of lies and deceit. Neil would threaten to expose me as a whore when, all along, I'd know that my husband knew. Neil would blindfold me, and Rod would fuck me from behind. A game . . .

'You're beautiful,' James breathed, finally sliding his cock out of my spunk-bubbling anal canal.

'And you're amazing,' I said softly, lying on my back beneath the sun.

'I think there's someone in your house,' he whispered, his dark eyes frowning.

'No one's there, James. Don't worry.'

'I think I'd better go home,' he said, zipping his trousers.

'All right. But promise me that you'll come back later.'

'Yes, I promise. But, if your husband –'

'I'll tell you what I'll do. If you see my handbag on the patio table, then it will be safe for you to come over.'

'OK,' he breathed eagerly. 'I'll see you later.'

As he slipped into the bushes and made his escape, I went into the house and headed for my bedroom. Whoever had been in the dining room would have gone. They'd have seen me and slipped out of the front door. It was all a game, I thought, slipping into a short summer dress. Spunk oozed from my anal iris, filling the tight crotch of my white panties.

I made myself a cup of coffee and sat on the patio.

I couldn't believe that Rod was the voyeur. It was impossible to accept that my husband had been in it with Neil and his blackmailing. But all the pieces of the puzzle appeared to fit and the picture was complete. Whether or not it was the right picture, I had no idea. Someone had found the key to the shed and taken the photographs; Sue had seen Rod and Neil together . . . Had I painted a true picture?

'Hi,' Rod called, closing the front door.

'Home again in the middle of the day?' I said as he joined me on the patio. 'Have you come back for your mobile phone?'

'My phone? I took my phone with me this morning.'

'I thought I saw it on the hall table earlier.'

'No, not mine. I might be a little late this evening. I should be home by seven.'

'OK, I'll have dinner ready for seven.'

'You'll be all right? I mean, you don't mind?'

'Of course I don't mind, Rod. If you have to work late, that's fine by me.'

'Neil might call in this evening. Is that all right?'

'No problem.'

'If he arrives before I get home . . .'

'I'll look after him, don't worry.'

'Thanks, love. Right, I'd better get going. I'll see you at seven.'

Neil might call in? I mused, as Rod left the house. What was the plan? Would Rod hide somewhere and watch his brother fuck me? Or was I very wrong about the whole thing? Sipping my coffee, I doubted that I'd ever discover the truth. Who was fooling whom? I wondered. Did it matter? As long as I had my lovers with their hard cocks and spunk-laden balls, nothing mattered.

Hearing James talking to his friend in his garden, I felt my insatiable clitoris swell. Two teenage cocks, I mused. Rod had gone back to work; the sun was shining in a clear blue sky, and I was desperate for more crude sex . . . I finished my coffee, and reckoned that the time had come to place my handbag on the patio table.

NEXUS NEW BOOKS

To be published in March 2005

TORMENT, INCORPORATED
Murilee Martin

Southern California, 1990s. Charlene and Ed run a very kinky business providing paid sexual domination for the jaded tastes of La-La-Land. With Ed behind the scenes and Charlene front of house, they make their clients' juices – and their money – flow. Ed thinks of himself as the gentle type but, when Charlene begins to take her on-the-job training a little too seriously, Ed must face how dominant his tendencies really are.

£6.99   0 352 33943 8

COLLEGE GIRLS
Cat Scarlett

Beth is an impoverished student at St Nectan's College, Oxford. When Dr Milton recruits her to an exclusive club for submissives and pony-girls, Beth's independent spirit soon gets her into trouble. Charlotte wants her last year at Oxford to be a memorable one. Lizzie wants Dr Milton all to herself. Beth just wants to pay the rent. Pony races, perverted parties and Victorian pornography combine to give these college girls a thoroughly indecent education.

£6.99   0 352 33942 X

THE NEXUS LETTERS
Various

Here, Nexus readers share their most intimate secrets – from the slaves who'll do anything they're told, to ice-cool supervixens; from husbands who like to watch, to the men – and women – who pleasure their neighbours' wives – it's all here, in our kinkiest and most perverse collection yet. Enjoy!

£6.99   0 352 33955 1

If you would like more information about Nexus titles, please visit our website at www.nexus-books.co.uk, or send a stamped addressed envelope to:
  Nexus, Thames Wharf Studios,
  Rainville Road, London W6 9HA